Advance Praise for *Anomalies*

"This book makes spirituality exciting and vibrant. I predict it will be so successful that we'll all have to learn how to pronounce 'anomaly' correctly."

—**Russell Brand**, comedian, author, and actor

"We get to see this unusual futuristic world through Keeva's smart and unapologetic eyes. *Anomalies* is a whirlwind adventure with deep meaning. It has smart writing, engaging characters, and a plot which leaves you hanging on to every word."

—**Max Beesley**, actor and musician

"The psychological goal for every teen is to resolve the separation process by emerging as adults with their own character, opinions, and belief systems. *Anomalies* explores the process of teenage separation from a new, fresh, engaging, and interesting perspective. A must-read for all teens and parents."

—**Dr. Fran Walfish**, PsyD, Beverly Hills child, adolescent, and family psychotherapist
Author of *The Self-Aware Parent*

"A fast-paced story which champions individuality and truth. Keeva is a compelling heroine who is relatable and strong."

—**Pamela Anderson**, actor, author, and activist

Anomalies

Anomalies

The Rise of the Underground

Sadie Turner and Colette Freedman

SelectBooks, Inc.
New York

This edition published by SelectBooks, Inc.
For information address SelectBooks, Inc., New York, New York.

First Edition

ISBN 978-1-59079-361-9

Library of Congress Cataloging-in-Publication Data

Names: Turner, Sadie, 1973- | Freedman, Colette.
Title: Anomalies / Sadie Turner and Colette Freedman.
Description: First edition. | New York : SelectBooks, Inc., [2016] |
Summary:
  In the future where no disease, war, or discontent exists, and all
  citizens are complacent members of the Global Governance,
  fifteen-year-old
  Keeva discovers that nonconformity will be punished, dissent is not an
  option, and insurgents will be destroyed.
Identifiers: LCCN 2015023368 | ISBN 9781590793619 (pbk. book : alk.
paper)
Subjects: | CYAC: Science fiction. | Identity--Fiction. |
  Conformity--Fiction. | Individuality--Fiction. | Government, Resistance
  to--Fiction.
Classification: LCC PZ7.1.T92 An 2016 | DDC [Fic]--dc23 LC record avail-
able at http://lccn.loc.gov/2015023368

Book design by Janice Benight

Manufactured in the United States of America
10 9 8 7 6 5 4 3 2 1

This is for anyone who feels different.
Who knows something isn't quite right.
This is for everyone who refuses to conform
and needs to Scream it. Shout it.
Shake it up. Twist it. Bend it, and shift the perspective.
This is for those of you who skip when others are walking
and who dive in while others are floating.
For those that have the courage to be true to themselves
no matter what.

This is for the exceptional.

Acknowledgments

SADIE WOULD LIKE TO THANK
Suzie for inspiring me every day,
Robert for always believing in me,
and Reagan, Todd, Stacy, Normandie, Randy, Russell,
Andrew, Pam, Adam, Trina, Nicola,
Stephen, Max, Clare, Sydney, Tania, Vin, Kaley, PK, Dorit,
Cindy, Paul, John, Jeremy, Fritz, Jen, Finn, Oliver, Kevin,
Akiva, Susie, Mum, and Dad for all the support, love,
and encouragement along the way.

COLETTE WOULD LIKE TO THANK
Brooke, for changing my life and encouraging me
to let my freak flag fly;
Nickella, Anne-Marie, Adam, Ronnie and the cast of
Serial Killer Barbie for reminding me how to have fun;
and all of the Anomalies: Scout, David, Kelly, Zac, Dylan,
William, Keb, Jade,
Franny, Nessa, Maureen, Christian, Max, Doug, Diane, Rooney,
Sean, Gillian, Jaret, Robyn,
Rebecca, Elan, Adam, Diana, Kerry, Jen P., Devon, Deb G.,
Emilie, Jackie, Tegan, Jhen
Lynn, Lynne, Fred, Jen L., Agatha, Michael Scott,
and Hannah Hope.
And, of course, Mom and Dad for everything and more.
So much more.

Sadie and Colette would like to thank our beta readers,
Fergus, Zachary, Max, David and Bob.
Stuart for introducing us,
Becky and Kate for believing in us, Savannah for our photos,
our fabulous editors, Nancy and Yoji,
and with gratitude to our agent, Bill, and our publisher, Kenzi.

Nothing is as it seems.

Prologue

The screams pierce through the early morning ocean air. I don't know if they belong to the baby or my mother, I just know that I have to get home. Immediately. I knew something was wrong the moment I got up that morning. I had one of my feelings. I shudder as I rub salty water away from my eyes. Mother isn't scheduled to deliver my sister for several hours. I thought I would have time to get in an early swim.

I thought wrong.

The wails are deafening as I get out of the water and race up the shore. As I push open the wooden door of our home, the first thing I see is my mother. She is lying on a bed in a pool of blood. A stranger dressed in white with a large turban is closing her eyes. What is happening?

"Mother!" I scream, my six-year-old voice shaking with fear and sadness.

The stranger tries to hold me, but I pull away. My mother is dead. Her blond curls are matted around her head, giving her a disturbing angelic look. A tiny baby lies quietly on the bed next to her. My father, my rock, is broken on the floor next to my mother's corpse. He is sobbing.

"Mother," my voice cracks. My life is over.

"You must listen to your heart, Keeva," the turbaned stranger warns, lowering his accented voice and forcing me to come closer to hear him.

"How do you know my name?"

He doesn't answer. Instead, he picks up the infant and slips into the back room.

Moments later, there is a knock at the half-opened door. Two officials enter. They are dressed from head to toe in black, the uniform of the Global Governance. Protectors. Sobek Vesely's men.

"A citizen has been born," the shorter man says. It is a statement rather than a question.

"She's dead," I immediately say, unsure why I am lying. I know my responsibility as a citizen is to confirm the baby's birth to these government officials so that they can record her in the census. Officials are always present at a child's birth. It is the law. Their job is to insert a small crystallized dot, called a Third, containing data for the encrypted codes of our Global Governance, between the baby's tiny eyebrows.

A strong instinct is begging me to justify the lie. "Please, just let us grieve," I implore, nodding to my wailing father.

The men respectfully bow and leave, recording on their data tablets what has transpired. They have no reason to suspect I am lying. Citizens of the Global Governance don't lie. It is not in our nature. There is no reason for me to lie.

The turbaned man emerges from the back room. He hands me my baby sister. Her fingers are so tiny. So delicate. Her eyes are so bright. She looks just like my mother.

For months, my mother and I had been talking about names for the baby. Now, my mother is dead. I digest the terrible reality and begin to cry. The stranger gently takes the baby from me, "You have sad eyes, Keeva. Sad eyes which will allow you to both observe the world and the truths within yourself."

I am in shock. I cannot digest what he is saying. I want my mother. I want my sister. I want everything to be fine and it never will be again.

"Everything will be fine," the stranger says kindly as if he can read my thoughts. "I am Harijiwan. I promise to protect her until you are ready. Be strong, Keeva." He swathes the baby in white, as if she is part of his costume, and heads toward the door.

"Her name is Sun," I call out before turning to comfort my distraught father.

1.

I am spinning.

Around and around, suspended from a vaulted ceiling, I am upside-down, watching the world turn around me. I close my eyes because I'm so dizzy and I call out for help, but no one is listening. There are grownups nearby, tall people in crisp black uniforms, laughing and ignoring my cries. They move fluidly, as if floating on air. I try to move my hands to stop myself from spinning, but they're pressed to my sides and swathed in silk. It is as if I am in a cocoon. Terrified, I finally open my eyes, which immediately rest on him; I see them reflected in his bright blue eyes. Silently, his look encourages me to be strong. He will be there for me. He will protect me.

And, although I can't stop spinning, I know that I am safe.

This has been a recurring nightmare throughout my life. At fifteen, I have the usual teenage bad dreams about falling or my teeth falling out, but the spinning nightmare is the most common. It is so real that it feels more like a memory, even though I can't remember anything like that ever happening to me. In a way, it feels even more real than the memory of losing my baby sister and the turbaned man who took her from me.

7

I know Sun is alive. Somewhere. Waiting for me. Sometimes I ask my father what happened to her, and he tells me she never existed. But I do have a sister. I know I do. Still, he never wants to talk about her so I don't press him. I have pushed the memory of her deep into my subconscious, so my dreams are only filled with spinning . . . and the nameless, blue-eyed boy who once made me feel safe.

Now, the only time I ever really feel safe is when I'm in the water. When I swim, I feel free. My mind is completely unfettered and the nightmares are distant memories. I swim before breakfast every day. It is a routine and I like routines.

Diving through the ocean's waves, I relish the feel of the cool, salty water as it drenches my skin. I can feel the morning sun breaking on my back as I swim parallel to the jagged shore. I take long, powerful strokes, enjoying my own strength and the solitude. At this hour, I am the only one out here. Soon, the ocean will be teeming with workers taking samples, children learning skills and fishers foraging for food. Right now, the ocean is my private pool and I'm loathe to get out.

This will be my last ocean plunge for almost a month. I'm leaving for camp in a few hours. I take one last dive and open my eyes as I scan the clear water, silently saying goodbye to familiar underwater plants, bright coral reefs, and schools of colorful fish. I turn toward the shoreline and swim underwater until I get to the sand. There, I burst out of the ocean and race home, allowing the wind to dry my body. By the time I jump the three steps of the small beachfront cottage where my father and I live, I can already smell the eggs and toast wafting through the air.

"Hurry Keeva, it's just about to start," my father warns.

As I enter the house, I grab a thick towel from the rack near the door and wrap myself in the heavy material. My father loads up my plate and pours me a cup of caffeine. I inadvertently rub my pinky on my Third, a tiny opaque crystalline diamond pierced in the center of my forehead in between my eyebrows. I received it as a baby. Every citizen has one. The news is sent directly to the tiny dot on our forehead through a complex satellite system, which both feeds us important news and tracks us in order to protect us. As the report starts, I slide onto one of the two tall metal stools next to the kitchen counter. This is our morning routine and we eat in silence as the mediacaster intones on a hologram across the room.

"Today, we begin another session of Monarch Camp and I am privileged to introduce the Leader of Global Governance, who would like to personally welcome you. Sobek Vesely."

The holo feed cuts from the mediacaster to our world leader. Sobek Vesely sits in a high-backed chair and looks directly into the camera.

"Welcome, citizens." His baritone voice immediately commands attention and I find myself mesmerized. In a clipped accent, he gives the world broadcast, announcing the opening of Monarch Camp's Summer Solstice Session, a session that my friends and I will be attending.

Unlike my muscular father, Johan, who is tanned from working in the sun every day of his life, Sobek Vesely's skin is so white it's almost translucent. His short-cropped brown hair accentuates his strong cheekbones and his black eyes are piercing. He is handsome, in an odd sort of way. Compelling. And extraordinarily tall. Even sitting down, his frame is barely contained on the holo projection.

Sobek Vesely is responsible for bringing our world back from the brink of extinction. He is our leader and I respect and admire him. Unlike my grandparents' generation, who lived in fear of war and disease and overpopulation and global warming, I live in a world without war. A perfect world where the citizens feel both secure and content. A world run by one united governance with no regional boundaries.

"And I look forward to greeting each one of my future citizens in three weeks as you leave your childhood and officially enter the new world as fully realized citizens." Our world leader finishes his brief welcome speech and the broadcast cuts to the local weather. Sunny and warm.

It's always sunny and warm in the Ocean Community.

I finish my breakfast and swing my legs off the stool, practically falling into my father. I love my father, but I don't understand him. Dr. Johan Tee is a marine biologist who spends all of his time consumed with his scientific experiments to keep the ocean clean. Personally, I don't think he's very happy. He wanted to be a surgeon, but instead he became a scientist. After the Great Technology War, he married my mother and moved to the ocean. I think his life is filled with regrets, as he spends more time talking about medicine than his work at the Desalination Plant. He is a man who has trouble expressing emotion, so when it comes time to say goodbye, he gives me the briefest of hugs. I cannot bear to abandon him, since I am his only family. I blink back tears, forcing my voice to sound casual as I quietly tell him that I'll be back in a few weeks.

Upstairs, in my small attic room, I change into a T-shirt and a pair of shorts. I sit down at my desk and stare at a picture of my mother on my tablet. It was taken just before she died. She was very pregnant and I had my arms wrapped around her belly. I fight back tears, still upset that I never got to say goodbye to her. I shut down my tablet and put both it and my identity watch in the desk drawer. While our Thirds are used to monitor and protect us, our watches are ways that we communicate with each other. They hold holos and memories. They are our lifeline to our friends and family when we are not with them. Yet I cannot bring my watch or tablet with me.

Electronics are not permitted at camp.

There is not a day that goes by when I don't miss my mother. I hope she is with my father's parents now. They died after the war, not from the floods, but from the disease that followed. They were not alone. Practically everyone over the age of twenty who was not protected with a data chip perished. It was Sobek Vesely, then a young technology whiz working for one of the major corporations, whose company had manufactured and distributed the Thirds before the war. Because of the former government's strict regulations, though, there were only enough data chips manufactured for unmarried citizens under twenty. When the war came, the Thirds helped ward off the disease that followed it. My parents were dating, but not married, so they received the chips. They were among the lucky ones.

Because of the success of the Thirds, Sobek Vesely became an instant celebrity. His technology was critical to the future growth and survival of the remaining citizens.

And while the old governments were collapsing, Sobek's star was rising. He became indispensable. Every survivor demanded his input. And he delivered, using his crucial technology to unite the world under one leadership. His leadership. He agreed to fully integrate his technology in exchange for appointment as world leader. People were ready to follow and Sobek Vesely was primed to lead. The survivors were desperate, and Sobek Vesely was a hopeful option. He was both a popular and a promising young man with bright ideas and a clear vision for the future. Because people were dying by the tens of thousands, there was no time for elections, so Sobek Vesely was appointed world leader and created a one-world government.

My grandparents did not survive; neither did my aunts and uncles. But everyone with a chip did, thanks to Sobek Vesely. He brought our world out of its misery into a new era. My friends and I live in a new world where we will never know hunger or poverty or unhappiness.

We are incredibly lucky.

I get up and survey my small room. Although I've been mentally preparing for this summer for my entire life, I'm still not quite sure if I've packed enough. I like to be prepared for anything and everything. My duffel bag is on the bed. Annika and Rane will be here any minute. For the next three-and-a-half weeks, the three of us will be attending Monarch Camp, the Governance's mandated camp for all fifteen-year-olds.

Since the Global Governance was established fifty years ago, all children are required to attend camp when they turn five and return ten years later, to be reunited with their intended partner and assigned to their new community. It's the single most important event of my life; yet as I scroll down the packing list, I don't want to think about my future . . . only my present. I wonder if I'm bringing enough stuff. In a pinch, I could always borrow bits and pieces from Annika or Rane, but I'm so freakishly tall, none of their clothes will really fit me. Most of my supplies are already crammed into my blue duffel bag, except the bandanna my father gave me. I've knotted it and wrapped it around my wrist, like a bracelet.

There are six work communities: Labor, Agriculture, Ecosystem, Renewable Energy, Ocean, and Academic. Like all members of the Ocean Community, I am identified by the color of my community. Sobek Vesely's rationale for assigning us a chromatic dress code is to help us understand that the community is bigger than the individual—that we are all united in working toward a collective goal. So, all of my clothes are blue. It's not that I'm particularly vain, but with red hair and light blue eyes, I lucked out. I sometimes wonder what it would have been like if I had to grow up wearing brown like the Agricultural Community or purple like the Labor Community. Hopefully, I'll never know.

Once I'm assigned to my future occupation community, a butterfly will be tattooed on my left shoulder with my community's signature color. My best friend Annika's older sister has a cobalt and sapphire-colored butterfly on her left shoulder, and Rane's mother has a gorgeous turquoise butterfly tattoo on her left shoulder. Most people who grow up in the Ocean Community are reassigned here, so I've been planning my exact butterfly tattoo color for most of my life. Annika and Rane both want azure, but I want aqua—the color of the ocean. That's where I'm happiest—it's where I feel safe.

Before the Great Technology War, the oceans used to be so polluted you couldn't even swim in them or eat the fish. Since Sobek Vesely and the Global Governance rebuilt our society, the waters have become a beautiful aquamarine blue, and completely clean. The ocean is the sole source for our water supply. At the Desalination Plant, where my father works, salt is taken out of the ocean water. Biologists, like my father, work hard to ensure that the water is always clean.

Footsteps stomp up the stairs before I hear my best friend's voice calling, "Hurry up, Keeva."

Annika barges into my room. At 5′3″, Annika Aames is nearly six inches shorter than I am and the clumsiest person I know. Still, I kind of envy her. At 5′9″, I am way too tall, way too skinny, and my hair is the color of the sunset. I'm not the kind of person who likes to stick out in a crowd; I've made it a habit to try to blend in for most of my life. It's easier that way.

"Where's Rane?" I zip up the duffel bag, after haphazardly stuffing it with more of my clothes. All blue.

"Downstairs. You nervous?" Annika's bright brown eyes scan my face. She can always tell if I'm lying.

"A little. But it's all predestined, right? So there's no point in being nervous." Even as I'm saying it, there is something dancing in the back of my mind . . . an idea I don't really understand, which is niggling at me. "Anyway, we're just being imprinted with our other half and then assigned to a community . . . and we're all going to be Oceans, right?"

Annika nods, her high ponytail swinging back and forth as she definitely bobs her head up and down. She, Rane, and I made a pact last week when Rane turned fifteen. Since we're all born in June, we are assigned to Summer Solstice Monarch Camp. The camp operates four times a year, and we're really happy that we get to go to camp when it's warm out. The camp is set in Mid-America and I hear it can get ridiculously cold during the Fall Equinox and Winter Solstice sessions. Annika, Rane, and I plan to stay in the Ocean Community, and it shouldn't be a problem because the Global Governance, or GG, always encourages pairs to relocate to the female's community.

"No matter what, I'm going to stay in the Ocean Community. Could you imagine working for Renewable Energy? Boring!" Annika paces around the room. She has a hard time keeping still.

"I think it sounds cool. Getting energy from natural sources."

"Or Ecosystem, yawn." Annika keeps talking, a mile a minute. She does that a lot when she wants to make a point. Nothing detracts from her focus. "But the good thing about Ecosystem is at least they wear green, and that would look great with your coloring, Keeva. Red hair, a million freckles—"

"A billion freckles," I interrupt.

"Exactly! You'd look gorgeous. Especially if you got a kelly-green butterfly tattoo."

"Why are we even discussing this?" I mutter. "We're both staying in the Ocean Community."

"Sure. Unless we're Anomalies."

We're quiet for a minute. There are horror stories about Anomalies: people who get to camp and cannot be reunited with their intended partners due to unforeseen circumstances. They either never come back from camp or are reassigned to other communities.

"Don't look so serious," Annika laughs. "We'll be fine. Though I barely remember my partner. Doug, I think, or Danny . . . Daniel . . . Dave? It's something that starts with a D." Annika shrugs, "It's weird that we're imprinted when we're so young. You'd think the GG would want us to hang out or something to make sure we're compatible."

"Everyone's compatible," I say. "That's why I'm not nervous, because the GG has done the research for us. Our genes match up with theirs. We'll have perfect kids and good lives. Although, all I remember about my intended partner is that he had blue eyes. The color of the ocean."

"We both have lousy memories," Annika laughs.

"Tell me about it." I can barely remember anything from my childhood, let alone my intended partner. We met at Monarch Camp when we were five, spent three weeks playing together and being tested for compatibility, but that is a faded memory. I can't even remember his name . . . only the blue of his eyes. Spinning . . . spinning . . . the memory forms and I push it to the back of my mind, "I just hope he's cute."

"I know!" Annika giggles. "All I remember is that Doug/Danny had a really big head."

"He was five. He's probably grown into it by now."

"Annika! Keeva!" Rane's voice echoes from downstairs. "Hurry up."

"Here's to the first day of the rest of our lives." I grab the duffel bag off the bed and easily sling it over my shoulder. Annika follows me down the stairs, toward our exciting future.

THE SECOND THE TELECAST WAS OVER, Sobek jumped up from his chair. He hated when studio people came to the Palace. He loathed faking smiles and wearing makeup to give his skin more pigment. What he really hated was these media messages, but they were necessary. His citizens expected him to feed them propaganda and he was king of the spin.

"Where's my son?" he barked to the mousy Academic woman who had been hired to organize the telecast.

"The virtual game room in the South Wing," she said before disappearing around a corner.

Sobek grinned. No one liked to be around him for very long. Humans were such sensitive creatures, and they didn't do well with criticism or harsh language. Sobek made it a practice to both criticize and speak down to his employees. He thrived on their fear.

It made him stronger.

He preferred this compound in Sabbatical City to his other palaces in the Asias and Australia. There was something sleek and glitzy about it that reminded him of his own planet so many lifetimes ago. His other two headquarters were located on the other side of the world: Pyramid City based in the Giza Pyramid in the former Egypt and Argyle City based in the old Argyle diamond mine where his workers crystallized the diamonds, along with his own secret compound, into Thirds.

Sobek looked around at his sumptuous palace in the heart of Sabbatical City. It was filled with statues of gods these people had worshipped centuries earlier. Before he took over the world, this used to be called Caesar's Palace and was located in a silly place called Las Vegas.

It was as if waves parted as Sobek stormed through the compound, looking for his heir. Calix had grown up alongside other children. He had schooled with them and played with them: this was important for his socialization. One can't control what one does not understand. But playtime was over and Sobek was ready to groom his son to take over his kingdom.

First, his son would have to be properly educated.

2.

I am flying.

Annika, Rane, and I board the helicraft outside our secondary school. The large black machine takes off quickly, leaving my beloved community behind. I watch the ocean disappear as the helicraft heads due east. I live on the coastline of West America, in a place that was once called northern California. I put my nose to the window and look through the dark glass as the terrain turns from green to brown. Once upon a time, this trip would have taken longer. That was before the war, when the world looked a lot different.

After the war, the polar ice caps in the North Pole melted. South America, Antarctica, and Europe instantly sank into the oceans, killing all of their citizens. The United States barely survived, left with only eleven of its original states. Our west coast and slightly inland survived and Africa's east coast and slightly inland survived. Canada and Mexico were similarly decimated. Only Asia and Australia remained completely intact, in a bizarre twist of fate where countries sank despite their mountainous regions. It was simply a matter of geographic placement.

The world was quickly redivided.

The former United States and Canada, only shells of their former greatness, were trisected into three parts: West, Mid- and East America. West America and East America are bordered by oceans. Mid-America is the section of land between. The Americas take up about a third as much land as they used to before the war because everything from the former East Coast all the way to Texas in the South and up to North Dakota sank underwater.

Monarch Camp is located smack-dab in the middle of Mid-America on the former border of Utah and Nevada. As we soar through the air, I see a never-ending expanse of brown, dry land beneath me. There are very few bodies of water as we fly farther inland. A lake here and a lake there but nothing significant. I squeeze my armrests and watch the white of my knuckles as I try to control my panic. I'm not sure what is happening to me; I feel a sense of dread knowing that I'll be landlocked for the next few weeks.

Rane, Annika and I sit in the helicraft's first four rows. There are three rows of three seats behind us. The helicraft carries twelve fifteen-year-olds from our community and one pilot. We don't speak during the ride. Each of us is too nervous about what we are going to find when we arrive at camp. Rane senses my anxiety and squeezes my arm. Her touch calms me. The bright royal blue of her fingernail polish contrasts sharply with the porcelain color of her skin. Throughout my life, Rane has always been there for me when I've been nervous. So has Annika. So what do I have to be nervous about? For most people, Monarch Camp is a solitary experience. I get to go there with not one, but two best friends.

I close my eyes and try to relax. There are ten heli-crafts in total from each community, each carrying a dozen teenagers. Math's never been my strong suit, but Rane, who's a whiz at everything, told us that there will be around 840 total campers at this session. Before the Great Technology War the population was out of control and there were over five million fifteen-year-olds . . . which means a few hundred thousand would have been attending the Summer Solstice session. Now, there are just a tiny fraction of those teens left.

That's why Sobek Vesely and his Global Governance have worked so hard to protect us from our past: to preserve our future.

And I know exactly what my future will be. Annika, Rane, and I will end up back in the Ocean Community. It is all I know and all I want to know. All three of our families have lived in this community since the war and I don't want to live anywhere else. The Aameses and the Crowleys have been like a family to me as long as I can remember. The three of us were raised like sisters, constantly sleeping over at each other's houses, swimming, and planning our futures together. After my mom died, I probably spent as much time at Annika's house as my own, and her big sister Quill and her sister's partner Jed have been like older siblings to me. I'm not as close with the Crowleys, Rane's parents, although I used to have a crush on Rane's older brother, Cannon. He went to Monarch Camp three years ago and now lives in East America in the Academic Community with his partner Jo. Even though he visits on the two prescribed visiting weeks each year, he already seems . . . different: like a foreigner.

So my plan is to have a fun three weeks, reunite with my partner and return to the Ocean Community to fulfill my destiny.

"Stop daydreaming," Rane nudges me. "We're here."

I look out the window. We are hovering in the air and there are helicrafts to our right and left. Below, a line of helicrafts land in an orderly fashion. The large, black, flying machines take turns landing on the designated heliport that sits in the middle of the mountainous range.

Once we land, we lug our duffel bags through a large tunnel, which has been carved through a mountain. We walk single file. Annika is ahead of me, Rane is behind. It is dimly lit and hard to see so we must take small steps in order not to trip, which Annika does—three times. We walk like this for almost a mile until we finally see the light. Just beyond the tunnel's exit is the camp. I blink several times as my eyes adjust to the bright sunlight. It is flatland as far as the eye can see. These parts used to be called the Bonneville Salt Flats, a densely packed salt pan that covered thirty thousand acres. There used to be little significance to the area before it became the site for the America's Monarch Camp.

Before the Global Governance built a camp on top of the salt pan, it was just loads of salt, a few abandoned government buildings and old airfields. There is now no longer a need for the government buildings. The old national government used to be based in a place called Washington, which sank during the polar ice melt and is now completely under water.

So Sobek condemned all the old government buildings because he had no need for extraneous government locations, including these former government buildings. He condemned the airfields on the Salt Flats where the former government carried out military experiments. Sobek doesn't believe in global warfare so once he came into power, all munitions and bombs were destroyed.

"The only weapons we need are our minds," is one of Sobek's mottos.

This motto is etched into our currency chips as a constant reminder of the importance of peace. In his palace in Sabbatical City, Sobek finds ways to keep the world at peace. I smile, lucky to be alive in a time when calm and nonviolence will always prevail.

"Welcome to Monarch Camp," Annika reads from the huge sign at the entrance of the camp. It is made out of sheet metal and there are seven colored butterflies hanging from the bottom of the sign, spinning in the wind. Each community's color is represented by a butterfly painted in purple, brown, green, red, blue, yellow, or black.

As we pass under the sign, we each tap our respective butterflies. Annika, Rane, and I reach up and hit the blue butterfly, which is hanging in between Renewable Energy's Red butterfly and Ecosystem's Green butterfly. I feel giddy as I share in the collective energy of the kids all entering camp. While I am making my official entrance, a boy knocks into me as he is hitting his red butterfly. He doesn't even apologize.

"Um, excuse me," I tap him on the shoulder.

"What?" he smiles as he spins around.

"You just bumped into me."

"Sorry about that, Beanpole, but how do you know you didn't bump into me?" He has full lips and a large toothy smile. He is much cuter than any of the boys at home, but I quickly dismiss this as I confront him.

"Beanpole?" He is as tall as I am and I glare into his mocking eyes. "You were the one who bumped my shoulder."

"And I'm saying, maybe you bumped my shoulder."

"You're being ridiculous." I don't have a lot of experience with boys outside of my community. I wonder if they are all this obnoxious.

"Maybe I did and maybe I didn't, but I definitely know that I'm not the one who is holding up the line." He grins again. Sure enough, there is a long line of Oceans waiting to pass through the opening, and I am holding them up.

"Whatever." I knock my butterfly and enter the camp. I want to scream at him but he is already ahead of me, surrounded by his posse of red. I won't let my first day be ruined. My life is about to officially begin and I couldn't be happier. It's weird that I can barely remember this place from my childhood. How strange that, as a five-year-old, I must have walked a mile underground without being afraid. Or taken a helicraft without fear.

It's odd, the things I remember and the things I don't.

Men and women in crisp, black uniforms herd us toward the flagpole where we will be assigned to our bunks. As we head to the center of camp, I see two dozen adults standing by officiously, wearing the colors of the seven communities. I hear one of the black uniforms tell a camper that these will be our counselors for the next three weeks.

"How soon do you think we can go swimming?" Rane asks as we walk.

"Huh?"

"Look, there's a lake!" Rane turns me clockwise and I immediately smile. There is a large man-made lake just to our left with several wooden cabins around it. I'll be able to swim! Sure, it won't be in my beloved ocean, but I will feel more at home. Smiling, I look over the rest of the terrain. There are more cabins to our right at the base of the mountain. There are playing fields behind us and just in front of us is a flagpole bearing the seven striped flag of Global Governance. I look back at the lake. Just beyond it is an imposing stone building which, judging from my history lessons, has the design of the Victorian period. I've never seen anything like it. It is completely out of place, but stunningly beautiful with tall stone structures with turrets.

"What's in that building?" Rane asks a passing counselor. While I am fairly shy around strangers, Rane has no problem letting her voice be heard, especially if she is curious about something, and Rane is always curious. She is one of the smartest people I've ever met in my life.

"It's part of MC-5," the counselor in black says.

"What's that?" Rane presses.

"Monarch Camp for five-year-olds. They come for the last week of the month. Just after you go home." He rushes off, trying to reign in a group of boys from Ecosystem who have wandered away from the pack.

"We should check it out," Rane impishly whispers.

"No way," I say.

"Way," she shoots back. "C'mon Keeva, aren't you even curious? We can see what all of the fuss is about. Check out the place where we met our intended partners ten years ago."

"I'm not planning to get into trouble while I'm here." It's not that I'm not interested, I am. But I want to stick to the program.

"Suit yourself. But when I have a free moment, I'm definitely going," Rane says.

"C'mon, let's get good seats." I pull Rane in the direction of the flagpole where everyone is congregating. Rane, Annika and I sit at the far left of the semicircle so that we can have a perfect vantage point of the entire procession.

A hard-looking woman in a black uniform walks up to the flagpole and I know that my session is about to begin.

"Welcome, Citizens."

Everyone quickly settles down and finds a patch of ground to sit on as the woman with short-cropped white hair and high cheekbones raps her ringed hand on the flagpole, making a surprisingly loud noise. Annika, Rane, and I sit side by side, holding hands and waiting eagerly for our fates to be decided. Annika's sister Quill told us everything that is about to happen, so we are prepared as we watch the announcements. Quill said that we should try to remember every moment from the second the Camp Director starts speaking. It is such a mind-blowing experience to finally be reunited with your intended mate that it's easy to get caught up in the emotion of it. Quill can still describe the first time she and Jed were reunited. Each moment. Each feeling. It's a story I've heard far too many times and I'm ready to have my own story to tell.

"Welcome, Citizens," the handsome woman repeats as the last few whispers quiet. "My name is Claudia Durant and I am your Camp Director. Welcome. Over the course of the next hour, I will be announcing each group of intended partners. As you know from your sociology lessons, these partnerships have been carefully arranged to ensure a long and happy life." She gives a practiced smile before consulting her digital tablet. "I will be calling you by the girls' bunk assignments. Girls Camp is located next to the lake and Boys Camp is at the base of the mountain. When you hear your name, please come forward. You will have two hours to reunite with your intended partner and explore the campground before continuing on to your assigned bunks. Nothing is off limits except the administration building." She points to the same Victorian building that Rane asked about. I feel Rane squeeze my hand, but I ignore her, focusing my attention on the Camp Director.

"When your names are called," Claudia Durant says, pausing for a split second to survey the entire camp before continuing, "you will feel something you have never felt before. It is OK. It is just part of the imprinting process."

Annika, Rane, and I sit nervously, surrounded by a group of kids from the Ocean Community. All the communities are huddled together. It is an uneven rainbow with blues, browns, purples, greens, yellows, and reds all assembled in patches. Only the Protectors, kids in sleek black outfits who look a lot more mature than we do, congregate in smaller groups, peppered among the larger cliques.

"Bunk 1 Girls! Annika Aames, your intended partner is . . . Dante Suarez from Bunk 1 Boys."

Annika jumps up and we all scan the crowd. At the edge of the red group, a caramel-skinned boy rises. He has thick black hair and a big smile. When they lock eyes,

I notice something quite remarkable. Annika's Third begins to buzz. I can hear the soft purr of electricity and I watch as she closes her eyes. Annika is momentarily in shock before she opens her eyes again. She shakes her head, trying to understand the new jolt of energy.

"What's happening?" I whisper.

"It's . . . it's incredible" is all she says. Her eyes glaze over and her pupils suddenly dilate. My usually klutzy friend doesn't trip once as she makes her way to the flagpole. The entire time, her eyes are locked on her intended partner who smiles widely at her as he deftly glides through the crowd. Dante Suarez's body has clearly caught up with his head and he is cute. Really cute. Annika's smile takes up her entire face and I watch as she grabs his hand and pulls him along to the lake area.

Claudia Durant keeps calling out names. First the girl's name, then her intended partner's name. It's a fascinating process to watch because no one has any idea who their intended partners are. As each girl's name is called, everyone murmurs and looks around before her intended partner's name is called. I feel privileged to be a spectator in such an important life event. The only person who seems unfazed by the activity is the Camp Director. Durant has clearly been in charge for a long time because she is almost bored by the task.

Claudia Durant finishes listing the partners in Bunk 1 and moves on to Bunk 2. Annika is the only person from the Ocean Community assigned to Bunk 1. It is filled with mostly Labor and Ecosystem girls. I can still see her in the distance by the lake and I try to suppress my jealousy. She has been assigned to someone who she likes.

ANOMALIES

With whom she seems completely compatible. I hope that I am equally satisfied.

As each of the bunks is called out, I observe the flashes of fear, uncertainty, and excitement on each of the intended pairs' faces as they are matched together. Then, I hear their Thirds buzz before a calm washes over them. I can't wait for the calm to wash over me. With each name Claudia Durant calls, I feel increasingly anxious. She finishes calling Bunks 2 and 3 and begins on Bunk 4.

Even though many of the matches are across communities, people seem generally suited to each other. A gangly girl from the Labor Community squeals with delight as she is partnered with a tall, athletic boy from the Agricultural Community. The Lauderdale twins, who are in my grade in the Ocean Community, are matched with a pair of identical twins from the Ecosystem Community. Claudia Durant calls out Bunks 5 through 15. More squeals of excitement, more future partnerships solidified. The Global Governance has taken all unknown variables out of partnerships and the result is a one-hundred-percent success rate for marital pairings. In my grandparents' time, more than half of the couples used to get divorced. Now, there is no such thing, because people are matched from the inside out, rather than from the outside in. Our DNA dictates our compatibility. The guesswork has been removed. I am so entranced by the process, I barely notice that neither Rane nor I have been called.

"What bunk are they up to?" Rane asks twisting her nearly white, blond hair around her finger. She always does that when she's nervous. Rane is almost as tall as I am and she wears black spectacles, which make her light blue eyes look enormous.

"No clue—16? 17?" I quickly count the number of bunks along the lake. Twenty in total. I look around at the remaining campers. There are no longer distinct assemblies of color, just a small circle of nervous faces scanning the crowd, wondering whom their intended partners will be.

"We'll be fine." I clasp my hand tightly in Rane's to comfort her, and before she can respond, her name is called.

"Bunk 19 Girls—Rane Crowley. Your intended partner is Edward Stoppard—Bunk 19 Boys."

I can barely stifle a laugh. Eddie is a member of the Ocean Community who lives half a mile up the shore. His father works with my father. Rane is being matched with Eddie, nerdy Eddie. I am still tightly clasping Rane's hand when she is imprinted. Suddenly, I feel a spark of energy jolt through my fingers. It is coming from her Third, and I feel the energy travel from in between her eyes through the rest of her nervous system, eventually shocking her hand, which in turn shocks my hand. I watch her eyes, magnified by the glasses. Her brown pupils get bigger and bigger, covering up most of the light blue. A wave of calm envelopes her body and she stands up.

Unflustered. Serene.

I watch the pair shyly greet each other, old friends who are now suddenly asked to change the entire nature of their relationship.

The pairing makes sense.

Both are smart, much smarter than the typical Ocean Community members, where physical strength is encouraged over mental acuity. They will be happy. They'll have beautiful towheaded kids and I guess they'll both end up as marine biologists. Again, I find myself filled with envy. The transition will be so easy for Rane. Not only will she not have to wait three extra years to be with her intended partner, she knows him already. She could have done a lot worse. Eddie, although a bit geeky, is a standup guy who is popular, smart, and really kind. My eyes follow them as they walk off toward the base of the mountain. Eddie gently grabs her hand, just a finger at a time until their hands are fully clasped. The blues of their outfits match and they look like a single unit as they walk farther and farther away, disappearing into the distance.

"Bunk 20 Girls—Keeva Tee."

I'm pulled out of my reverie when I hear my name. My Third will soon buzz and I will soon find satisfaction in my intended partner. I stand eagerly, waiting for Camp Director Durant to say, "Your intended partner is," but those words never come. Instead, she reads off a list of two more names in Girls' Bunk 20 and four more names in Boys' Bunk 20: "Mikaela Fleming. Blue Patterson. Kai Loren. Burton Skora. Genesis Kraft. Radar Morton."

There must be a mistake. Shock spreads across my face as I look around at the remaining seven campers. Two greens, a red, a purple, a yellow, a brown, and me.

Anomalies.

"WHY AM I HERE?"

Calix was irritated. He had reluctantly left the game room where he was playing laser holo tag with his friends. His team was winning by two points and he hated leaving his friends in a lurch. But when Sobek beckoned, Calix had no choice but to comply. He followed his father from the ground floor up one hundred levels to the penthouse suite. Sobek's office overlooked the entire city, but Calix was unimpressed by the view. He scanned the city below that was teeming with people. He wished he were one of the masses and could just disappear rather than be the son and sole heir of the world leader. Calix slumped into a leather chair, wondering if his team was still winning. He much preferred hanging out with his friends than his father.

"You need to cut your hair," Sobek snarled.

"I don't need to do anything." Calix undid his ponytail, shaking out his long black hair, which framed his strong jaw. He grinned defiantly at his father.

"It's your choice . . . for now. But all Protectors have short hair and you'll be eighteen soon." Sobek sighed. He was used to his son's recalcitrance and, in the past, he hadn't discouraged it. All leaders need an unbreakable spirit and he had spent the last seventeen years raising the strongest heir he could. Soon, Calix would be tested and if his son could survive the test then his options were limitless.

Sobek waved his hand across the 360-degree view of the city and thousands of holos appeared over the window.

They showed different communities, different cities, different territories.

"How did you do that?" Calix was stunned. He didn't know his father had so much access.

"The information from the satellites is projected here," Sobek replied.

"This is your office?"

"Everywhere is my office, son. In our new, technologically advanced age, I can set up a command center from wherever I am." Sobek held up his wrist. On it he wore a sleek identity watch. "Satellites collect information from every citizen's Third. The information is sent to my identity watch and I can watch who I want, when I want."

"So, you're spying on everyone?" Calix got up and slowly wandered around the perimeter of the room, trying to view the thousands of changing holos.

"Spying is such a negative word," Sobek said.

"What would you call it?"

"Observing. Gathering. Protecting." Sobek looked at his son, "How do you think we keep everyone safe?"

"I don't know."

"Start thinking son. There is a complex system set into place and it will need a complex mind to control it."

"Like I said, you spy on everyone."

"There isn't enough time in the day. I have underlings who do that for me. They are located on floors 88 to 90. They collect data and send the critical information directly to me." Sobek watched his son's amazement as he tried to take in all the holos. "I'm planning to give this to you."

Calix stopped at a holo. His dark green eyes settled on a small group of teenagers standing in a cluster in what looked like a large campground. "Exactly what are you giving me?" Calix finally asked, his eyes glued to the tall freckled redheaded girl with the sad eyes who stood in the center of the circle.

"The world, my son." Sobek grinned, "The world."

3.

I am stunned.

We all are. Our silent shock is interrupted by the petite girl in the green overalls who won't stop crying. No one moves to her, no one helps. Our lives have all been seemingly condemned with this unexpected new label.

"How can I be an Anomaly? I'm so popular," she spits out between sobs, not caring how ridiculous she sounds. She curls up on the ground in a ball, bawling so hard it looks like she is about to throw up.

"Popularity has nothing to do with it, Mikaela. Don't you know your history?" A boy in drab olive-green work clothes mutters as he protectively puts his arms around her, enveloping her in his large frame. I admire the way he instantly comforts her, as if he is rescuing a wounded bird. The boy with the square jaw is also an Anomaly, yet his concern is not for himself but for her. A selfless act. They are both from the Ecosystem Community and they practically blend in with the environment. Two small dark figures camouflaged by their green clothes in the tall grass.

"The person you're supposed to imprint with is probably dead. That's why you're here. It's why we're all here. We don't have a partner. We're individuals. We're not connected to anyone," he says, gesturing around to the rest of our ragtag group.

"But it's not fair, Genesis."

"Life isn't fair," Genesis immediately replies. His voice is soft, so that we must strain to listen to him. He has broad shoulders and the muscles of someone who has spent his young lifetime working in the fields. I watch Genesis kick the small patch of grass at his feet until the earth turns over and makes a brown hole of dirt. I see an almost imperceptible twitch in the corners of his almond shaped eyes. He looks like he is going to cry, but he is clearly trying to stay strong. Ecosystem is the most emotional community and Genesis and Mikaela express themselves immediately while the rest of us are still trying to process. I am envious of them. I want to scream, cry, explode. Instead, I just stay silent and look at my feet.

I don't want to know these people. These Anomalies.

"This wasn't what was supposed to happen." Mikaela continues, "What are my parents going to say?"

I think about my father. What am I going to tell him? Will I even have an opportunity to tell him anything? I am no longer certain of my future. I take in deep breaths, trying to control my fear. I close my eyes and pretend I am swimming. Long rhythmic strokes. Holding my breath for ten, twenty, thirty seconds. I imagine I'm underwater, racing a school of blue-lined snappers. I'm surrounded by the yellow and blue fish, darting in and out of brightly colored coral. I'm . . . I'm . . . I open my eyes. I'm sitting in the middle of nowhere, redefining my life.

I'm an Anomaly. I let out a sudden gasp, the realization finally sinking in.

"There is nothing to worry about," Claudia Durant says. She never looks up from her digital tablet. She forces a smile while simultaneously typing notes. "Ninety percent of Anomalies are quickly imprinted and reintegrated into society."

Before any of us can ask the unanswered question about what happens to the other ten percent, Claudia Durant finally looks at us, as if we are an afterthought to the day's events.

"Like I said, it is all going to be fine." She pats Genesis on the shoulder and it seems like an awkward action for her. She is forcing a compassion she clearly doesn't possess. "I'll be right back. Please stay put. I have to finish some administrative duties and then I will show you to your cabins. We have plenty of time." She gestures to the rest of the camp who has gone off into pairs, "Everyone else is getting acquainted. You might as well do the same."

She turns and I watch her white hair bobbing away into the distance until we are alone. Seven misfits. Everyone else has been paired off and is wandering around with their imprinted partners, buzzing away, feeling good. Rane and Eddie are most likely already kissing by the base of the mountains, and Annika and Dante are getting to know each other—shyly asking each other questions as they collectively begin their life's journey together. All around the camp are pairs of twos who are happily embarking on their futures. The joy is tangible; you can almost feel it in the air. Almost. It is absent in our miserable group of seven who are sitting and standing next to our duffels in the middle of the pitch, waiting.

This has to be a mistake.

Other than Mikaela's incessant sobs, it is almost silent except for the sound of the camp flag flapping in the wind: seven colorful butterflies set in a circle across a stark white background with a not-so-subtle GG in the middle. When I entered the camp an hour earlier and first saw this flag, I had believed that my destiny was set. I would be imprinted with my blue-eyed partner and return to the Ocean Community, marry at eighteen and become a productive citizen. That is what was supposed to happen. I have been preparing for it since I was five. This is supposed to be the best moment of my life.

Instead, it has become the worst.

I'm not alone. The rest of the Anomalies are either staring off into the distance or suspiciously sizing each other up, trying to figure out what to do. How to manage the incomprehensible situation. Finally, a tall boy with bright red high-tops and a booming baritone voice jumps up.

"Well, we might as well introduce ourselves," he says. "I'm Kai."

I quickly realize it's the obnoxious boy who bumped into me. He winks at me, also remembering our initial introduction. I look away. My bad day has just gotten worse.

Kai wears a red tracksuit and red sneakers with white laces, a small act of rebellion considering that we are supposed to dress head to toe in our assigned color. "I mean, we're all probably gonna die, so," he says, imitating Claudia Durant's clipped accent, "*Everyone else is getting acquainted. We might as well do the same.*"

"I don't want to get to know you," I say.

"You've hurt my feelings," Kai jests as he mimes stabbing himself with a sword and dramatically says, "*No, 'tis not so deep as a well, nor so wide as a church-door; but 'tis enough, 'twill serve: ask for me to-morrow, and you shall find me a grave man."*

"Stop it," I find myself shouting. "Can't you see she's scared." Sure enough, Mikaela has gone into a full-blown panic attack and is having trouble catching her breath.

"We're all scared, Beanpole. I thought a little gallows humor might lighten the mood."

I glare at him.

"What? You didn't like my performance? I played Mercutio in the school play last year. I was told that I am an excellent actor."

"I give you two thumbs down." I wish he'd just be quiet.

But he's just starting. He leans over Mikaela, "The only thing we have to fear is fear itself." Kai looks up at me and winks again, pushing a long curly lock of brown hair away from his brown eyes. He grins, an uneven smile revealing dimples and perfectly white teeth.

"You're quoting ancient history," I snarl. He is incredibly arrogant.

"History has a dangerous way of repeating itself, Beanpole." He stands next to me. Way too close. I'm not comfortable when people invade my space.

"Beanpole. Really, you want to go there? You're just as tall as I am."

"Yes, but you're a girl. Didn't know they grew them so big in the Ocean Community."

"Didn't know they grew them so obnoxious in the Renewable Energy Community," I say. This boy is infuriating, and for the second time today, I stand eye to eye with him. The tips of our noses are almost touching: his is long and sharp while mine is short and narrow. I can feel the warmth of his breath and I want to hit him. Now, I'm not a fighter, but if he provokes me, I know that I can take him. I match him in height and I know I am stronger than he is. I'm an athlete and he's just tall. Tall and lanky. Tall and lanky and utterly irritating.

"Relax, Beanpole. I'm just trying to get us to talk to each other. Sitting here quietly isn't going to help us. You know, it's a sin to be silent when it is your duty to protest."

"Protest?" I say quietly, looking around to make sure that there are no Protectors in earshot. "Be careful, talk like that will . . . ."

"Will what? Get me killed? Looks like I'm headed down that road anyway." Kai smirks, "Relax. I'm just trying to make conversation."

"It's not even your own conversation," I snap back. "Now, you're quoting Abraham Lincoln. Isn't that a little old school?"

"I've always been old school. Nothing like learning from the past to better understand the future. Though, I must say, I'm impressed. I thought you Ocean types were all brawn, no brain. Not bad, Beanpole."

"Stop calling me that. My name is Keeva."

"Finally, an introduction! It is a pleasure to meet you Keeva. I'm Kai. Kai Loren. I live about an hour from here in Mid-America. How about the rest of you?"

The girl in purple stretches her legs. She is absolutely stunning. So pretty, in fact, that she almost makes Annika look dull. Almost. Somewhere in her past she has been from part of the Asias. She has long jet-black hair, heavy bangs and her emerald eyes complement her velour mini dress . . . fairly inappropriate attire for a camp. "I'm Blue Patterson." She nods at Kai, "I'm not too far from you. Did you take a helicraft here or drive?"

"Drove. Borrowed my cousin's motorglide."

"Cool," Genesis says.

I roll my eyes. Boys and their cars.

"I'd love to see it," Blue flirts. I have no idea why she is wasting her time with this arrogant boy, unless she is already playing the game of seeing whom she will be imprinted with. She can have him. I have no interest.

"Sure, I'll take you for a ride," Kai says, "Where do you live?"

"Sabbatical City," Blue says noncommittally before adding, "Actually, my family works at the Caesar."

That quiets us. The Caesar is where Sobek Vesely stays when he's in the Americas. It is an enormous palatial structure, which is in the heart of Sabbatical City.

"Do you know him? Vesely?" Kai asks.

"Hardly," Blue says, batting her stunning eyes at him. "My father's the caretaker and my mother's one of five hundred staffers. The place is enormous, I think I've seen him maybe twice in my entire life." She sighs, "It's ironic, me being a Caesar girl and ending up an Anomaly. Though, I think I must have always known. I mean, I was always . . . different from everyone else."

"How?" The short stocky boy in yellow asks, in a genuinely curious voice.

"I dunno. I mean, all of my friends always seemed so . . . content. So happy. Even though we're Labor and mostly work with our hands, I was never into that kind of stuff. I was always more interested in science like the

Ecosystem Community and art and music like the Academic Community. I suppose I was dissatisfied. I never felt whole. But my friends were always fulfilled, like they always had everything they ever wanted. I'm not talking about money or stuff, I'm just saying . . . jeez, I don't know what I'm saying—"

"That you feel incomplete," the boy dressed in yellow interrupts.

"Exactly."

"Me too." He gives her a reassuring look as he squints up at Kai and me. "I'm Burton," he says in a raspy voice. "I'm the only one here from the Academic Community . . . which doesn't surprise me. I mean, our community rarely produces Anomalies and when we do, well . . ." he leaves the sentence unfinished.

"Why are you being so pessimistic?" I say, "We just have to get imprinted with someone new and then we'll be like everyone else."

"Is that what you want to be?" Kai asks, "Like everyone else?"

"Of course," I quickly say. "It's what everyone wants."

"Is it?" Kai locks his eyes with mine. He is really working my last nerve. Why can't he just leave me alone? I wish Claudia Durant would come back already and tell us what the next steps are.

I hate not knowing.

"Look around," Burton says running his hand through his hair . . . well at least what is left of it. Like Protectors, the Academics, both men and women, wear their hair very short. Burton's spiky black hair is so closely cropped to his head he almost looks bald. "The only ones we have left to imprint with are each other. Not much of a selection. And, in case you haven't noticed, there are three girls and four boys. The odds aren't so good if you're a guy." He looks at Kai and Genesis and then over to a muscular boy leaning on his brown duffel who hasn't spoken yet.

We all turn to the boy who is busy with his hands, twisting and tying something. Finally, he stands up and walks over to Mikaela, handing her the object. She stops crying for a second to examine it. It is a beautiful necklace neatly braided together with long grasses and daisies he found next to him in the field.

"I'm Radar," he says, shyly smiling at Mikaela as he gently puts the necklace around her neck. "And if we're going to be imprinting, I want you."

"**D**O YOU LIKE MS. SINGH?" Sobek asked his son when he had finally sat back down.

"She's fine." Calix wondered why his father was asking about his intended partner. It had been two years since Calix had attended Monarch Camp and his father hadn't asked him once about Sarayu. She was a pretty girl from the Academic Community and he spent the requisite time with her: talking on their tablets, looking at each other's holo on their identity watches and planning their futures. Well, he wasn't much on planning . . . Sarayu spent most of the time talking. She'd like to talk for hours discussing their futures, preparing her move from East America to Sabbatical City to be with him. Calix liked her well enough and was content to spend his life with her, but he was currently far more interested in the holos projected on his father's windows. He wondered how he could access them.

He wondered how he could steal his father's watch.

"Just fine?" Sobek lifted his eyebrow. "Isn't it odd that the rest of your friends are . . . what is the term you use? Head over heels. Yet, you feel your intended partner is 'fine?'"

"I suppose. I mean. I've never really thought about it."

"Did you ever wonder why your Third didn't buzz when you were at camp?"

Calix absentmindedly touched his Third, which was encrypted with his father's nanotechnology. Thirds allowed Sobek to gather and disseminate information through the satellites. A way in which citizens could both observe and be observed

"No. I mean, I assumed it didn't buzz because there was a glitch."

"A glitch? My technology doesn't have glitches. I run a well-oiled system."

"Of course you do, sir." Calix wondered how much longer his father was going to take. Usually their father-son chats didn't last more than five minutes. Maybe he could get back to the virtual room before the game was finished.

"These Thirds saved this planet."

"I know. You're a genius, Father." Calix said trying to force an awe he didn't have. He barely knew this man who was responsible for half of his DNA. Calix had mostly been raised by his mother while his father was busy running the world.

"What is the purpose of the Thirds?" Sobek asked.

"Thirds are used to collect data and to connect to holo transmissions," Calix's answer was rote. "They track visuals. The Thirds make every citizen responsible for his and her own actions." He'd been learning this information since he was a child. His mind wandered back to his friends. He wondered if they had started a second game. He was happiest when he was playing virtual games with his friends. It was one of the only times he could escape the reality that he was Sobek's son. He preferred to be a regular teenager. He wanted to fit in, like everyone else.

"Son. Are you listening?" Sobek's voice was hard.

"Yes, sir. Look, I'm royalty right? I suppose my intended mate is inconsequential. So it doesn't matter if she's fine or fantastic. And Sarayu is fine. She's great even. But she will simply breed my children. My primary purpose will be to eventually help you run this place, right?"

"This place?" Sobek looked at his son. Could he really be that daft? "When you graduate next year, all of your friends will join their intended partners. What will you be doing?"

Calix thought for a moment. He had never considered that. He just assumed his father had a plan for him. He now realized, his father was revealing the plan. Calix settled back into the chair.

He was never going to finish the holo laser tag game.

4.

I am a pariah.

An outcast. A reject. Persona non grata. We all are. We are kept separate, as if we are diseased.

We sleep separately, eat separately, and do separate activities. Although it is by chance rather than fault that our predestined matches have passed away, we are misfits in the system, and we have to be reprogrammed to survive in the new world. We have to start over.

Claudia Durant does not go into details, but she assures us that it is not our fault that we are Anomalies. We are simply operating outside of a very well-oiled system, and it is her intent to integrate us as quickly as possible. Durant explains that we will soon be imprinted with a suitable match, and we will lead lives as productive as those of our friends who have already been imprinted. The unfortunate thing, she tells us, is that protocol dictates we must take a series of tests to determine for whom we are best suited. This means we will not have a "normal" camp experience; rather, it will be filled with tests to assess our compatibilities: both with a community and with our intended partner.

Our instructors are all Protectors, the elite unit that enjoys a higher status than the six work communities, Labor, Agriculture, Ecosystem, Renewable Energy, Ocean, and Academic. The Protectors are all employed in different levels of the Global Governance from mediacasters up to Sobek Vesely's high-ranking bodyguards. Only one in one hundred people is asked to be a Protector; you are either born into the community or handpicked by the world leader himself. Protectors are the eyes and ears of Sobek Vesely, and my entire life I have grown up slightly in awe—and in fear—of them.

Now, they are my counselors.

Claudia Durant instructs us every morning. We wake at six for a jog around the perimeter of the camp, eat a quick breakfast, and then suffer through monotonous morning sessions filled with the history of the GG. I've heard all of this before, but that doesn't seem to matter to Claudia Durant. Every morning, she drones on and on about people's selfishness and how it almost led to total world annihilation. She explains to us in a patronizing tone how the Great Technology War, also known as China's war with the US and Russia, was over in a matter of minutes. The actual "fighting" was made up of three sides pushing buttons and millions dying—dying over ignorance and greed. She reiterates how the nuclear fallout of The Great Technology War nearly destroyed our oceans and animals, and how Sobek Vesely stepped forth and offered us a solution: a new world without war. A world where dissent is a thing of the past and everyone is compliant, happy, and satisfied. A world where information and protection come from a new form of technology

ANOMALIES

called a Third, the technology that Sobek patented and generously gave to the world.

On day four, Claudia shows us a propaganda holo, the same one I've watched every December on Emancipation Day, showing Sobek introducing the data chip which, in addition to connecting them to the mainframe satellite system, uses a newborn's DNA as a way to imprint the GG citizens with an intended partner who will satisfy and complete them. The holo shows satisfied couples all over the Americas smiling with their newborns as each baby receives his or her Third. The film ends with everyone holding up their fists and repeating Sobek's most famous motto: *With satisfaction comes happiness, and with happiness comes peace.*

Today is the sixth day of listening to these endless lectures and I want to scream. I get it. I've seen it. Why do I need to hear it again? I just want to find Annika and Rane and talk to them. I want to go home to my father. Since the minute I was old enough to understand language and use my Third, I've been listening to how Sobek Vesely and his Global Governance saved our planet from destruction. So why am I forced to review the lesson? Is this because I'm an Anomaly? Is that why I need to hear about this repeatedly? Are they so afraid that I am going to revolt because I am different? I feel just the opposite: I just want to fit in, to get imprinted, and forget this ever happened.

Forget that I was ever different.

Every day that Claudia drones on and on about our history I want to shout out that I am bored. That I know every fact she is going to say about our past. But I stay quiet. We all do . . . except for Burton, who antagonizes her by ceaselessly asking questions. I suppose it's in his nature because he's from the Academic Community, but it's not good to stand out so much. Yet Burton refuses to stay quiet. I know he's annoying her because every day she shows less patience with him. And Protectors are known for their patience.

It's what makes them so dangerous.

In the afternoons, Claudia's sub-instructors give us a series of daily tests that are meant to assess both our inclination toward a Community as well as our affinity with each other. Inelia is an older woman with gray eyes and long silver hair, which she wears in a tight braid. I guess she missed the memo that says most Protectors have short hair. Hers is gorgeous and hangs defiantly down the center of her back. She has a slight limp and uses an ebony cane, the color of her skin. But Inelia isn't an invalid, she's just the opposite. Even though she is one of the oldest counselors, she is unusually spry. In martial arts training, she uses her cane with the skill of a practiced black belt. Even Radar, who is a Krav Maga expert, is no match for Inelia who flattens him every time we do hand-to-hand combat.

I've never done martial arts; luckily I pick it up unusually quickly. I learn better by observing, and I realize that combat is less about my own strength than anticipating my opponent's moves. Within a few days, I can beat everyone, including Radar. I'm not sure why I've absorbed the skill so quickly, but I know that if I look into my opponent's eyes, I can predict their moves just seconds before they act. So I react and deftly take them out. Kai is the most fun to beat and I flatten him every time. His cockiness irritates me, and on the mat, I can let out my aggression.

Inelia instructs us in all things physical: archery, martial arts, rock climbing, cliff rappelling, and swimming. I'm the best at swimming, naturally, and easily win every race. Kai is a distant second simply because he's a good athlete and the rest of the Anomalies don't even come close. Most of us lap Mikaela, who can barely doggie paddle. Seriously, what kind of fifteen-year-old doesn't know how to swim? Though I'm not sure how being a great swimmer is going to help me imprint. It just proves that I belong in the Ocean Community. As far as imprinting, well, the prospects of who I can imprint with are weak.

Max is the other instructor. As kind as Inelia is, Max is the polar opposite. Tall, dark, and extremely handsome, Max's beauty belies his brutality. He too carries a cane, but it isn't to help him walk. If we hesitate even slightly during mental acuity tests, he whacks the back of our legs and arms with the stick. It is a sadistic and antiquated form of punishment, but Max prefers it over the more sophisticated methods, such as electric shocks or neurotransmitter therapy. Most Protectors are old-school barbaric that way. They prefer the intimacy and immediacy of inflicting physical pain. It's why all executions, and they are quite rare, are hangings. There are gallows in every city to remind citizens of the consequences if they challenge the Global Governance.

The last three hangings all involved people from the Academic Community who questioned Sobek's authority. Poor Burton, clearly a product of his community, suffers the brunt of Max's wrath because he drives Max crazy with his ceaseless questions. Burton's skinny little legs are covered with welts from Max's stick. It's savage, but Protectors have a reputation of being savage. Kai has somehow become Max's favorite, and the rest of us fall somewhere in between the two extremes.

What I like most about Max's lessons, however brutish they may be, is that they challenge my mind. Each day, he concentrates on a different skill which I have never learned. Which I never thought important. Skills the average fifteen-year-old would have no clue how to handle.

"What is your name?" Max snarls as I sit across from him at the class on Interview Skills.

"Keeva Tee." I respond, looking out the window where Blue is giggling with Kai. I can't explain why she bothers me so much. Maybe, it's because she seems to be throwing herself at him. It's gross.

"Focus." Max snaps. "When you interrogate someone, eye contact is important at all times."

"I thought this was a lesson on interviews, not an interrogation." I respond.

"What's the difference?"

"Well, an interview is to learn about someone and an interrogation is . . . ." I hesitate. I've only seen interrogations on vids. Usually it involves terrorizing a helpless victim to get information from them. I'm not sure what to say.

Max stands up, waiting for me to answer. He walks around the table, standing behind me. I am sufficiently intimidated and can feel the hairs on the back of my neck stand straight up as he leans on my chair, breathing down my back. I cannot see him, but imagine the scowl on his face.

"It's . . . an interrogation is . . . ."

Thwap. Max's cane comes down on my hand causing the skin to immediately welt up. "What's an interrogation, Keeva?"

"It's when someone uses scare tactics to gather information." I try to control my breath, I don't want to cry in front of this man. In front of this monster.

"Now was that so hard?" he says.

I leave my hand on the table. I won't give him the satisfaction of seeing me in pain.

"Interviews are standard Q-and-A sessions where you get information. Interrogations are where you get the truth," Max says simply as if the earlier moment had not transpired. "They are interchangeable when you learn how to do them correctly, and the key skill, on either side of the table, is eye contact. When you look someone in the eye you can tell if they are lying. Now, lie to me."

"What?" Is this guy for real? Is he looking for another excuse to smack me with his cane?

"I'm going to show you how I know you are lying. I'm going to ask you three questions. Lie in two of them, and tell me the truth in one. First question: what is the name of your best friend?"

"Um . . . Cecily."

"No." Max snaps, "I'm not going to even count that one. Don't 'um' before you answer, it immediately gives away the fact that you are lying. You also had a verbal disconnect. You were nodding as if to convince me it was the truth. It was not. Next question. Who is your least favorite person at Monarch Camp?"

"You."

Max laughs, surprised and seemingly impressed by my answer. "Truth. Tell me about a time you did something you shouldn't have done."

"My father said not to swim past the reef until I was ten, but once at the age of eight, someone challenged to see if swimming past the reef was possible. And it was hard to resist. The current was really strong and a fisherman had to come to my rescue."

"Lie."

"How do you know?" I am amazed. I had looked into Max's eyes and felt very convinced as I told the story. It could have happened. My father did warn me not to swim past the reefs, and a fisherman had saved Annika once from almost drowning. I just combined the stories.

"You rarely used the word "I." Most teenagers start every sentence with I. You were psychologically distancing yourself from the lie. You also fidgeted. Next question. Tell me your scariest memory and why."

I answer immediately, careful to use *I* in my sentences, and not to nod my head or fidget, "I am terrified of snakes. I was once hiking in the caves with Rane, and when we sat down to rest, a snake was coiled up next to me. I was so scared, I screamed. It wasn't a poisonous snake. Rane knew because she knows everything, but I was terrified."

"Lie."

"How can you tell?" I am now annoyed. I thought I was lying perfectly.

"One. You cleared your throat before you started as if you were performing. Two, you pulled on your ear."

"I don't understand, you could tell I was lying by the way I pulled on my ear?"

"Ear, hand, lips . . . any of those are a tell. A change in your behavior that gives clues to what you're doing. I asked you a question, you had anxiety when coming up with the lie, and anxiety triggered your autonomic nervous system to go to work to dissipate the anxiety. So, while you were lying, blood drained from the surface of your face, ears, and extremities and created a sensation of itchiness. You didn't realize it, but your hand inadvertently went to the area." Max is so smug that I want to grab his cane and hit him. Instead I obediently thank him.

"Lesson over for the day. Now send the next Anomaly in."

On the seventh day, I finally get to see my friends. They do their best to cover their disappointment that I'm an Anomaly, but I can see it etched in their faces. I bite the inside of my cheek to stop myself from crying.

"I'm so sorry," Rane and Annika say in unison, rushing up to me. It's cinema night, and it is the first time we are allowed to mingle with the general camp population. Most of the kids are inside the theater with their imprinted partners, but we remain outside. Inside the auditorium, I can hear their terrified screams. They are watching some old-fashioned vid involving chainsaws and blood. I'm not in the mood for a horror film, especially when my own life is turning into a horror story.

I've been so lonely that when I hug my friends, I don't want to let go. I have so little in common with the other Anomalies. Mikaela, when she's not crying, is fairly stuck-up and narcissistic. Blue is so busy playing the game of who she is going to imprint with that she has little time for me. She has her sights on Kai because he's cheeky and fun; however, Genesis is handsome and down to earth, and she seems to like him too, so she's playing for both of them. I'm not drawn to any of the boys. Burton talks too much, Radar only has eyes for Mikaela, Genesis is too shy to get a read on, and Kai is . . . well Kai is the most irritating boy I've ever met in my life. It is as if he has made it his life's mission to antagonize me.

"It's fine. It will all work out," I say stoically to my best friends, knowing that my life will never be the same again. Sure, for the next three years I'll go back to the Ocean Community to finish secondary school, but once I turn eighteen I will be reassigned to my new partner and my new life. Anomalies never follow protocol and instead are usually reassigned to a different community.

I sit on the picnic bench and look down. Even I don't believe my lie. It won't work out. There is no way I will be assigned to my beloved Ocean Community.

My friends hold my hands, silently giving me strength. I have to figure something out. I can't just wait for my life to be dictated to me, I have to take some action. At least Genesis lives in West America, which is sort of close to the Ocean Community. He works on a farm in a place called Cabo San Lucas; it's only a few hours on the bullet train. I convince myself that it doesn't matter if I don't connect with the shy boy from the Ecosystem Community; he will have to do.

"I'm probably going to be imprinted with Genesis. He's nice. Quiet, but nice." I hesitate as I think about the possibilities of sharing a life with Genesis. I know it could be a lot worse. "He's very kind. I mean, he's always helping everyone else and he's also cute. He's definitely the cutest of everyone. He's strong and it would be nice to have an intended partner who could carry me over the threshold when we get married." I can't help myself as I giggle over the antiquated notion.

"But Keeva," Annika whines, holding the sound of the 'a' at the end of my name like a screaming banshee, "We're all supposed to stay in Ocean together."

"I know," I say trying to keep a stiff upper lip. "So, no chance in you guys switching to Ecosystem, is there?" I ask hopefully, knowing their answer.

"Dante's from Renewable Energy, but he wants to come to Ocean," Annika says, almost apologetically.

"And Edward's already an Ocean, so . . ." Rane leaves the obvious answer hanging in the air.

"I know," I say, forcing an enthusiasm I don't feel, "Just thought it was worth a shot. Hey, at least I'll still be near the water. There's an Anomaly who actually lives in Mid-America. Landlocked, ugh."

"He's not the tall boy, is he?" Annika asks.

"Yeah, the rude one who bumped into me that first day. Why?"

"He's gorgeous." Annika blushes before quickly adding, "I mean, my Dante is handsome, and I'll be completely devoted to him, but . . . wow, that guy is so good looking. I mean, he's gorgeous."

"He is?" I ask in disbelief. I've never thought of Kai as gorgeous.

"Have you even looked at him?" Annika asks incredulously.

"Looked and listened. He never shuts up and he thinks he's so much smarter than everyone else."

"Who's so much smarter than everyone else?" Kai walks by and interrupts our conversation.

"You are," I say, turning my back to him.

"Actually, Keeva was just talking about you," Annika says mischievously.

"She was?" Kai grins and my friends practically swoon. I have no idea why they think he is so cute. I just don't see it. He's tall, and I suppose there is something charming about his crooked smile. Maybe I just can't get past his arrogance.

"Well, I hope she's not boring you by talking about how much she likes me." He playfully pushes me on the shoulder and starts to leave.

"Shouldn't you be watching the vid?" I ask.

"Shouldn't you?" he grins.

"Where are you going?" I ask.

"I want to check out MC-5." He points to the Victorian building, which stands ominously in the distance. "I mean, aren't you guys curious what goes on in there? Why it's off limits?"

"No," Rane says. "We were told not to go there, so why would we?"

"Wait," I turn to my friend. "The first day of camp you said you wanted to check it out. You were insistent."

"No I wasn't." Rane looks at me like a stranger.

"Rane, it was one of the first things you wanted to do. You told me you were definitely going to go there. You hate when people tell you that you can't do something."

"I didn't."

"But . . ."

"Don't put words into my mouth, Keeva." Her words are clipped, tinged with an anger I haven't heard before.

"OK, my mistake." I say carefully, unsure of what has happened to my once overly curious friend. I was standing next to her exactly a week ago when she was determined to check out the building where we spent time when we were five.

"So, you guys coming or not?" Kai asks.

"Not," Annika and Rane say in unison.

"Not," I repeat, although a part of me wants to. I'm not as comfortable with my friends as I thought I'd be. Something is *off* with them.

"Suit yourself, Beanpole." Kai smiles and walks toward the building.

"Ha," Rane giggles. "He has a crush on you. You guys would be perfect together."

I don't understand. A second ago, Rane was yelling at me for putting words into her mouth and now she's pushing me together with Kai.

"First," I say angrily, "Kai Loren is the last person in the world, I would ever imprint with, and second, he's an Anomaly. He couldn't have a crush on anyone if he tried. Neither can I. We don't fit in. Our Thirds don't buzz. We won't achieve true happiness and tranquility. Until we're fixed, we're enemies to the Global Governance. Worse than that . . . we don't count."

I guess my retort is a little angrier and more pathetic than I think because both Annika and Rane give me a funny look. Maybe it's the first time that it really sinks in how different I am. How different my future will be. We hug goodbye, and they go into the building to find Dante and Edward. In a few minutes, they'll be screaming like everyone else. In a few hours, they'll be back in their beds with the other normal campers. Tomorrow, they'll participate in usual camp activities like bonding on the rope courses, building fires and making macramé bracelets: activities regular campers do. And I'll go back to my indoctrination. Claudia's lectures. Inelia's workouts. Max's mental tests.

So much for a relaxing summer camp experience.

"**W**HAT DO YOU INTEND TO DO with your last summer before graduation?" Sobek asked. He sipped the tea his third assistant Rika brought him. He liked the girl. She was young and ambitious. The way he wished his son were. "I'm waiting."

"I've been working on my technologies," Calix said excitedly. He had inherited his father's scientific skills, and he loved engineering new technology in his workroom. He also loved hacking into the palace's mainframe computer, but he elected not to share that particular information.

"The time for play is over," Sobek announced.

"It's not play, father, I'm discovering—"

"The only thing you have to discover is your place in this world. And this summer, I'm taking it upon myself to educate you . . . properly."

"What does that mean?"

Sobek tossed his tablet to his son. Calix caught it easily, snatching it out of the air with his left hand. He had always had lightning-quick reactions, a skill that helped him in his favorite mental and physical games.

"Type in 09-21-2047," Sobek instructed.

"That's my birthday," Calix said, quickly typing in the number.

"And people accuse me of not being sentimental," Sobek grinned as he looked at his watch, typing in a few numbers himself.

"What are you doing?"

"Transferring the data from my watch to the tablet. It's just about time. Now, type in Academic. That's 2-2-2-3-3-6-4-2."

"About time for what?" Calix said as he typed.

"Your first lesson." Sobek smiled and looked up at the monitors as the thousands of holos disappeared, giving way to one image.

Calix looked up at the holo. He saw a lone young woman standing on a platform with a noose ringed around her throat. She was in her early twenties and stood fearlessly, her face set in a rigid mask. Calix could not identify exactly where she was, but there were mountains behind her. A group of citizens, mostly clad in yellow, stood around the platform, and Calix's eyes immediately went to a man, not much older than he was, who was standing off to the side. He was trying to remain stoic; yet Calix could see his red-rimmed eyes beneath his spectacles.

"What has she done?" Calix asked his father.

"Dissented," Sobek replied. "She is a secondary-school teacher who was advocating revolt. She was the head organizer of an insurrection against the Global Governance."

"She's so young." Calix could not get over how proud she looked. Unapologetic. He had never seen anyone face death before, and he hadn't imagined it would be like this.

"Do not let her youth fool you. She is extremely dangerous. The woman was tried by the Protectors and found guilty. Her act of rebellion will be a lesson that her community will learn the hard way."

"What lesson is that?"

"Type in your name, son: 2-2-5-4-9."

Calix did so. When he punched in the last number, the trap door under the condemned woman's feet slid open. Before Calix realized what he had done, before he digested the atrocity his father allowed him to commit with his own hand, the condemned woman fell through the trap door.

And her neck snapped.

5.

I am nervous.

After only one week, Mikaela and Radar imprint and leave the group. I'm there when it happens. All the Anomalies are. We are eating breakfast as Claudia Durant enters with a huge smile taking up most of her mannish face.

"The test results from week one are in. And congratulations are in order." Claudia Durant never stops smiling. "We have our first match. Mikaela Fleming, your intended partner is . . . Radar Morton."

Mikaela is sitting next to me and she lets out an excited squeal. I then hear her Third buzz and watch as a deep serenity spreads over her face. I quickly grab her hand. On the surface, it appears like I am congratulating my fellow Anomaly, but the reality is I want to feel the vibration. To try to understand what is happening. Sure enough, once my fingers clasp hers, I can feel the energy radiating from her Third down to her fingertips. It's the same buzz I felt when I was holding Rane's hand. How does this happen? I understand that our Thirds are used to collect data and to connect to holo transmissions . . . but I've never seen them alter one's personality. This must be part of the imprinting method. When two people are so connected that they cannot live without each other, their Thirds have a reaction. Out of the corner of my eye, I see that Kai has his hand on Radar's shoulder. Is he conducting his own experiment? I guess I'm not the only one who has noticed the odd behavior. Kai looks at me and I nod, giving him silent credit for also figuring out the strange phenomenon.

Mikaela and Radar stand up and hug each other, and we all clap half-heartedly for their success, biting back our jealousy. Blue doesn't even hide her frustration. She simply sits there and sulks. Mikaela and Radar's match only magnifies the fact that the rest of us are still failures in the new world's perfect system.

"Mikaela, you will be reassigned to Bunk 7 Girls, and Radar, you will be reassigned to Bunk 7 Boys. You will have two hours to reunite with your intended partner and explore the camp before continuing on to your assigned bunks."

I'm surprised by Claudia Durant's phrase. They've already been "reunited." They've known each other for a week. Why do they need two more hours? I don't understand. She said the same thing to them as she had to the rest of the campers on day one. No changes. No permutations. The same speech.

When Claudia finishes reciting her monotone pronouncement, she excuses the new pair. Mikaela and Radar smile giddily, grab hands and leave the dining hall.

And then there were five.

Five square pegs trying to fit into round holes. By the end of the second week, Claudia Durant's lectures are over because there is no need for them anymore. Time is a luxury we no longer have: it is ticking away and more than half of the session is over. We have less than a week to imprint.

Our days are filled with tests. Max takes us through mental calisthenics that continuously increase in difficulty. I don't know what is worse, Max's nearly impossible mental acuity tests or the insanely boring multiple choice questions we fill out every day. They are so lame and monotonous that I practically fall asleep trying to answer them all.

The simple questions are all formulated to ask me about . . . me. I'm fifteen years old, how am I supposed to know who I really am? Most of the questions give three choices:

Are you A. talkative, B. silent, C. a combination of both?

Are you A. frank, B. secretive, C. a combination of both?

Are you A. adventurous, B. cautious, C. a combination of both?

Are you A. sociable, B. reclusive, C. a combination of both?

I have absolutely no idea so I keep choosing C.

As simplistic as the multiple question tests are, Max's mental tests keep getting harder. One day, he tells us to pay attention as he shows us a vid of a group of children playing under a wind turbine. It is a ten-minute vid that starts off innocently enough. It has music that sounds like an old-fashioned carousel, and shows a boy whose friends leave him alone in the desert, where he befriends an inanimate wind turbine. The music then gets darker to show the boy's fear and confusion. Suddenly, the turbine comes alive and speaks in a robotic voice, giving the boy confidence and encouraging him to enact revenge on his bullying friends. The turbine then uses his energy to kill the boy's mean friends for abandoning him.

When the lights come up, I look around. Everyone seems highly disturbed by the vid. What was the point of Max showing it to us? Our instructor hands out tablets on which we are to type five answers. If we answer correctly, the rest of the day is ours to do with as we please. If we answer incorrectly, we will watch another video and the process will be repeated.

I smile. How hard can the questions be? As disturbing as the vid was, it was fairly ordinary, and I both understood it and paid attention to it. It should be an ordinary comprehension test, yet Max's questions are anything but ordinary.

"What color shorts was the lead bully wearing?"

What kind of question is that? How can I remember the shorts color? It wasn't part of the story. Still, I put down red for renewable energy as the boys seemed to all be from that community.

"What time was it on the main boy's watch when the bullies left him alone?"

"Wait a minute. How are we supposed to know that?" Burton asks.

"Because you were supposed to pay attention," Max barks, before clipping him on the shin with his cane. He doesn't even wait before asking the next question.

"How many turbines were in the closing sequence?"

I want to scream. The closing sequence of the vid must have had over a dozen turbines. The question has nothing to do with the story. Frustrated, I put down "many."

When the exercise is over, none of us have gotten all five questions right. All of us got the first one right and

Kai and Blue each got three right, Burton got four, and Genesis and I each got two right.

So, we watch another vid.

This goes on for close to ten hours. Each vid is progressively more disturbing, and I try to tone out the warped messages, which is usually some variation that one needs a partner to survive in the world. Instead, I concentrate on the minutiae, counting stripes on shirts and paying attention to numbers and colors and details.

Burton is excused after three videos when he gets a perfect score. Blue is excused after four videos. Kai, Genesis, and I are coming closer and closer, but still not attaining perfect scores.

"It's past dinner time," Genesis finally complains. He rarely speaks up, but he is voicing what we are all thinking. How can we concentrate if we are hungry?

"One final vid. No, actually, you three seem to be incapable of simple detail recollection, so let's see how you do with emotional recollection."

"What do you mean?" Kai asks. He is tired. We are all tired.

"Turn your chairs away from each other. Now draw the person in this room who evokes the strongest emotional bond. Couple your heart and your mind to recreate the person. Do not look at each other. You have fifteen minutes to draw your interpretation of the person. If you are successful, you can leave."

Fifteen minutes later, we stop drawing on our tablets. We hold them up for Max's inspection. I have drawn Max, capturing not only his beauty—his tousled hair, his penetrating eyes, his full lips, his high cheekbones . . . I have also managed to accurately capture his compassionless brutality. His cruelty. His savagery. His evil.

Both Kai and Genesis have chosen the same person. Thick red hair, light blue eyes, a narrow nose and hundreds of freckles. They have both chosen me. Like my depiction of Max, they have captured something inside of me. Something which they have brought out through their pictures.

Genesis has captured my beauty, but Kai has captured my strength.

After scarfing down a cold plate of leftovers in the dining hall, I enter Girls Bunk 20, the designated Anomalies bunk, which now seems even emptier since Mikaela left. The wooden bunk at the end of the lane is sparsely decorated and most of the metal bunk beds are empty. There are now only two girls in a bunk meant for twenty. I nod to Blue who is painting her nails and I change my clothes next to the wall of shelves. I fold my blue outfit neatly into the assigned cubby and put on my sleep suit. Blue has already changed into a purple lacy nightgown. The girl has the weirdest fashion sense. With all of my blue clothes and all of her purple clothes, the shelf looks like a big bruise.

"How was the rest of your day?" Blue asks. She seems distracted.

"Long. Kai, Genesis, and I pretty much failed Max's attention detail test, so he finally gave up on us. I'm zonked." But rather than go directly to bed, I take her attempt at conversation for an invitation to chat. When

Mikaela was also in the bunk, she was the buffer between me and the usually standoffish Blue. Now, we have to fend for ourselves, and being polite will cause the least amount of conflict. I even join her on her bottom bunk bed. She offers me a bottle of nail polish.

"But it's purple," I say.

"Look again." She smiles. I examine the bottle and sure enough it's an eggshell blue.

"What are you doing with this?" Like our clothes, we are relegated to accessories in the color of our Community.

"I have the entire rainbow." She smiles and pulls out a small, purple polyurethane bag from under her pillow. Every color is there: yellow, red, green, orange. . . . It is beautiful.

"You could get into so much trouble." I pull out a bottle of bright orange and giggle.

"I could. But I think we're both already past the point of no return." She grabs the orange from me and defiantly paints her pinky. She then grins at me, waving the brush, and with competition in her voice says, "Dare you."

I don't hesitate and I paint my thumb orange. We start laughing and pulling out all the bottles, rebelling in our small way by painting each of our fingers a different color. To anyone observing, we'd look like two teens giggling before bedtime.

Only we know how precarious our situation has become.

"We're not like other people, you know," Blue says, blowing on her fingers to dry them.

"I know." The brief moment of levity has been ruined. Every day I am reminded that I am an Anomaly; I don't need Blue to reiterate it for me. I concentrate on my maroon ring finger, enjoying the beauty of the rich velvety color. "Yesterday, Annika barely looked up when I passed by. It's like she's totally moved on. And she's my best friend."

"*Was* your best friend," Blue interjects. "Friendships get redefined when one of them is an Anomaly. So do families. My sister is a bigwig in the palace; she's going to absolutely freak when she finds out I'm an Anomaly. She could even lose her job. My parents too. This is a huge black mark for my family."

This is the first time I've seen Blue unguarded. She's almost likable.

"What about your friends?" I ask.

"Just like yours. They're all brushing me off. I came to Summer Solstice with four kids in my class at secondary school. They're not my best friends, but they're friends. Good friends. Kids I've known my whole life. I even play in the band with two of them."

"You play music?" I realize Monarch Camp is nearly over and I know virtually nothing about Blue.

"Played music. I don't think they'll want me in the band now. I play both acoustic and electric guitar. I'm pretty good, but that doesn't matter when you're an Anomaly. The guy who plays keyboards is already snubbing me. When I get back, they all will. I don't even bother any more. It's like this camp has created all of these cliques. Your Bunk, your Community, your intended partner's Community. I suppose it all comes down to two-person cliques, and I'm not a part of any of them."

"You're an elite member of our clique of five," I joke. But it's not funny. Blue, Genesis, Kai, Burton, and I are definitely members of a club no one wants to join.

"What happens to us when camp is over, Keeva? What are our options?"

"I don't know. I mean, I guess I haven't thought about it that much. I suppose I haven't wanted to think about it."

"Start thinking," Blue says as she hands me nail polish remover. She's already wiped off her rebellious colors. I reluctantly wipe mine off as well, first taking a mental picture of what it looks like to be multicolored. To express my individualism.

"Did you know your grandparents?" Blue asks.

"No." I wonder where she's going with this. "They died in the Great Technology War. All old people did."

"Or did they?" Blue pulls out a worn photograph which is rolled up in one of the nail polish lids. She hands it to me. I see a smiling young man, who looks a lot like Blue.

"Who is this?"

"My grandfather." Blue hesitates.

"Tell me, what are you hiding? I promise I won't tell anyone."

Blue wavers before eventually confiding in me. "My grandfather is alive, Keeva. I don't know where he is, I think somewhere in the Asias. But he's alive." Her eyes are filled with hope.

"How do you know?"

"I get . . . messages from him. I can't explain it, maybe they're just feelings. But I'm telling you he is alive. Sobek tried to wipe out our past so that he could create a new future, but in doing so, he wiped out generations of knowledge."

I'm in shock, still trying to understand how Blue's grandfather is still alive. We are only two generations removed from The Great Technology War. Could there be others out there? Survivors?

"Keeva, focus. There is so much we don't know, except that we have to be matched with an intended partner to get out of here. We have to survive this."

"What do you mean, survive this?"

Blue looks around, to make sure no one is listening. But the bunk is still silent. She beckons to me and I follow her as she gets down on the floor, wiggles underneath the bed and shines a headlamp on words delicately carved into the wall. Three words of warning carved by a previous tenant of the bunk. A previous Anomaly.

Conform or die.

"SHE'S DEAD?" Calix asked in disbelief.

"And you were the one who killed her," Sobek said.

"But I . . . I . . . ."

"What? Didn't think she deserved it?" Sobek asked cruelly. "You have no idea what people deserve and what they don't. You've built up too much compassion living here."

"What are you talking about? Why did you make me do that?"

"It's time to make a man of you, Calix. Your mother has coddled you for too long. You have a destiny, and it's not hiding in your little workroom trying to break into the mainframe."

Calix looked at his father in disbelief. "How did you—"

"What? You think I didn't know? I know everything. I am right about everything. I am beloved by all. And soon, very soon my son, you will be, too."

Calix was fairly sure his father was wrong about that.

I am changing.

We now spend more time on mental tests than physical ones. I am beginning to ace Max's tests. I can spot a lie, recall details, and quickly process situations and problems. When our instructor is finally satisfied by our newfound skill set, he turns us over to Inelia for a daylong hike.

The area is beautiful and for a short time, I try to forget I am an Anomaly. I attempt to ignore that my life is in an upheaval. I just enjoy the fresh air and beautiful mountains. Even Kai doesn't annoy me as much as he usually does. We are the most athletic of the bunch and race each other on the trail. The others are far behind mostly because Blue wears sandals instead of sneakers and everyone keeps waiting for her. Everyone except for me and Kai. He's almost tolerable as he makes me laugh, telling me stories about his six younger brothers back home who are desperate for him to become a Protector so they can have bragging rights.

"Do you want to be a Protector?" I ask as we wait for the others at the base of the mountain. I hadn't even considered that option for myself. It could definitely be a way that I could return to the Ocean Community. I never really saw myself as one of Sobek's crème de la crème, but it would certainly allow me to gain back some normalcy. I could live near my ocean. Near Annika and Rane. Near my father. Protectors live among the communities as Sobek's eyes and ears. They enjoy elite status as bankers, media, governance officials, and politicians.

"I don't know," he says earnestly. "My parents have a lot of mouths to feed and we're not exactly rolling in money in Renewable Energy. Everyone uses solar power; it's not such a lucrative field. I never really envisioned myself working in a factory my whole life, making solar panels, and I hate the thought of my younger brothers being stuck indoors. They're so active and full of life. If I can, I'd like to help them."

For the first time, I detect vulnerability in "Mr. Know-It-All." When Kai lets down his guard, he can be somewhat charming. Even likable.

"Everything has a price," I think aloud. "I'm sure being a Protector comes with its own baggage."

"Maybe, but at least the Protectors don't have boundaries. Sure, they report to Sobek . . . but they have a lot more freedom than the other communities."

"I have freedom in the Ocean Community," I say defiantly.'

"Do you?" His eyes almost dance when he talks. They are a deep chocolate brown and I suddenly notice small specks of gold in them. "I mean, the ocean is magnificent, but it's also your prison. You're tied to it. You can't go anywhere else. You can't do anything else."

Instead of waiting for my response, Kai starts the climb up the mountain. That's the kind of boy he is, someone who makes a ridiculous, definitive statement and then leaves me to figure it out. I turn, wondering if we should wait for the rest of the group. We've already hiked ten miles, and Inelia told us that we were going to climb to the top of the summit. But we are supposed to climb as a group. As a bonding experience. I sigh. Maybe it's better not to follow the rules all of the time.

I follow Kai.

At first it is a gradual incline and I easily keep up. Yet, as the path narrows toward the top, it becomes almost vertical. I glance down and can see the rest of the group starting the ascent. They look like tiny specks in the distance. I quickly turn back to my task so that I don't get dizzy. I have a slight fear of heights, which I would never let on . . . especially to Kai. I don't like anyone to know my weaknesses. Slowly, I scale the rocks, hand over hand, until I reach him. We climb together and, after being cooped up with so many tests, I love feeling the strength of my own body as I navigate up the rocks. Then, as we are nearing the top, I slip. My foot misses the toehold and I am thrown off balance. My arms flail, trying to grab a piece of shrub, a rock, anything. As I am about to fall, several thoughts rush through my head including the fact that I'll never see my father again, never grow up, never have a family of my own. . . .

"Got you, Beanpole." Kai's large hand grasps my small wrist, preventing me from falling to my death. I start to panic, breathing quick shallow breaths, but he never loses his calm as he reaches for my other hand.

"Look into my eyes," he says calmly. "And don't forget to breathe."

Yet, I seem to want to look anywhere but those chocolate brown eyes. Instead, I turn my head and manage to fix my gaze on the ground, which looks a million miles away. I start to feel faint. My other hand feels sweaty, and I am losing my grip. I am going to fall. I don't have to worry about being an Anomaly because I won't be around to see what happens.

"Keeva!" This time Kai is shouting. I can feel him squeezing my hand, his fingers digging into my palm, hurting me. The pain focuses me and I quickly turn my attention back to his eyes. Only then am I able to reach my other hand up to him. Slowly, Kai lifts me up to safety and deposits me in an indentation in the rocks.

As I catch my breath, Kai's large hand never leaves mine, quietly steadying me. I am grateful for the support.

"You OK?" he asks.

I nod, not trusting my voice. "Thank you," I finally say shakily. "I think you just saved my life."

"I suppose I did." He grins, "Guess you owe me one." He resumes climbing. I don't hesitate too long, afraid if I do that I will lose my courage to continue the climb. I can see the rest of the group behind me. I doubt they even know how close I came to plummeting past them. Slowly, hand over hand, foot over foot, I ascend until I get to the top. Kai wordlessly hands me his canteen and we drink in silence, overlooking the vast expanse as we wait for the rest of the group.

Inelia is the first to arrive and the rest of the group is just behind her. They have no idea that I almost died and we don't tell them. Instead, everyone makes small talk until Burton finally brings up the question we are all dying to ask, "Inelia, what happens if we don't imprint?"

We all look at our instructor, who hesitates a bit too long before answering. She wipes the sweat from her brow,

"There are a few rare reasons that Anomalies don't imprint. Sometimes your Thirds aren't functioning properly. Sometimes your DNA is compromised. Sometimes . . . ." She lets her sentence trail off as if she is lost in thought, but she quickly recovers. "Look, you are all going to be fine."

"You didn't answer my question," Burton pushes.

"Didn't I?" she asks a bit too glibly. "Look, just stick with the program." Inelia says this as a warning, a way to end the conversation; yet Burton has zero social skills and doesn't stop talking.

"What does that mean?"

My instincts are instantly on high alert and I can suddenly read Inelia's thoughts. They are clear as the ocean. Burton is going to die. There is a high chance of it. Kai and I are next in line. Genesis and Blue are less likely, but the possibility is there. I look around. Is no one else hearing this? I watch as Inelia purposefully does not answer Burton's question, instead, she nods to the far side of the mountain. It is an easy jaunt, and the five of us follow her over the makeshift path through the shrubbery and rocks. I spend most of the climb trying to engage Genesis in conversation so that I don't have to deal with the information I just discovered. How did I hear that? Inelia didn't talk. She didn't even look at me; yet, I heard her thoughts . . . clear as day. I use all of my energy to feign interest as Genesis tells me about his farm. He is a genuinely nice kid, and I concentrate on how to pair up with someone whom I am not in the least bit attracted to. This focus keeps me from questioning my own sanity and the voices I heard.

Finally, at the far side of the mountain, we rest and wait for Inelia to tell us more. We drink water from our canteens as Inelia furtively looks down at camp and then back to us. She motions for us to cover our Thirds and she does the same. Technically, it is not legal to do this, but since Inelia is a Protector we obey her without question.

"What's going on?" Kai asks. He looks silly with his thumb covering his Third.

"Thirds don't work on the periphery of Monarch Camp."

"I thought they worked everywhere." Kai says.

"Sobek would like to make you think so," Inelia smiles, "But there are certain dead zones. Remote areas the satellites can't reach. Underground, the desert, certain parts of the forest. . . ."

"—But Sobek wouldn't let that happen." Blue insists.

"Technology is a rapidly evolving beast. There is so much data to absorb already that having a few places off the grid isn't necessarily a bad thing."

"But it doesn't make sense." Blue says, "How can he run the world if he has blind spots?"

"Because it also means that Sobek has a few areas where he is unaccountable." We let that information sit for a bit. What Inelia is saying could be considered treason. It means that Sobek could potentially do things so terrible that even he does not want someone to possibly monitor them.

"If we're off the grid, than why are we still covering our Thirds?" I ask. "Because you can never be too careful." As if heeding her own warning, Inelia lowers her voice. "One of the reasons that the Global Governance has been successful is that there is no dissent," Inelia whispers even though there is no one around for miles. "In the GG, there is no room for independence or discord. In the rare cases of dissent, people are punished by the Protectors, who operate with impunity. They answer only to Sobek, who is accountable to no one. However," Inelia lowers her voice even more, as she says, "There are Underground Societies around the world. People who are unhappy with Sobek's rule. People who want their independence back. They are members of secret societies who are planning a revolt."

I am shocked. This information was never given in our history lessons. We've always been told that the reason we live in peace is that our society works. Sobek's Monarch Camps ensure that we imprint with our perfect mate and create perfect children. These successful pairings have ensured a world devoid of violence, disease, hatred or impurity. This is the first time I am hearing about secret underground societies, and I am stunned into silence. So is everyone else.

"I've heard about the Underground Cities," Burton finally says. "It's rumored the main one is right in Sabbatical City."

"Yes," Inelia says quietly, even though there is no one around for miles, "It's led by Sobek's sister."

"What? Whoa. How come we were never told this," I blurt out. I am shocked my instructor, my Protector instructor, is sharing subversive information.

"No one knows about the Underground except the Protectors, whose mission is to eradicate it. To stomp it out."

"Why would people want to revolt?" Blue asks.

"Because this world is not meant to be perfect." Inelia sighs, "Creativity, innovation, and abstract thought all work when people don't think alike. Sobek is creating a submissive culture of people who all think the same."

"What you're saying could be considered treason," Kai interrupts.

"Yes," Inelia agrees, "it could. That is why I am warning you all that you must conform to the system or you will be—"

"Recycled." I find myself saying the word that Inelia is thinking.

"Yes." Inelia smiles at me, unconcerned that I have just read her thoughts. "You must assimilate if you want to survive."

"Conform or die," Blue says, echoing the warning in our bunk walls.

"Yes. You must conform, otherwise, you will be recycled. Sobek will find a place for you, but I promise you that it is a place you never want to be. Physically or mentally. Look, I've already said too much, but you need to know that you can choose to fit in. It's important that you know you have a choice," Inelia warns before motioning for us to move our hands away from our Thirds.

And she gives us something to consider that we've never had before.

A choice.

"Keeva." I feel someone shaking me. I am sound asleep and I don't want to get up. "Keeva, get up." I open my eyes. Kai is standing over me.

"What are you doing here?" I whisper, quickly looking around the quiet bunk. Blue is sound asleep. "You shouldn't be here, Kai. You could get into trouble."

"I know." He smiles mischievously. "C'mon, it's our last night of camp. Let's go have some fun." I barely hesitate. I slip into a pair of shoes and pull a sweater on. Even though the days have been hot, the nights have been incredibly cold.

Kai and I sneak out of the bunk and walk silently through the dark camp.

"Where are we going?" I ask when we are out of earshot from the bunks.

"You'll see." Kai pulls me past the helipad toward the empty government buildings. Lined up against the closest building is a row of motorglides.

"I promised you a ride," Kai says as we get to his bike.

"Actually, you promised Blue a ride," I say, remembering their flirtation the first day of camp. Blue has barely left Kai's side all week, probably hoping that the instructors will take note of how good they look together. I'd be the first to admit that they make a striking couple. So why isn't Blue here with him instead of me? More importantly, why did I agree to come?

Kai doesn't argue. Instead, he smiles his cockeyed smile and pulls off the tarp covering his motorglide, an aerodynamic black machine with silver handlebars. He pulls out two bright red helmets from the tank bag and hands me one.

"You think I'm gonna trust you to ride that thing?" I say. Am I flirting with him? Where is this coming from?

"If you can't trust me, who can you trust?" Kai continues to hold out the helmet. I hesitate.

"What are you so afraid of?"

"That I'm going to die," I say, before realizing how silly that sounds. My fate is going to be decided in just a few hours and death is one of the options awaiting me. I roll my eyes as I realize the irony of my statement. "Sure, why not." I grab the helmet and put it on.

I watch as he easily swings his long legs over the sleek machine. I get on behind him, gently putting my hands around him.

"You're going to have to hold on tighter than that, Beanpole," he says as he floors the engine.

I am almost thrown from the seat by the instant speed, and I wrap my arms tightly around his waist as we fly across the salt flats. It's exhilarating. Kai drives over a hundred miles an hour, and it's the closest thing I have ever felt to flying. Every problem, every worry, and every thought flees from my head as I feel the cool wind and the thrill of the speed. Finally, after about twenty minutes, he stops. We are in the middle of nowhere and probably violating every camp rule possible, but I don't care. Kai climbs off the bike, but instead of helping me down, he gets right back up behind me.

"What are you doing?"

"It's your turn."

"No way," I protest, trying to shimmy off of the bike, but Kai holds me tightly. "Live a little, Keeva. What you don't try can't hurt you."

"That's what I'm afraid of!" I say, but I relax onto the bike and let Kai teach me. "All you need to know are the clutch and the brake." Kai moves my left hand over the handlebar. His hand envelopes mine. "This is the gear and this is the clutch. The left side is for shifting."

"Let me guess," I say, "The right side is for braking."

"You are a remarkable student, Miss Keeva Tee."

"Thank you, Instructor Kai Loren. What else do I need to know?"

"That's pretty much it. Release the clutch and hit the accelerator. Oh, and don't forget to breathe."

"Breathe. Sure. No problem," but I take a deep breath and then slowly let the clutch out. "We're moving!" I scream.

"We are," Kai is amused. "Now, you know how to drive a motorglide. Wanna go faster?"

"OK." I let go, relishing the feeling of being in the moment. Most of the time, I feel like an observer. I watch everyone and everything, never quite belonging anywhere. Well, anywhere except for the ocean. But swimming is something I do, riding like this is something I am. I am one hundred percent a part of the action and it is overwhelming . . . in a wonderful way.

I feel so alive.

Finally, I brake the bike, and we both climb off and lay down on the salt flats, looking up at the unadulterated sky. There are billions of stars twinkling above us. It is spectacular.

I feel free.

We lie in easy silence for a long time before Kai finally speaks. "These used to be called the Bonneville Salt Flats, and it was one of the best race tracks in the world. Drivers used to come here from all over the world to try out their cars here."

"How do you know?" I ask, though I shouldn't be surprised. Kai has clearly studied history, both the approved and the unapproved version. "My grandfather used to race," Kai says sadly. "Before the Great Technology War, he was one of the best in the world. Built his own machines. Our family lives so close to the flats that he used to bring my dad here all the time when he was a little boy. Being here, I feel closer to him. I never knew my grandfather, but I don't think he'd approve of what's happened with the world."

"What do you mean? The world is fine."

"Is it?" Kai sighs. "I'm not so sure. I mean, look at the rest of the campers, Keeva. It's like they've been brainwashed. I've noticed it with most adults, frankly, with most people after they get back from camp. Their Thirds buzz and then . . . ." his voice trails off.

I want to tell him that I've noticed the same thing. Annika and Rane are like different people. Come to think of it, most adults are that way: happy, compliant, satisfied. I sense Kai wants to talk some more. So I just listen.

"Theoretically, I like the idea of a world without war. But a world without conflict? It scares me to death. As humans, we're not wired that way. We are meant to feel and think and have opinions and disagree. How can there be progress if everyone's purpose is to serve the same philosophy? I think . . . I think Sobek Vesely and the Global Governance are dangerous. After camp, I'm going to try to find the Underground City."

"What if something happens to you?" I say before realizing how invested I have become in this boy. I turn and study his gold-speckled brown eyes, trying to figure him out. He's like an older brother. Why do I suddenly care so much about him? I don't know, I just do.

"I can't keep living this way, Keeva. It's a lie. I have to do something. I can't just sit by and watch. I have to take responsibility."

I'm not sure how to respond, but when I feel Kai's hand slip into mine, I don't resist. We look up at the stars. Holding hands. Thinking. My mind drifts as I connect the stars into patterns, remembering my lessons on planets and constellations. I am aware that I am conflicted with new feelings. Is this possible? Am I suddenly feeling emotions for the arrogant boy who rubbed me the wrong way from the second I met him? No. He is a friend, a brother, a fellow Anomaly. Nothing more. But I feel safe with him, and there is a comfort in that safety.

We lay there for the next several hours, enjoying the peaceful quiet. Just before sunrise we get back on Kai's bike and speed back to camp, getting back to our bunks with minutes to spare before wake-up.

"**M**OTHER!" CALIX BURST INTO HIS APARTMENT and immediately wrapped his arms around his mother's waist. He could not stop crying.

"Shh. What happened?"

"He's a tyrant," Calix managed to blurt out between sobs.

"Do you want him to see you like this?" But Anya Vesely did not pry off her son's arms, instead she let him wail into her. "Shhh. Shhh. It's going to be fine. You are going to be fine, my boy."

"Mother," Calix said again as he suddenly ripped himself from the protective embrace. His anger was taking center stage over his disgust and horror. "Do you know what he's capable of? Do you know what he does? Killing innocent people—"

"How do you know they're innocent?" Anya asked softly.

"That's not the point. He doesn't even have the courage to kill with his own hand. He's . . . he's a coward."

Calix did not expect the slap from his mother that cracked across his jaw.

"Why did you do that?" Calix reached up to his stinging cheek.

"Sobek Vesely is not only the world leader; he is your father and I will not have you say anything incendiary about him." Anya then nodded to her house servant who excused herself and left the living room. Anya returned her attention to her son, kneeling down so that she could look directly into his eyes.

"Listen to me very carefully, Calix," Anya said, an urgency entering her voice. "Your father and I had a deal–"

"What do you mean?"

Anya sighed. There was no easy way to break the news to her son. She'd been wanting to tell him for weeks, to warn him, but she hated the idea of him losing his innocence, so she remained silent. But now the time was here. Sobek had played his hand by involving Calix in an execution. It was typical of Sobek, not playing by the rules. She sighed again. She had already lost him. Anya stood up and surveyed her boy who was on his path to manhood. "Your father wanted to indoctrinate you into the ways of leadership when you were young, a child of five or six. However, I convinced him to let me raise you until you were well into your teens. I wanted to give you a normal life, son. I wanted you to have normal friends, normal experiences before. . . ."

Anya let her voice trail off. This was not going to be easy.

"Before what?" Calix demanded.

"You are the heir apparent, Calix," Anya said mustering all of her strength. "And with great power comes great responsibility. From now on, your life as you know it will no longer exist. There will be a new normal for you that you must accept, embrace, and excel at. I have done my part in giving you a well-balanced perspective so that, perhaps when the time is right, you will instinctively know the clear path to take."

"I don't understand, Mother." Calix felt as if this were a goodbye. The one constant in his life had been his mother. Why was she speaking to him so strangely? What was she saying?

Anya walked over to the windowsill of the large ground-floor apartment. She stopped in front of a bright white flower, sitting in a crystal bowl of water. It was in full bloom. "Remember what I told you about the lotus flower, Son."

Calix rolled his eyes. For as long as he could remember, his mother had taught him about plants. He knew how to use them to heal, to kill, and everything in between. "Of course. The *Nelumbo nucifera*, or the lotus flower, can live for over a thousand years and has the rare ability to revive after stasis."

"Yes." Anya reached into the pocket of her black tunic dress and pulled out a small pouch with a string around it. She placed it around her son's neck. "The lotus seed. For you to always remember that in the deepest darkness can come the most beautiful light. The greatest gift of the lotus flower is to bloom brilliantly, even though it grows out of the mud." She put her hands on Calix's shoulders and looked into his deep eyes. "You are now on a journey, Son. And like the lotus flower, it may sometimes feel as if you are surrounded by mud and darkness . . . but know that you are capable of growing beyond. Don't let your eyes fool you. For sometimes deep below, can rise up something quite magnificent. Sometimes, it is only when you become blind that you can really see."

As if on cue, the house servant entered from the bedroom, carrying two packed duffel bags, which she placed by the front door.

Anya gave her son one last hug before stepping away. "You are to live with your father from now on. You have a world to run and it is agreed that Sobek will be the one to show you how to run it."

"But I don't want to, Mother," Calix insisted.

"I don't care what you want," Anya said, willing a harshness to her voice which she didn't feel. "Get out. It's time for you to stop being so soft. You're nearly eighteen. It's time to start being a man."

Calix didn't recognize the cruelty coming from his mother. Her words were more painful than the slap. He tried to look into her eyes to find a glimmer of kindness; yet there was none. Eventually he picked up his bags, hesitating at the door. "Goodbye, Mother."

Anya turned, not trusting herself to respond. She did not want her son to see the tears streaming down her face. She had made a deal with Sobek, and he had come to collect. All of her hard work in raising her son with love and empathy was now in the hands of Sobek. She only hoped she had given enough goodness to Calix that he could endure his father's evil.

When Anya heard the door shut behind Calix, she returned to the windowsill and picked up the beautiful bowl that hosted the lotus flower.

And smashed it into the ground.

7.

I am excited.

The entire camp is gathered in the auditorium for Sobek Vesely's visit. Most of us have never seen the world leader in person, and we line up at the helipad awaiting his arrival. Some of the campers have been up since daybreak, claiming their places in line closer to the landing pad to catch the first glimpse. The Anomalies are standing near the back. It's not that I'm not curious; I am. I just don't want to lose any more precious sleep just to stand in line and wait. It seems silly. Plus, today my fate will be decided, and I really don't want to have a few extra hours to worry.

I can see the helicraft as it comes over the mountain. Everyone cranes their necks to watch the sleek black metallic craft as it descends onto the pristine salt flats. The dichotomy of nature and technology is almost unnerving as the craft descends. For a moment, the bright sun reflects off of both the helicraft and the flats, causing everyone to shut their eyes. It feels almost as if the craft is trespassing. Almost. I feel Kai's hand grab mine and I don't pull away. I smile gratefully at Kai, gaining comfort from his touch as the whirring blades echo noisily.

Holding hands like everyone else, we almost blend into the crowd of two by twos.

The doors of the helicraft open. Like everyone else, I am excited to meet Sobek Vesely. It is tradition that he visits every session of Monarch Camp and gives a speech to the campers on the last day. After the craft settles, I can easily make out Sobek's tall stature. He steps out, quickly followed by two Protectors. A helicraft landing just behind him holds four more Protectors who quickly form a perimeter around their leader. The minions are all burly men and women clad in black, boasting stern expressions. Even though he is surrounded, Sobek Vesely stands out in his small crowd. He is a head taller than his bodyguards and is unafraid to smile. As he bobs his head up and down, acknowledging everyone, it doesn't take me long to realize that the smile is a lie.

Sobek Vesely is standing forty feet away from me. My world leader is a great and powerful man. At least I have always believed so because I have been told this in my history books. My teachers have preached it. The media has supported it. My father has confirmed it. Yet, looking directly at him, I am quite aware that there is something slightly off. Sure, he is composed, attractive, and certainly radiates power, but he is devoid of emotion. Despite his enormous, hundred-watt smile, his eyes are completely dead.

I watch closely as he walks from the helipad to the auditorium, blatantly ignoring the campers who have lined up to see him. He is the biggest celebrity in the universe, and kids have been waiting since early morning just to have a chance to catch a glimpse of him up close. I see a thin girl, a shy brunette whom I slightly know from the Ocean Community, step out of the line and attempt to approach him. Sobek's goons quickly box her out, causing her to trip. Sobek Vesely doesn't even turn around. The girl's intended partner helps her up, but neither one of them seems upset by what has just transpired. They don't seem to notice his behavior. I do.

I've been noticing a lot of things lately, especially about my instructors. I've never really had any experience with Protectors before Monarch Camp. The ones in the Ocean Community mainly spend time at the Desalination Plant and keep their distance from the rest of us. I always thought it was because they were better than we were, but maybe it is something more. I've had a lot of time to observe my instructors up close and all three of them, even Inelia, behave differently than everyone else. They are more defined as individuals. Also, I never see their intended mates. All the other counselors seem to pair off, but not my instructors. They all operate on their own, without someone else helping to define who they are.

What is it about being connected to one's intended mate that makes one lose his or her identity?

Ever since they've been paired up, the other campers seem to have a collective docility. I suppose that it's fine that they are always content to be with each other, but their contentedness has dulled their curiosity and spontaneity. The first day of camp, only three weeks ago, everyone was buzzing with anticipation: a bunch of strangers and individuals. In less than a month, the atmosphere is much different. The campers have become unemotional. Detached. Self-Absorbed.

"Sobek's not what I expected," Kai whispers as we enter the crowded auditorium, finding seats in the back row.

"I know. He's . . ." I can't find the right word. It's treasonous to speak ill of our world leader; yet, every instinct I have makes me want to run as fast as I can from the camp. Where is this instinct coming from? I want to leave; however, there is nowhere for me to go. We are surrounded by a mountain on one side and acres and acres of salt flats on the other three sides. It's topographically impossible to escape . . . unless I was a practiced mountain climber or could live without food and water for a month. I take a few deep breaths, trying to control my spontaneous panic attack. What am I freaking out for? I shake it off and smile at Kai, aware that several campers are within earshot. "He's certainly a surprise." I turn my attention to the world leader and wonder what he is going to say. Sobek stands behind the dais, waiting for everyone to stop their chattering. When the room is finally silent, he begins his speech.

"Butterflies begin their lives as worms," Sobek Vesely smiles a toothy smile, "and worms are . . . ugly." He pauses, waiting for the requisite laugh and the audience easily complies. Vesely is quite charming. His disarming nature allows him to easily win over the crowd who are intoxicated by his casual manner and dulcet voice. "Worms represent undeveloped potential. Just like the potential I see in all of you." He winks while gazing at the front row where Annika is sitting, and I see her blush.

I miss Annika. I miss my best friend. I haven't really spent time with her since our interaction at cinema night

ANOMALIES

and it's not like I haven't made the effort. I sneak away to her cabin every chance I get, but she's far more interested in her relationship with Dante than spending time with me. She's changed. A lot. Rane has, too. My best friends still look the same and have the same character traits and quirks, but they have become completely self-absorbed, both in themselves and in their future spouses. Dante and Edward have become their entire worlds, and I am just a nuisance, an outsider they politely tolerate.

"Metamorphosis. Life is about metamorphosis," Sobek continues, adeptly speaking to the entire crowd of campers and counselors, making sure to make eye contact with each person. "And life truly begins once you have made the transformation from an immature form to a fully realized adult. After insects cocoon, they are reborn as beautiful butterflies. Citizens, you are now butterflies. Your parents have all attended Monarch Camp and were imprinted to create you, my beautiful butterflies. And one day, you too will create your own beautiful butterflies."

Wait. Did he just call us beautiful butterflies? Seriously? I look at Kai and he rolls his eyes. He is just as baffled as I am. This is our world leader? He sounds crazy. Beautiful butterflies? We're not small children, but he's talking to us like we are imbeciles. Yet, everyone seems to be lapping it up . . . campers and counselors alike. I feel like there is this daze over everyone at the camp as they are nodding idiotically at our leader.

"Today, you will receive your butterfly tattoos. I know how exciting this is for all of you. A day you have been waiting for your entire lives. With that tattoo, comes your official entrance into the GG: A society free from the threat of terror. Safe from war and secure in our quest for peace. One world. A single universe run by the Global Governance. Nurtured and commanded by me."

Sobek is clasping his hands together over his head, cheering for himself. I can feel the lust of power radiating from him. What is wrong with him, and why can't anyone else see it? Are they so brainwashed that they don't know he sounds like a dictator? They are just sheep, following the herd.

"What if we don't want to enter the Global Governance?" a solitary voice asks. The entire camp turns and looks at Burton, who is now standing just a few seats away from me and addressing the world leader. Burton is not intentionally defiant, just genuinely curious.

"What is your name, Son?" Sobek asks, the practiced smile never leaving his face.

"Burton Skora . . . Sir." He adds the sir as almost an afterthought.

"Well, Burton Skora. There is always a choice." Sobek exchanges looks with Claudia Durant, who gives the leader an almost imperceptible nod. "Why don't we have a chat about it later?" Sobek returns his attention to the captive audience and continues to spew his propaganda. "Across the world, in the Asias and Australia, children are at Monarch Camps. They are also receiving their tattoos and officially becoming citizens of our new world. International brothers and sisters joining us on our universal quest for peace. I welcome my new citizens, just as I welcomed your parents and will welcome your children."

He bows and everyone jumps to their feet. Kai, Burton, and I are the last to stand and I only do so when I feel Inelia pinch the back of my neck so hard that I have no choice. Blue and Genesis stand without any prodding. They seem to be buying into the system.

So why can't I?

After Sobek addresses the camp, he meets with the five remaining Anomalies separately. Apparently, this is customary. Our entire fate is decided in one ten-minute interview. Talk about needing to make a good first impression. We are prepped before the meeting: Max preps Kai and Genesis, Claudia Durant preps Burton and Blue, and Inelia preps me.

Inelia and I take a walk along the perimeter of the lake. She puts her arm on my shoulder and the touch is electric.

"It is time for you to overcome your ego, Keeva," Inelia says quietly, even though we are alone.

"What do you mean?"

"If you erase the self, there is no you, just infinite possibility."

"Wait, why are you talking in riddles?" I ask. "This is the most important meeting of my life. You're supposed to be helping me."

"I am, Keeva. Stop questioning and start listening. When you meet with Sobek, you need to think beyond the small picture of yourself. Beyond your own wants and needs. You have an opportunity here, which few people have. Especially the few daughters of the Ocean. It is finally time for you to listen to your heart."

"But . . . how do you know?" I blurt out, but Inelia only smiles and continues to walk. I've never told anyone about the instincts I have—not even Rane and Annika. Definitely not my father. It's like a psychic ability where I sometimes know things are going to occur before they do. This doesn't happen all the time, but it's been happening more and more . . . especially since I've come to camp. For most of my life, I've worked so hard to silence this instinct so that I can be like everyone else that I often forget it's there. But Inelia knows. Somehow, she knows.

One of Sobek's bodyguards appears in the distance and beckons to us. It is my turn to meet with the world leader. Inelia suddenly speaks to me with an urgency I've never seen before.

"We're counting on you, Keeva. All of us. You have no idea how incredibly special you are, but it all comes down to this moment. This is your final test and you must listen to your heart. Trust yourself."

She escorts me to Claudia Durant, who is waiting for me just outside of the cafeteria. The camp director gives me a terse smile before opening the door. I don't think she likes me, but there is nothing I can do about that. I guess if there is anything I've learned from Monarch Camp it is that it doesn't matter if anyone likes you. Burton and Kai certainly don't seem to care if they are liked. They just are who they are. And the rest of the campers only seem concerned that they are liked by their intended partner. No one else. I used to be so desperate to be liked by everyone. To fit in. Now, it all seems so pointless.

I follow Claudia Durant into the cavernous room where I immediately see Kai sitting at a far table with Sobek Vesely.

He looks completely at ease. They both do, and I swear they are laughing. I can feel myself holding my breath. I'm surprised that what I am most worried about is not me, but Kai. I don't want anything bad to happen to him. There are rumors, terrible rumors, that if Anomalies cannot reintegrate into society, they are recycled . . . which I believe is just a euphemism for killed. I don't want Kai to die. I feel a lump at the bottom of my throat. Kai is the only person I can really relate to here. Kai and Inelia. I shudder, thinking about my conversation with my instructor. I can't get her warning out of my head. The last person who told me to listen to my heart was . . . no, there can't be a connection. I close my eyes and try to rid myself of the memory of my baby sister and that horrible morning all those years ago.

I wait in the corner of the large room and watch as Kai and Sobek Vesely shake hands. Annika was right—Kai is handsome. So tall and self-assured. And when he smiles, there is a mischievousness behind his eyes. I feel lucky that he is my friend. As if he can read my thoughts, Kai looks in my direction and winks at me before he leaves the cafeteria. I find myself blushing. Why am I blushing? I don't have feelings for Kai. He is just a friend. Then why am I blushing? I don't have time to question my newfound feelings. Claudia Durant is at my side, walking me over to the world-leader's table.

"Have a seat, Keeva," Sobek gestures to the chair across from him.

At a nearby table, Sobek's six bodyguards play holo cards. They furiously tap the air as holographs of cards spread out on the table into formations, and the Protectors slap at the transparent cards to claim their win. I'm a bit awed by the entire situation and I stand there stupidly. He motions again for me to sit down.

"Caffeine?" He nods to Claudia Durant, who is still standing at attention. She brings me a steaming cup and leaves. "Three sugars, right?" he asks while dipping a silver spoon into the sugar bowl and doling out three spoonfuls.

"How did you—"

"I'm the world leader; I know everything." He looks serious before cracking a smile, "Your instructors told me. I'm a bit of a sugar addict myself. Tell me about yourself."

I drink my caffeine, using the action to stall, a tactic I learned from my father. I don't want to talk about myself. Is the point of this interview simply to exchange pleasantries, or is it to determine my future? I feel incredibly tense and the immediate caffeine and sugar rush isn't helping.

"There's not much to tell. I'm from Ocean, which you obviously know. I love to swim, which is fairly obvious. I live with my father. We're . . . happy." I stare into the world leader's eyes, somewhat entranced by them. This close, I notice they are almost oblique. Sobek's eyes are completely mesmerizing and once I lock into them, I have trouble pulling away.

"You're an Anomaly. Are you really happy?" he asks scanning my face for a reaction.

"You're the world leader. Are you really happy?" I say without thinking. I don't mean to be sassy or snarky, it just comes out—a gut reaction in a stressful situation.

Sobek laughs, a loud baritone laugh. "Indeed. But I know my place in this world. The question is, do you know yours?"

I pause for a long time before answering. I have another sip of the warm, sweet caffeine. There are so many things I want to say. I want to tell him that I don't trust him. I want to ask why people have Thirds and why they buzz. Why my friends seem to have different personalities now that they've imprinted. I want to scream that I remember the boy who was supposed to be my intended partner. The boy with the bright blue eyes. And if I could just find him, then we can be imprinted, and I can be normal. I want to shout to the entire camp that it's not my fault that I'm an Anomaly, that I can be a good, productive citizen. But my heart is telling me to say something else. And, for the second time in my life, I listen to my instincts.

"Sir, I believe I was made an Anomaly for a reason," I say confidently, silently praying that Kai has given the world leader a similar speech. "I don't know what happened to my intended partner and, frankly, I don't care. I believe that I am meant for bigger things than working in the Ocean Community. I know I can be an outstanding member of the Global Governance if you will give me the opportunity."

"What opportunity is that?" Sobek asks, almost amused.

"Look, I'm stronger than practically everyone I know, and," I hesitate just ever so slightly, "as a member of your Protectors, I believe that I will be an asset to the Global Governance."

"So you think you're Protector material?" Sobek asks.

"I do. People trust me. People like me. I can be your eyes and ears in my community and ensure that the resistance is squashed."

"There's a resistance?" Sobek leans in. It is clearly a test.

"There is. No one talks about it, but we all know it's there. People who are not happy with one world order. Although why people wouldn't be satisfied with world peace is beyond me."

Sobek's eyes gleam. This is the exact thing that Sobek wants to hear. He smiles brightly.

"I've been looking for someone like you for a long time, Keeva."

"Thank you, sir." I smile with false bravado, trying to hide the fact that I am shaking inside. "I believe in peace." I then hold my hand up into a fist, punch it straight up into the air over my head with my first two fingers slightly open into a peace sign, and repeat Sobek's motto, "With satisfaction comes happiness, and with happiness comes peace."

I shake Sobek's hand and smile at Burton, who is waiting for his interview. I barely make it out of the cafeteria before I throw up.

"**H**OW WAS YOUR DAY OFF?" Sobek asked his son.

"Fine," Calix said. His father had gone on one of his routine visits to Monarch Camp and had finally left Calix alone. In spite of this, rather than playing games with his friends, Calix had stayed by himself in his workroom. He could not get the image of the woman out of his mind. The woman he had murdered. The woman his father had manipulated him to kill. And it was all with the swipe of a few numbers. Whoever knew the codes could possibly override the controls. Could possibly save lives. Calix was furious at his father, but he knew he was a dangerous man. And without his mother to guide him, Calix felt alone and unequipped to handle his father's unpredictable savagery. So Calix practiced a trick his mother had once taught him. He masked his anger with aloofness. "No big deal. Did some work. Hung out."

"Did you talk to Sarayu?"

"Sure. We talk most nights." Calix paused, "Father, you asked me why I'm not smitten with my intended partner."

"I did," Sobek said carefully.

"Well," Calix hesitated, "why aren't I? I was talking to her, and she was going on and on about which part of the palace we'd live in and how she wanted two girls and a boy and other trivial things and, well, I didn't really care. I mean, don't get me wrong, I like her . . . but I'm not in love with her. Not even close. What's wrong with me?"

Sobek laughed. He enjoyed the sensation. He rarely laughed, and now he had two belly laughs in less than twenty-four hours—first with the red-headed Anomaly from Monarch Camp and now with his son. "There is nothing wrong with you, Calix. In fact, if you did have feelings for Sarayu, I'd be upset. It would mean that your mother did her job too well in raising you."

"That doesn't make any sense."

"Not yet, but it will," Sobek said. "Tomorrow, your re-education begins. You will be attending the week-long session of Monarch Camp for five-year-olds that begins when regular camp ends. The MC-5 program."

"But I'm seventeen," Calix said.

"Indeed. But you were never properly indoctrinated. Future Protectors rarely are. But to see what kind of world you will command, it is important that you go through the twinning process."

"Twining process? But that would mean I would need a partner to be twinned with."

Sobek smiled. Perhaps his son was not as daft as he thought. He pressed a button on his tablet, and he heard Rika's melodic voice on the other end.

"Yes, sir?"

"It's time," Sobek said, and turned his attention back to his son. Calix was a good-looking young man. Tall and strong with a well-defined jaw and deep-set eyes. He would have a strong media presence in the world. The citizens would definitely respond to him. Sobek's eyes never left his son's face as he waited for the office door to open, until a slight woman with thick black hair rushed through the door and threw her arms around Calix.

"Sarayu? What are you doing here?" Calix's words were muffled through his intended partner's tight embrace.

"Your father wanted to surprise you," she said sheep-ishly. "Are you surprised?"

"Yes," Calix said. His eyes locked with Sobek, silently questioning his father's motive.

"Isn't this fun," Sobek said a little too eagerly. "Tomor-row, we're going to visit Monarch Camp. See the wee ones play. Maybe we'll even stay a few days. Won't that be a fun trip?"

Calix shuddered, ignoring Sarayu's squeals of delight. He had a feeling the trip was going to be anything but fun.

8.

I am optimistic.

I think I may have a chance to still be happy. To be like my friends. If I imprint with Kai and am invited to be a Protector, I can possibly continue my original destiny. I can proceed with the plan I had outlined my entire life. I can go back to my community, and life will go on close to the way it was before.

I am hopeful for my status quo. After my meeting with Sobek, I sit with Blue and Inelia in a small room, waiting for Claudia Durant to tell me my fate. Inelia is nervous about something, and although I want to ask her, something tells me to stay quiet. Suddenly, I hear her voice in my head.

"Can you hear me?" Inelia says. Only she is not speaking. She is looking at me, but her mouth is not moving.

"Yes," I say out loud.

Blue looks at me. "What?"

"Um . . . nothing. Sorry." I turn back to Inelia who is just looking at me. Waiting. I try again. Thinking rather than speaking. *"Yes, I can hear you. What is this?"*

"You have an ability Keeva. It's like a form of ESP. You can hear thoughts, when you are open to hear them. When

you are mentally available, you can get hunches, intuitions, gut instincts that will guide you. Now listen to me very carefully. You are about to be imprinted. Most likely, your Third will not buzz. Your psychic energy is too high. Your brain instinctively knows how to short-circuit the Third so that you can think independently and not be manipulated by the chip. Certain Anomalies are the same way. You must protect yourself."

"How?" I am still stunned that I am having a conversation without opening my mouth. That we are communicating in front of Blue who cannot hear us.

"You know what it looks like when someone's Third buzzes. You felt it with your friends and then again with Mikaela. Act that way. Pretend it is happening to you."

Our silent conversation is interrupted when Claudia Durant enters the room. She is not alone. Kai and Genesis are with her. She is all smiles.

"Bunk 20 Girls—Keeva Tee, your intended partner is . . . ." I look at Kai, smiling because I know that I will not have to pretend with him. He's my best friend here, and even if I don't have romantic feelings for him, we'll have fun together. Even if my Third doesn't buzz, I will be happy to be imprinted with him. I start to stand, but sit back down when I hear her say, "Genesis Kraft—Bunk 20 Boys."

What has just happened? This is not the way it is supposed to be. Clearly, Kai Loren and I are supposed to be together; yet I have just been officially imprinted with Genesis. Destined for a life together.

Destined to be satisfied. Destined to be happy. Destined to find peace.

My Third isn't buzzing and I'm pretty sure why. Genesis is a great guy, but we have no connection. Not the way Kai and I do. I think about Annika and Rane and their intended partners. They are thrilled to spend the rest of their lives with Dante and Edward. The thought of spending the rest of my life with Genesis, instead of Kai, makes me sad.

"Guess it's me and you, Keeva," Genesis smiles as he takes my hand.

"Guess so," I say. I am anxious. Incredibly anxious. The last few hours have been a blur and I can't quite get a grasp on what is happening. Claudia watches us, expecting us to do something. I quickly remember Inelia's warning and plant a smile on my face and will a serenity to flood through my body. Genesis then shyly gives me a kiss on the cheek. This action seems to satisfy her.

"Bunk 20 Girls—Blue Patterson. Your intended partner is Kai Loren—Bunk 20 Boys."

Blue squeals and rushes over to Kai. I stand there stupidly, smiling at them even though inside, my heart is breaking. And why does Kai seem genuinely happy? He looks thrilled that Blue is his partner. Fine. If I mean nothing to him, I can force myself to believe that he means nothing to me.

"And now for the most exciting part," Claudia Durant looks at us, then continues, "The four of you have been invited to join the Protectors."

Everyone smiles, except for me. I am still furious about Kai's excitement over being imprinted with Blue. But I have little time to stew as Claudia Durant quickly rushes us to the flagpole, where the last campers are finishing up getting their butterfly tattoos. Genesis and Blue get their tattoos first. As we wait, I purposefully bump into Kai.

"Hey, you just bumped into me."

"Sorry about that, Beanpole, but how do you know you didn't bump into me?" I say, replaying our first conversation at camp.

"What's the matter, Keeva?" he says. His voice is tinged with something. Is it sadness? Is he in any way upset about his match as well?

"I'll tell you later," I say. But I know I won't, and I sit down in the chair Blue has just vacated.

"Ah, Protectors," the tattoo artist says knowingly as I sit down to be marked. She is the counselor from the Academic Community. An artist. Burton said his mother was an artist. Where is Burton?

I grimace as the jet-black butterfly is tattooed on my shoulder. The needle pierces through my skin and burns me as the black pigment is etched into my left shoulder. I bite my lip in order not to scream. Protectors are tough, so I must now be stronger than I've ever been. This is not the butterfly I want. This is not the life I choose, this is not the intended partner I wish, but I force a smile as the tears gather in my eyes. The artist finishes and moves on to Kai, who is next to me. He elects for a black butterfly with tiny red dots on the wings . . . to honor his original community. Why didn't I think to do that? I could have had blue dots to remind me of the Ocean. Frustrated, I look at the deserted flats. Everyone is packing, readying themselves for the trip home. Was it only three and a half weeks ago that I was declared an Anomaly? It feels like a lifetime ago.

"Do you have any blue left?" Kai is asking the instructor.

My ears perk up and I watch as she opens her ink kit, revealing a rainbow palate of blues from navy to robin's egg. I can't help myself and I start to cry. This is what my life was supposed to be.

"Hey," Kai says, "I thought this would cheer you up, not upset you. Come on, pick the color of the ocean and add it to your tattoo."

Gratefully, I point to the bright aqua in the center of the palate.

"Where do you want it?" the tattoo artist asks. She is bored and clearly ready to pack up.

"Can you make a few droplets of water around the butterfly, like she is shaking it off?" Kai asks.

"That's not really protocol."

"Are you questioning a Protector?" Kai's voice is suddenly authoritative.

"No, sir."

"Good," Kai smiles and looks at me. "Keeva, you're going to get your ocean after all."

Five bright aqua drops of water later, I am done and the four of us walk hand in hand in pairs to the bunks.

Kai and Blue.

Genesis and me.

All three of our instructors pop by to say goodbye as we pack. Inelia gives me a long hug while Max and Claudia Durant shake my hand proudly and welcome me to the elite community. Claudia Durant warns me that none of my relationships will ever be the same. People react differently to Protectors. She shares that she used to be from Labor, and none of her old friends trusted her once she was promoted.

"I've never heard of Labor being Protectors, it's too—"

"Low brow?" Claudia Durant laughs, making her entire face seem soft for the first time all session. "It's true, Labor rarely become Protectors. This happens only on rare occasions."

"Wait," I say, suddenly realizing, "you were an Anomaly?" I am shocked. My perfect instructor seems like she was born into her role.

"All the Anomaly instructors are. Takes one to know one, right?" She smiles, "Anomalies can go one of two ways. They can imprint immediately like Mikaela and Radar. Or, if they are so special that they truly don't fit into any of the communities, Sobek Vesely personally invites them to join Protectors."

"So, you've been where I am?"

"Twenty years ago. In this exact spot." She lowers her collar and shows me a beautiful ebony butterfly with a streak of gold across its right wing. "I was given the gift of joining the Protectors and have dedicated my life to helping other Anomalies."

"But you said there were two ways Anomalies can go. What about Burton? Has he been—"

"We've talked long enough, Keeva." Claudia Durant's eyes close over into small slits, and all traces of conviviality are gone as she cuts me off. "Best of luck to you." She shakes my hand officiously and leaves me both afraid and intrigued by our conversation.

On the helicraft home, Annika and Rane treat me like royalty. In their eyes, I've catapulted from pariah to princess. After a while this gets annoying and I close my eyes, pretending to sleep. Everyone on the helicraft is being extra nice to me. Somehow I have managed to rise from outcast to celebrity in a matter of hours. I am now one of Sobek's elite, a future leader of the Global Governance with a higher status than my friends. A higher status than my father.

I race home to my father who hugs me and congratulates me on successfully completing Monarch Camp. He hands me my bathing suit, knowing how desperate I must be to jump back into the water. How desperate I must be to feel ordinary again. Still, I feel anything but ordinary. As I swim out toward the reef, I try to ignore the raw skin on my newly inked shoulder. With each lap, as I swim farther from shore, I digest what has happened to me and contemplate what will happen to me. For the next three years, I will finish my schooling in the Ocean Community, and then I will imprint with Genesis and we will be assigned to one of Sobek's Protector squads. It all seems so simple. So normal.

But everything is anything but normal.

At night I go to sleep in my own bed and listen to the ocean crashing to the shore. This sound has been like a lullaby to me for my entire life. Yet as soon as I am asleep, suppressed memories come flooding out. I have disturbing nightmares so real, so vivid, I wake up screaming.

Every morning, I awaken in a pool of sweat and am afraid to go back to sleep. My father holds me, stroking my sweat-soaked hair, but that doesn't protect me from my subconscious. The nightmares are the same:

I'm spinning around and around, suspended from a vaulted ceiling, watching the world turn around me. I close my eyes because I'm so dizzy, and I call out for help, but no one is listening. There are grown-ups nearby, tall people in crisp black uniforms, who are laughing and ignoring my cries. I try to move my hands to stop myself from spinning but they're stuck, pressed to my sides and swathed in silk, as if I am in a cocoon. Terrified, I finally open my eyes, which immediately rest on him. His bright blue eyes reflecting in my own. Silently, his look encourages me to be strong. He will be there for me. He will protect me. And, although I can't stop spinning, I know that I am safe. But the boy starts crying. Suddenly, the pain is too much for him. I see hands choking him, and I feel hands choking me. Why? I just don't understand why this is happening. Just when I am sure I will die, the hands let go. I feel a piece of myself leave my body, gone . . . never to return. Someone has stolen a piece of me, a piece of my energy. They are feeding on it, using my energy to make them stronger.

I wake up screaming for them to stop. Begging for them to let me go.

This happens night after night. I can't swim; I can't focus on school or on my friends, only on the dark nightmares that invade my psyche. My mind is opening in ways I don't understand. I see things that are not there. I remember things I shouldn't. I think I'm going crazy, but I'm afraid to say anything. Oddly, the one person I want to speak to is Kai. Unfortunately he is miles away in Mid-America. We do manage to talk every night. We either 2-D face talk on our tablets or I tap his code into my identity watch and his holo pops up so that I can see him in 3-D. We talk, although it is never about anything of consequence. Even though we are not imprinted partners, we are friends. But I am careful what I say to him. I know the Global Governance taps our watches and tablets, and the things I want to talk to him about are too dangerous to be monitored.

What I really want to know is if he too is dreaming about Sobek Vesely feeding off his soul.

"I **T'S EXACTLY AS I REMEMBERED IT,"** Calix said as he looked around Monarch Camp. "Without the campers, of course."

"They're just little kids," Sarayu murmured. "It's late. They're probably already sleeping."

It was past nine o'clock when they arrived at Monarch Camp and Calix reflectively felt himself reach for Sarayu's hand as they exited the helicraft. They had flown alone as Sobek had come to the camp on an earlier craft.

During the short ride from Sabbatical City, Sarayu talked nonstop; yet it wasn't annoying. Calix now found himself somewhat attracted to his intended partner. Sure, he wasn't head over heels in love with her. But anyone could see that she was extremely beautiful. She was also exceptionally smart and immensely curious. Perhaps he could enlist her help in figuring out how to undermine his father's operation. Calix smiled. One step at a time.

"Should we wander around?" he asked Sarayu, squeezing her hand.

"I'd love to, but your father said we should go straight to MC-5," she said nervously.

"I'm not a big fan of doing exactly what my father wants," Calix grinned, stepping closer to Sarayu. They were right in front of the flagpole. He vaguely remembered seeing something about a flagpole in one of the holos his father had shown him a few weeks earlier. Shaking the image from his mind, he concentrated on his intended partner. Sarayu's eyes were tiger-like, green and yellow and constantly moving. Calix wanted to calm her frenetic eyes, which were now clouded with worry.

"Besides, there's nothing more romantic than a moonlight swim. Trust me," he leaned down and kissed her, feeling the warmth of her lips as she kissed him back.

"OK then." She smiled. "Sobek may be my world leader, but you are my future spouse. Let's go exploring."

Calix grabbed her hand and led her toward the lake.

9.

I am terrified.

I smell the smoke before I see the fire.

I am enjoying an early morning swim after having had my first nightmare-free sleep since I've been home. I crept out into the crisp morning, the unusually strong wind whipping against my back as I walked into the water. The cool water feels like a needed salve and, like riding a bike, my muscles remember exactly what to do. I suppress a suspicion that something is wrong. I had a feeling when I got out of bed, but I ignored it. I wanted to simply enjoy the morning.

My mind is completely clear as I focus on my strokes. I've been swimming for close to an hour when I instinctively know that something is truly wrong. My suspicions are confirmed when I come up for air and the smell suddenly hits me: the putrid stench of gasoline and smoke. I turn to my beloved home and see it engulfed in flames.

My father, I have to get to my father.

I pray that he has gotten out, but I can't see him through the thick smoke. What if he is still sleeping? Ever since I've been home, he's been acting strangely. I assume it's because he's worried about me, but he's been up late every night working, which is uncharacteristic of him.

If one word can describe my father it is predictable. He is completely ordinary and predictable, a punctual man who always goes to sleep early and rises early. Yet, the past week he's been up into the late hours of the morning. He keeps mumbling something about being on the brink of a discovery, but when I press him, he doesn't answer.

My arms feel leaden as they try to push against the choppy surf. I swim as fast as I can, all the while watching helplessly as my home goes up in a blaze. I choke on the salty water, trying to swim faster than I am physically able. Breathe, Keeva, just breathe, I say to myself, trying to calm down. When I finally get to the shore, I race to the cottage where I finally see my father. He's behind what's left of the house near a thicket of bushes, unsuccessfully trying to quench the flames. Once he sees me, my father races toward me with a black knapsack clutched in his hand.

"Keeva, you're alive." My father envelops me into his big arms.

"What happened?" I wrench myself free, watching my beloved home go up in smoke. All of my possessions . . . my clothes, my tablet, holos of my mother . . . .

"We don't have much time." He pulls a small object from his bag, "I'm sorry, but this will only hurt for a second." My father turns on a switch on a small handheld electric rod the size of an old fashioned screwdriver. Before I know what is happening, he puts it on my Third and I feel a burning zap that quickly fells me to the sand.

"What was that for?" I say angrily.

"I've disabled your Third."

"That's illegal," I say with disbelief. I'm a Protector now. I not only have to follow the rules, I have to monitor others. I could turn in my father for such a blatant act of treason. Is this a test? I could never hurt my father. But why is he disobeying the law?

"Keeva. I had to do it. This way they won't be able to track you. You have to become invisible," my father says hurriedly, scanning the empty shoreline. He presses a makeshift Third onto my disabled one. A crystalline dot which looks identical to my original Third. "This is for design only, it doesn't work but it looks authentic. They won't be able to track you. Now, you have to go. They'll be here soon."

"Who will? Dad, you're scaring me," I cry and start to shiver. I'm still dripping from the cold water. The air is thick with smoke and gray ash flies off the house, clinging to my wet body.

"Listen to me very carefully." As he speaks, my father takes off his blue sweatshirt and puts it on me before I can protest. "I've been working on a project which is not exactly in compliance with my job as a marine biologist." He pushes the knapsack into my hand. "I just finished last night. I spent a lifetime figuring out the exact answer. It's all here. The contents are invaluable." The wind whipping against the fire is drowning out his voice. "You have to find the Labyrinth."

"Labyrinth?" I can barely hear my father.

"Go to Sabbatical City, Keeva. Listen to your voices."

"I don't understand." What is my father talking about? My father is a rule follower. Someone who preaches protocol. Someone who has spent every day of his life in the ocean, working in the Desalination Plant on toxicology. Now he's suddenly disabling my Third and telling me to listen to the instinct he's refused to accept my entire life. It doesn't make any sense.

"It's a lie, Keeva. It's all a lie. Sobek and the Global Governance aren't protecting us from extinction. They're keeping us docile and complacent. The camps, the water . . . ."

My father's furtive words are now completely drowned out by the hum of a nearby helicraft landing on the beach. "Go. Now. Become invisible. You're not safe, Keeva. You never were."

He quickly hugs me, and then pulls me along to the safety of the bushes. I hide behind the scratchy shrubs, which cut my bare legs with their sharp branches. Through a small break in the undergrowth, I watch as he walks determinedly to the helicraft. I hate how vulnerable he looks. His thin T-shirt is whipping in the wind. The smell of the smoke is unbearable, but I can't leave. I have to see what happens.

My father puts his hands up in the air as the door opens, and two burly Protectors jump out and tackle him to the ground. One of them, a tall, bald man, looks in my direction and starts to walk toward me. My father screams, writhing out of the other man's grasp, as he tries to escape. The first Protector turns back and tasers my father, who crumbles to the ground.

I cover my mouth to prevent myself from crying out as the men lift his broken body onto the craft and fly away. But I know they'll be back. Whether it's for me or for the contents in the knapsack, I don't know.

All I know is that I have to hide before the helicrafts return.

"**D**O YOU THINK YOU CAN GO one day without disobeying me?" Sobek asked.

"I'm not sure," Calix said.

Sobek's men had found him and Sarayu swimming and ordered them to come to the Victorian building, just beyond the lake. But Calix was having such a good time racing his intended partner that he had waved them away.

"Again," Calix said once the men had huffed off. He pushed off the side of the dock and got a head start as he swam across the lake.

"Remember, I live in East America," Sarayu said at the far side of the lake as she beat him for the third time in a row. "I have a bit of an advantage over a landlocked boy from Sabbatical City."

"But I'm the only son of the World Leader," Calix boasted.

"Doesn't make you a better swimmer than I am," Sarayu teased as she splashed him with water.

Calix felt at ease, playing in the water with his friend. He could definitely see a future with this funny girl who wasn't afraid to challenge him. Yet their laughter had been short-lived. Suddenly Claudia Durant appeared at the end of the lake. Reluctantly, Calix and Sarayu swam toward her; and this time Calix purposely swam as slowly as he possibly could.

"Ah, Mr. Vesely. What a pleasure to see you again," Claudia Durant said when they reached the edge. She waited for the pair to climb out of the lake and tossed them each a towel.

"I wish I could say the same, Instructor Durant," Calix said. "But I have a feeling this camp experience isn't going to be as pleasant as the last time."

"Why would you say that?" Claudia Durant demanded. "It seems to me like you are having fun."

"That's because I haven't seen my father yet. I assume he's here."

"He is. He's waiting for you in MC-5."

"C'mon," Calix grabbed Sarayu's hand, only to be stopped by Claudia Durant.

"It is just you whom your father wishes to see right now. It's late. Ms. Singh will be joining Girls Bunk 8."

"She's staying with five-year-olds?" Calix laughed. "That's ridiculous."

"Not too ridiculous. You'll be staying in Boys Bunk 8. I suggest you get going." She nodded to the tall stone building in front of them. "I can tell you from personal experience your father does not like to be kept waiting."

Calix shook his head. He hugged Sarayu goodbye and headed toward the imposing Victorian building. He lifted his head to scan the top of the turret and saw a flicker of movement at the window. He could see his father looking down at him.

Sobek had been watching him the entire time.

10.

I am running.

There are already people starting to mill around, trying to sort out what has happened, and I need to hide before someone starts asking me questions. I need somewhere quiet to think until I can figure out what to do. There's only one place I can go, and I have to get there before the sun rises. Clutching my father's knapsack, I race down the shore, away from the houses toward the jagged cliffs. Ten minutes later, I am around the bend and the houses are completely out of sight.

The Cliffs are an area you can only reach at low tide, either in the early morning or in the early evening. Here the rocks are bigger and obstruct the shoreline. I gingerly climb the side of the cliff, putting my feet into the worn crevices I have climbed for years. When I am about halfway up, I rest on a large rock that juts out and I twist my body behind the ragged formation just to its left. There is an almost invisible entrance to a cave that one has to be quite thin to fit through. I pull the bag in behind me, trying not to fall. The entrance to the cliffside cave is slippery. I've been playing here since I was a little girl, and years of water splashing against the rocks has made my rocky path smooth and slick, especially in bare feet.

I easily find my way to my hiding spot in the back of the cave. After my sister was taken, I used to spend hours in here, hiding from the world. I would cry uncontrollably, unsure how to control my emotions. The cave seemed like the safest place to vent my frustrations and pain. My father refused to acknowledge my sister's existence and no one else knew. They assumed she had died like my mother had, in childbirth. They believed what we had told them.

But I knew she was alive. In my cave retreat, I drew pictures of her that I would one day give her. To make her seem real, I even celebrated her birthday every year. I hadn't been to the cave since Sun's last birthday, her eleventh, and it is crowded with bugs and twigs and mossy grass. Once I climb safely inside, I reach into a dry opening in the back of the cave, which is covered with a moveable boulder. I heave the big rock aside and pull out a candle and flint.

Once I light the candle and set it down in the middle of the cave, I take inventory of my father's knapsack. It is mostly filled with notebooks containing scientific equations, which I don't understand. I flip through the pages until I come to an illustration of the Desalination Plant. It is hard for me to look at my father's precise drawing, not knowing where he is or what he is doing. Why does he even have this notebook? Regulations dictate that all research material is to be kept in the labs, under strict Global Governance guidelines. Why would he break the law? I study the picture, which shows a maze of pipes underneath the water. They are all gray pipes with several colored caps: They are mostly silver, with a couple whites and one red.

Because the oceans make up 97 percent of the world's supply of water, Sobek's desalination plants use seawater reverse osmosis to develop viable drinking water. After the Great Technology War, Sobek created three solar-powered plants to immediately address the health issues faced by contaminated water. One for each of the new territories. So much of the population had died in the war, and the remaining citizens became sick from the toxic water. Radioactive particles released from the explosions at the nuclear power plants had threatened to destroy the entire world's seafood supply. Sobek's advanced scientific technologies quickly fixed the problem by neutralizing the toxin and gave us clean drinking water. My father was one of the masterminds behind the plant. So, why is he in trouble? I keep looking at his illustration, trying to see the problem. There is nothing out of the ordinary. It is simply a complex maze of pipes running along the bottom of the plant. He has color-coded each one and put a series of equations beside it. It is all terribly scientific and I don't understand it. I clearly cannot see anything covert or out of place. What is my father trying to tell me?

I pull out the rest of the bag's contents: There is a standard identity watch; yet when I put in the holograph identity chip, it is not me. It is my picture, but not my name. There are six chips in total: three for me and three for my father, all bearing the authentic data encrypted scanner codes . . . with fake identities. My aliases are Kallie, Kenzie, and Kiara. I have no idea who I am anymore.

Why does my father have secret identities for me? Is this what he meant about becoming invisible? Becoming someone else? There is also a wallet filled with currency chips, a packet of vitamins, and a necklace that belonged to my mother. I put the notebooks and the vitamins back in the knapsack and shove it into my hiding place. I put on my mother's necklace, a locket which I know encases pictures of both me and my father. I then set the identity watch to the "Kenzie" chip and put it on before shoving the currency chips in the pocket of my father's sweatshirt. I am still freezing. The sweatshirt hangs down to my knees, but I need some proper pants and shoes. All of my things are gone. I pull myself into the fetal position on the dry floor, hugging myself to get warm. How have things gotten so messed up? Usually at this time I'd be wolfing down an enormous breakfast and going to school. My eyes feel so heavy.

Maybe if I just close them for a minute, I can think better.

"Keeva, follow me," the voice says authoritatively. I somehow know I am dreaming . . . yet, I can't wake myself up, so I give in to my subconscious.

I am walking through a long, dark hallway. It is cold and made completely out of stone. I'm nervous, but the boy with the blue eyes next to me keeps squeezing my hand to give me strength. I turn to look at him. He is my height, about four feet, which is quite tall for a five-year-old, and he is wearing a knee-length tunic similar to mine. Only his is brown and

ANOMALIES

mine is blue. We walk hand in hand behind the tall woman with the short brown hair. When we get to the big room, she gives us each a cup of water and instructs us to drink. I don't want to drink the water because it tastes funny, but the look on her face scares me, so I drink it all.

I feel a little fuzzy, but before I can say anything, the short-haired woman starts to wrap a rope around the boy and me. Why is she doing this? I don't like it. The rope wraps tighter and tighter around us and I have trouble breathing. "Please stop," I beg. But no one is listening. The boy with the blue eyes is also crying. Between my tears and my inability to breathe, I think I am going to die.

I don't think it can get any worse until I feel myself being lifted in the air. I am terrified as I feel my feet leave the ground and I am hauled high into the cavern. There is some kind of pulley on the wall and a large man is turning a wheel and hoisting us to the high ceiling. It is so dark. I want to go home to my parents. My mother is pregnant and I want to talk to her belly. I want to talk to my baby sister. Why am I here? Suddenly, we are flipped over and as I scream in terror, I feel all the blood rushing to my head. Just before I pass out, I see a black butterfly fluttering around my face.

I jolt awake, bathed in sweat, trying to get my bearings. The guttering candle makes ominous shadows around the cave and for a moment I'm not sure if I am still trapped in my dream. I peek outside and see the full moon low on the horizon. I have slept for most of the day. I stretch my arms and roll my neck a few times, stiff from sleeping so long on the hard cave floor. My stomach is growling. I need food and a better place to hide, but I don't know where to go.

In the moonlight, I climb down from the cave and find myself constantly looking over my shoulder as I take back roads into town. Before I realize it, I am at Annika's house. I stand in front of the burnished steel door—the same door I've rushed through every day of my life. And I wait. I can hear Annika's family laughing in the dining room, plates clattering as the family eats dinner. I tentatively lift up my hand and knock, waiting nervously until Annika's mother opens the door.

I can only imagine how terrible I must look—wet, bedraggled, and barefoot, and wearing only my father's sweatshirt. But my fears are assuaged when Annika's mother sighs with relief, pulling me into her welcoming arms.

"Keeva, we've been so worried about you, honey," Mrs. Aames says softly.

Without preamble, I start to bawl.

"**W**ELCOME TO THE HEART OF THE OPERATION," Sobek said as his son followed Claudia Durant through the silver metal doors to the inside of the observation room.

"What operation?" Calix walked up to the dark window that served as a two-way mirror. On the other side, he could see butterflies. Hundreds of butterflies darted through the air as Protectors busily prepared ropes that were dangling from the ceiling.

"What is this, father?" Calix demanded.

Sobek's eyes danced merrily. "Have a seat, Son. It's just beginning. You'll see the first pair from Bunk 1 in mere minutes." He turned to Claudia Durant. "It never gets old, does it Claudia?"

"No sir," she smiled before turning her attention back to the play in front of her.

11.

I am safe.

"Tell me everything," Annika insists when we get to her room.

"I will," I promise, "but I have to take a shower first." I grab the one-piece bodysuit that Mrs. Aames has given me along with a pair of snuggly boots, and I walk down the hall to the bathroom. It feels so good to stand in the shower stall and instruct the heater to go up to 110 degrees. My hair is covered in ash and I wash it twice to get out all the soot. I want to stay in the stall as long as I can. I need a quiet place where I can digest everything that has happened, but my best friend is waiting for me. Annika was quiet all through dinner; clearly her mother had instructed her family to give me space. Mrs. Aames is a teacher at the secondary school and knows how to handle crisis situations. Once I finally stopped crying, she brought me into the dining room. She filled my plate and told me to eat until I was stuffed. I was in no mood to argue, as I was famished. I shoveled the chicken and mashed potatoes and garlicky mushrooms into my mouth as fast as I could. I knew Annika was dying to know what had happened, but she dutifully obeyed her mother's request.

Reluctantly, I step out of the shower and squeeze the water out of my hair. After I dry myself off, I change into the sleepwear and put a disposable head on the solar toothbrush so I can brush my teeth. Feeling warm and cozy, I go back to Annika's room and slide into bed.

"Everyone thought you were dead," Annika says when I come into the room. Her tone is accusatory but soon softens. "I mean, I didn't. I never would."

"Good." I'm not sure what to say.

"Besides, they never found the bodies, either yours or your dad's, so I knew you were alive."

"Who is everyone?" I ask.

"The mediacasters. It's been on the news all morning. There are never fires around here, especially so close to the ocean, so it's been on the same loop all day." Annika clicks the remote and the small hologram appears on the wall. There are pictures of where my house used to be and the smoke. So much smoke. Annika taps her Third and looks at me, expecting me to do the same.

"Um, it got messed up in the fire," I lie as I rub the imposter Third. "I'll get it fixed first thing tomorrow."

A flicker of suspicion crosses Annika's face before she nods and snaps off the screen. "You're not missing much, it's the same thing over and over. Early morning fire. Missing family. No bodies found. Blah, blah, blah. Now tell me what happened!"

"Honestly, I don't really remember." I say, not prepared to tell Annika the truth. Even though she's my best friend, I feel like my conversation with my father is too private to share. I am not ready to tell Annika about his secret papers or the fake identity chips or the brutal Protectors who tasered him right in front of me and then took him away.

So I start with the truth.

"I was swimming early. You know I've been having these crazy nightmares since camp, and it was the first time I slept through the night. So I went out for an early morning swim. I had been gone almost an hour when I smelled the smoke. It was awful. The closer I got to shore, the harder it was to breathe. There was a slight wind, so the fire felt even bigger than it really was. When I got back to the house, it was completely engulfed in flames."

Now, the lies. As I speak, I concentrate on my finger-nails, which still have soot in them. Remembering Max's interrogation lessons, I speak slowly and confidently. "I . . . I couldn't find my father anywhere. It was so early and there was no one around. I kept screaming for him, but he didn't answer. I even tried to go into the house, but the fire was everywhere. I guess I must have inhaled too much smoke looking for him that I got really dizzy and disoriented. I kind of remember walking on the beach for a while, but I honestly don't remember where." I look up, the next part is the truth. "And I guess I fell asleep."

"For the whole day?" Annika asks.

"Yeah. I was freaked out that I couldn't find my father and that my home had just burned down. I mean, nothing was left." I feel myself tearing up, "Not even a holo of my mom. I honestly just got away from the smell of the smoke and walked down the beach a bit before curling up and going to sleep. I came here the second I woke up."

"Why were you wearing your dad's sweatshirt?"

"He gave it to me." Another truth. I just hadn't specified when exactly he had given it to me.

Annika seems satisfied and puts her arm around me. "You know you can stay with me as long as you want. And I'm sure they'll find your dad. Maybe he got disoriented and wandered off also."

"Maybe," I say and then spend the next two hours listening to her moon over Dante. She shows me all the holos from him on her identity watch. He is cute and funny and Annika is charmed . . . almost beyond words. Every time she watches one of his holos, her Third buzzes. It is strange to see her so satisfied. So happy. So content.

She has completely forgotten my situation and is engrossed in her own.

CALIX KNEW WHAT IT MUST FEEL LIKE to be a lab rat. He sat between his father and Claudia Durant, behind a secret two-way mirror as pairs of children were paraded in front of him. They were clearly half-asleep and unaware of what was happening. He watched as a small, blond boy and a petite, mocha-skinned girl were led into the cavernous room. Hands clasped together, they each wore knee length sleep tunics. His was red and hers was purple. A Protector gave them each a cup of water and the children drank.

"What are they drinking?" Calix asked, but both his father and Claudia Durant ignored him as their eyes were glued to the scene.

After drinking the liquid, the children blinked their eyes several times, immediately dizzied from the drugged potion. A Protector then wrapped a thick rope around the small couple, binding them together. The dazed children quickly began to cry, but everyone ignored them. As the first Protector finished knotting them into a tight cocoon, another Protector turned a large metal wheel as the pair was slowly hoisted up to the ceiling.

"What is this, Father? Stop. They're crying." Calix jumped up and banged on the wall, but no one could hear him. No one could see him. He watched in horror as the children were flipped over so that they were suspended upside down.

And then they began to spin.

12.

I am awake.

The soft murmur of voices wakes me up.

I click on my watch . . . "Kenzie's" watch. It's 4:30 a.m., far too early for anyone to be up. I creep out of bed and open Annika's door. I hear distinct voices at the bottom of the stairs. Judging from the chorus of voices, they are more people than just Mr. and Mrs. Aames. I kneel down on the landing and crane my neck to peek through the banisters. I can see the backs of Annika's parents, who are standing at the door. They speak in furtive whispers.

"Do you know what time it is?" Mrs. Aames demands.

"We don't want to risk losing her again." I recognize the big bald Protector from the previous day.

"Her Third has been deactivated," the smaller Protector says.

"I know. That's why I called you. But I didn't think you were going to wake us up in the middle of the night. I was planning to bring her in after breakfast."

"We can't risk it, Citizen Aames. She's a person of interest and considered dangerous."

"Keeva?" Mr. Aames chuckles. "I've known that girl since she was a baby, she wouldn't kill a fly."

"She's an Anomaly, sir. Nothing is as it seems." The Protector is trying to push his way in the door, but Mrs. Aames blocks him.

"My house. My rules," she barks at him, before adding, "My prisoner."

I'm stunned. Did Mrs. Aames just call me her prisoner? And why would she call the Protectors on me? Last night, she was so nurturing, she made me feel so safe.

"Did she have anything with her?" the Protector asks, interrupting my thoughts.

"Nothing." Mrs. Aames moves to let the men in. "Now, just relax. I don't want to spook Keeva, and I certainly don't want to upset my daughter. Honey, make the gentleman a cup of caffeine. I'll go get her."

I quickly retrace my steps to Annika's room, slip under the covers and pretend that I am asleep. Seconds later, I hear the door open and Mrs. Aames's feet padding on the carpet toward the bed.

"Keeva, sweetie, wake up." Mrs. Aames's touch is gentle and I feel her push a strand of hair away from my face.

"What is it?" I feign the crackly voice of someone who had been unceremoniously awoken.

"They've found your father." She smiles, "You can go see him now."

Why is she lying? Mrs. Aames has been like a mother to me ever since I lost my own mother. Why is she betraying me like this?

I force a smile back and say, "Sure. Just give me two minutes."

She gets up and goes to the door, lingering for a second. "Everything's going to be all right, Keeva."

"I know," I say tersely, watching her shut the door. The second she's gone, I put on the boots and go to the window. Annika is still fast asleep, snoring so loudly she doesn't hear me as I pry open the window and climb out onto the ledge. I easily jump onto the nearby branch of the oak tree just outside Annika's bedroom window, the same one we've used to climb in and out of her house since we were kids. I shimmy down the tree and race out into the darkness of the early morning. I can't stay here. Nowhere in my beloved Ocean Community is it safe.

I have to get to Sabbatical City and find Labyrinth.

"I CALL IT A TRAUMA-BASED, mind-control technique," Sobek said proudly once the first set of children were released and sent back to their bunks.

"It's psychotic." Calix was stunned by the events unfolding in front of him. Another pair of children was being led into the room. It was like an assembly line. The pairs were brought in, drugged, bound together, hoisted to the air, spun around and around, and then released. "What's the point?"

"The point? The point?" Sobek uncharacteristically raised his voice. "The point, son, is that my technique uses a combination of psychology, neuroscience, and ritual to enslave the initiates and create compliant citizens of the Global Governance."

"They are five years old!" Calix screamed.

"Indeed. Their minds are at their prime. They are most open to be manipulated. They are ideal candidates."

"So, you hang them upside down and torture them?"

"Torture is such a primitive word." Sobek grinned, "I prefer 'educate.' We are educating them to be productive citizens."

"How?"

"Watch." Sobek pointed to another part of the room where two children were being choked. Protectors put their large hands around the childrens' small throats and throttled, strangling them in short shakes, until their victims passed out. In another section of the room, children were being dunked in water tanks and held under until they almost drowned. Calix felt extremely nauseous; however, his anger was stronger than his revulsion.

"You need to stop this right now, Father. It's sick."

"It's protocol," Sobek said, and nodded to Claudia Durant.

"Calix, your father has created a brilliant way to form a productive and compliant society," Claudia Durant insisted. "These children don't remember any of this. MC-5 is simply a blur for them. Maybe they remember painting or kickball or arts and crafts. This part of the camp is so deeply embedded in their subconscious that they will have no memory of it. You see, we are using these methods to block the victim's capacity for conscious processing, and then we are able to implant thoughts, directives, and perceptions in their unconscious mind, which helps them feel, think, and perceive things . . . such as their need for an intended partner. That need becomes so deep that they have little time to dissent as their sense of wholeness and purpose is completely wrapped up in their future spouse."

"Don't you people see what's wrong with this?" Calix sputtered. He started to choke.

Claudia Durant quickly poured him a glass of water.

"There is nothing wrong with creating a peaceful world without dissent."

"Well, I dissent. I won't stand for this," Calix said as he downed the water in one gulp.

Both Sobek and Claudia Durant watched Calix as his eyes quickly became glassy.

"What's happening?" Calix mumbled through a dry mouth. He looked at the empty glass. He was having trouble focusing. "What did you do to me?"

"We're educating you."

13.

"I am Kenzie."

I smile at the chunky lorry driver.

Truckers are constantly stopping at the diner stops along the route to Sabbatical City. After leaving Annika's, I take back roads to the highway and duck into the first roadside diner. I sidle into an empty leather booth and survey the truckers. Most are from Labor Community, who have come from as far south as the tip of Old Mexico, hauling water or goods from Agricultural Community. They are loners, usually singles whose intended others have passed on. They are mostly older, around my father's age. When I enter the diner, there are six truckers in the middle of their meals. Four male Labors and two women from Agricultural Community. I pick the one who is just finishing up her lunch and follow her to the charge station where she is unhooking her truck. She is dressed in a brown uniform, complete with a baseball cap that says Orchard Harvest. When she sees me, she gives me the once over before I introduce myself.

"You need a ride, kiddo?"

"I do."

"Then you've come to the right driver. I was getting tired listening to the media waves. Could use some human conversation."

"You don't mind?" I'm tentative. I'm not really in the mood to be chatting.

"Not at all. Hop on in, Kenzie, I'm Harrigan McFeely." The ponytailed driver smiles and we step up to her eighteen-wheeler labeled "Oranges."

"You from around here, Harrigan?" I make small talk, hoping that she is unfamiliar with the Ocean Community and the missing Anomaly whose house has just burned down.

"Nope. Down south. Been on the road for two days. Heading to the capital, than over to East America to pick up another load, then back south. How about you?"

"I'm just passing through." I climb into the tall lorry. It is immaculate, the dashboard filled with a holo map of the entire route.

"How many hours, d'you think?" Harrigan asks. If it is longer than two, she will need to log me into the data center, chronicling my time on and time off. Those are the regulations of the road. Hitchhiking is common practice in the New World. It is a safe and reliable form of transportation. Unlike the former world where gasoline emissions choked the air with noxious fumes and drivers spent large chunks of their lives stuck in traffic, there are now fewer cars, and all run on a combination of solar power and clean energy. Vehicles are distributed to citizens on a need-only basis. Citizens whose jobs require them to have cars, like most of the Labor Community, have one. I study Harrigan's face. There is no sign of doubt or suspicion. I take a

ANOMALIES

deep breath. Why should there be? Hitchhiking is commonplace, especially along the route to Sabbatical City.

"How far to the next rest stop?" I ask.

"About an hour and forty-five minutes."

"That'll be perfect." I drop a currency chip into her tip jar and settle in for the journey. I need to cover my tracks and do not want my journey chronicled in any way.

"Where you headed?" Harrigan asks. She is not prying, just making conversation.

"The capital, eventually," I admit, "but I'm meeting my father there and he's not expecting me for a few days, so I thought I'd take in the sights."

"Not many sights between here and Sabbatical City," Harrigan says.

"I know. But I'm working on a desalination project for school, so studying the desert's topography is important."

"How old are you?"

"Fourteen. And a half," I lie.

"You're tall for fourteen."

"I've been this tall since I was eleven," I smile. "My best friend calls me Beanpole." I smile, thinking about Kai, remembering the first insult he hurled at me.

"Ah. When are you scheduled for Monarch Camp?"

"This winter." I close my eyes, hoping to politely end the conversation before I start having to remember the lies I am spewing so that I don't start backtracking. I can't afford to get caught. With one push of a button, Harrigan can report me.

"Best summer of my life." Harrigan gets nostalgic and starts to wax on about her intended mate while I drift in and out of sleep.

For the next two days, I travel at night and sleep during the day. I keep to back roads and alternate between walking and hitchhiking inland. At the various diners which pepper the main byway, I easily hail one of the many truckers who are carting foodstuffs to the capital, pay a small passenger fee and spend a couple of hours in the cab before moving on. I am careful to not stay in one vehicle too long, lest they report a minor passenger. As long as a passenger rides for two hours or less, it is considered a "favor" rather than a "job." And I need as many favors as I can get as most of the journey is across a desert, which is virtually uncrossable during the day. As each trucker lets me off, I backtrack a little to cover my steps and find another vehicle.

Once the sun comes up, I locate a pocket of protected shade: an abandoned barn or thicket of remote trees, and curl up and sleep. Though I use the term sleep loosely because my slumber is anything but relaxing. With each dream, the nightmares are getting worse. They always begin the same; I follow the woman down the hall. But the tortures became progressively more awful. Some-times, I am hanging upside down; sometimes I am being choked within an inch of my life. And just at the moment of my greatest sensation of fear, I pass out . . . as if some-thing is pushing me to my furthest point of pain and then feeding off of my terror.

Sabbatical City is the heartbeat of the Americas. It's located in the middle of the desert, in a place that used to be called Las Vegas. I visited once with my parents when

I was a little girl, although I hardly remember it. But I've seen plenty of pictures, and Rane's brother Cannon sent her holos from his honeymoon there. It is the most popular sabbatical spot in the Americas. Most people honeymoon in Sabbatical City because there is so much to do. So many cultures and so many artifacts of days past.

The last truck, a twelve-wheeler filled with technology chips imported directly from the mines in Argyle City and operated by a Labor called McGee, drops me off in the center of the city. McGee is a grandfatherly type who gives me a few pointers of what to see and where to eat before he drops me outside the main strip. He warns me to keep my eyes open for thieves who are rampant in the city. Young hooligans, he calls them. I promise to be careful and wave goodbye as he heads off to the Caesar where he is dropping off Third components for Sobek's personal scientists.

Alone, I am immediately confronted by a deluge of sights and sounds. It is overwhelming simply to look up. While my Ocean Community is mostly flat and vast with both the ocean and the sky uninterrupted for miles, this area is compacted into a city in the clouds. Every space seems to be filled with buildings and helicrafts and passageways in the sky connecting the various edifices. The citizens in Sabbatical City all live in very tall structures that used to be called casinos. More than half of the population of the Americas live in this city. It was one of the only areas untouched by the Great Technology War because when the floods came, it was so far inland and most of the buildings so high that the entire area was not affected. So, it's almost retro compared to the rest of the

Americas. Old school. From a different time, except that the Global Governance built it up even further, and all the buildings' roofs serve as landing and takeoff pads for the Protectors' helicrafts.

I'm grateful to be wearing Mrs. Aames' Lycra one piece. It is oddly fashionable, and I do not seem out of place among the hundreds of people busily walking on the street. I am suitably invisible. Sure, I am one of the few people wearing blue since I am now so far inland, but no one gives me a second glance. They probably think I am a tourist on sabbatical. Most people who live in Sabbatical City belong to the other six communities, especially Renewable Energy and Academic Communities. I see more red and yellow than any other color. Although there are also a fair number of greens and browns and purples. And Protectors.

There are always Protectors.

Still, I decide to change in case they are looking for me. Even though it is easy to get lost in this city, a tall, redheaded girl in blue stands out like a sore thumb. I check my currency chips: I have enough money to survive for a week, which will hopefully be long enough to find what I am looking for. Hopefully.

There are many souvenir shops along the road and I'm not sure which one to enter. As I survey the long row of shops, I see a small, blond girl across the street. She smiles at me and I smile back. She wears her long hair in two braids, and she looks no more than eight years old. I wonder if she is lost because usually minors are accompanied by their parents. But there are no adults anywhere near her. She is also wearing blue, one of the only Ocean Community citizens on the busy street. I watch as she leans against a storefront, looking incredibly self-assured. I cross the street, strangely drawn to this girl. The moment she sees me, she darts into the store. Clearly, her parents told her never to talk to strangers. I follow her into the store. It is a huge wardrobe shop and I scan the vast isles, looking for the blond girl with the long braids.

"Excuse me, did you see a girl just come in here?" I ask the bored clerk.

"I see hundreds of girls come in here," she says, not even looking up from her tablet.

I do one last survey of the premises, but the girl is nowhere to be seen. She probably ducked out a back door. I shrug. If she needed my help then she would have stayed to talk to me. Besides, how will talking to some kid help me find Labyrinth? I look at the wardrobe choices. Inside the enormous emporium are rows and rows of clothes in all seven colors. I wonder which color will make me look most inconspicuous, and then I realize I don't even know my fake identity in order to make the purchase.

Hiding behind one of the tall racks, I examine each of the identity chips my father set for me. Kenzie is a member of Ocean Community. Kiara is Labor and Kallie is a Protector. How could my father know that I would be a Protector? There are so many unanswered questions, and I wish I could talk to him. I shake off my moment of self-pity, put the Kallie chip into my watch, and walk determinedly to the back of the store.

I ignore the salesclerk's suspicious stare as I head over to the rack of black clothes. There is an enormous selection to choose from, although most of them are highly impractical, such as shimmery mini dresses and five-inch black heels. I find a pair of black jeans, black work boots, a few black T-shirts, undergarments, and a black leather jacket with a softly lined hood. I bring my selections up to the counter.

"Don't you have to try them on?" she sneers. The clerk wears dull purple, a member of Labor. She clearly has a distaste for Protectors.

"I know my size, thanks." I smile politely. "Do you have somewhere I can change into these?"

"You have to purchase them first. Can I see some identity, please?"

"Of course." I click on Kallie's holo, projecting my face and community onto the counter. Yet, the woman hesitates. Perhaps she senses my nervousness.

"I'm going to need to see a second form of identity."

"But this is all I have," I panic. If she reports me, I won't be able to help my father. His capture will have been for nothing. "Wait," I say before she can reach for her security button, "I can show you my tattoo. I just graduated from Monarch Camp. That's why I'm a little out of my element," I add with an uncomfortable laugh before unzipping my bodysuit and revealing my newly inked butterfly.

"Well, that certainly solves that." She smiles. "Didn't mean to question you, but you can never be too careful these days. Especially with so many people pretending to be Protectors."

"Why would they do that?" I ask.

"Who knows? There's a whole shoplifting gang here. Been working the strip the last few months. I suppose they think they're the least conspicuous of the communities.

In any case, we've been told to double and triple check anyone who comes in. Especially people claiming to be Protectors. But your tattoo is definite proof. Most thieves run off after the second ID. You can change in the dressing room. It's just through the back."

I take my new clothes to the large dressing room and put them on. I turn around, admiring myself in the mirror. A pale redhead dressed head to toe in black. I try to stifle a laugh. I look . . . tough.

I look like a Protector.

A FEW HOURS LATER, Calix and Sarayu were sitting in chairs in what appeared to be a waiting room. They were both dressed in black tunics. Calix couldn't remember how he had gotten here, but Sarayu had been wakened in the middle of the night and brought here. She was terrified.

"Calix, what's going on?" Sarayu said.

"I don't know," Calix lied. He had seen what his father had intended for them. That sick bastard was going to make him and Sarayu, two teenagers, endure the torture the children were experiencing.

"Just drink the water. When they ask you to drink the water, drink the water. It will make you forget."

Just then, a Protector nodded for them to follow him down a long hall. Calix clasped Sarayu's hand, trying to protect her, but really trying to calm himself down. When he left this place and returned to the Caesar, he was going to find a way to disappear. He was done taking orders from his father. He was done being his puppet.

The pair reached the end of the hall and were led into the cavernous room filled with butterflies. Claudia Durant appeared and handed Sarayu a cup of water.

Calix whispered, "Drink it. In one gulp."

He watched her terrified tiger-like eyes as she lifted her shaking hands up to her mouth and drank the drugged concoction. Her eyes quickly glassed over as if she were in a trance.

"Where's my drink?" Calix demanded.

"Your father thought you would benefit more if you were fully conscious," Claudia Durant said cruelly.

Calix felt a rope being tied around him and Sarayu, binding them together. He barely managed to turn his head to look at the two-way mirror, imagining his father's glee on the other side of the wall.

Just before he was hoisted into the air, Calix looked at his father and mouthed five words, "I'm going to kill you."

14.

I am desperate.

I'm down to my last currency chip and I still haven't found Labyrinth.

I've been in Sabbatical City for a week and am no closer to finding him/her/it than when I got here. My frustration level is enormous, as I have spent my currency chips on food and clothes and a place to stay, and now I am almost broke. Every day, I roam the streets, overwhelmed by the noise and frenetic energy. I can barely hear myself think. I keep looking, looking, looking—trying so hard to find something that I have no idea how to find.

I look at my last currency chip, turning it over and over in my hands, and I almost feel a sense of relief. I've failed. Both my father and myself. I couldn't do it. Everyone told me to listen to my voices; yet they haven't been talking since I've arrived in this loud, crazy city. They've given up on me and now I've given up on myself. Whatever was supposed to happen, did not.

I sit down at a swanky outdoor cafe and order a large steak. I might as well have a good last meal if I am about to be penniless. Knowing my entire journey has been for naught allows me to relax for the first time since I've been in Sabbatical City. No longer looking over my shoulder and wondering if I'm being followed, I take a deep breath and just sit. Relax. Breathe. Take in the sights. The entire outdoor restaurant is packed. The concierge at the casino hotel told me it has the best food in Sabbatical City, so I decide to treat myself. After all, I have nothing left to lose. The waiter brings me the sirloin, and I savor each bite, torn between laughing and crying at my predicament. The whole situation is almost comical—my brave attempt to help my father when I didn't have a clue how to begin. And now, a complete failure, I know exactly what is going to happen: I will finish my exquisite meal, get a lift from a lorry driver directly to Ocean Community, not caring that my trip will be recorded on their holo, go back to Annika's, and get taken in by the Protectors. The end. I will do whatever it is they want me to do and, hopefully, see my father again.

Who was I kidding? A whole bunch of people, including Inelia, thought I was special. My father clearly believed in me as well because he entrusted his precious secrets to me. Little good that did him. I guess they read me wrong. I'm not someone who can save the world; I can barely survive in it by myself for a week. I want to go back to the Ocean Community and turn myself in.

I want to give up.

I hate myself for feeling so much self-pity, but I am suffocated by it. And because I don't try to fight it, I relax even more. I let go. Resolved to surrender to my miserable fate, I try to enjoy my last bit of freedom as I watch the other diners . . . mostly Renewable Energies and

ANOMALIES

Academics who are all engrossed in conversations, oblivious to the world around them. Everyone seems so happy, so resolved, so clueless. It's as if an entire tranquility has settled over the diners and I am the only outsider at the party. I am invisible, which is what I suppose I had always wanted to be; yet, lately, I have felt like I was meant for something more. But no one sees me. I am flanked by tables where people are engrossed in their own stories. Next to me, parents dining with their small children are cutting their meat for them. Renewable Energies gesticulating animatedly as they discuss a new theory on thermal energy. I find myself smiling sadly, wondering what it's like to really belong somewhere. To be seen.

Suddenly I feel a chill on the back of my neck. There is someone else who is crashing this party of normalcy. I slowly turn my head and see the perpetrator. It is the same blond girl I noticed my first day in the city. She is now dressed in black and is accompanied by a gangly older boy. As I continue my meal, I watch them, completely engrossed with the young pair who skulk near the restaurant's periphery. To anyone else, they might just seem absorbed in their conversation; however, to me, they are definitely lurking. Is it just a coincidence that the last time I saw her she was dressed in blue and now she's dressed in black?

Is she hiding like I am?

I watch as they easily amble up to a table on the perimeter, approaching a pair of tourists whose table has the requisite cartograms and travelogues. I noticed the table when I first sat down, since they were fairly loud, and the corpulent man was showing off for his mousey bride by ordering practically everything on the menu. They had caused noise pollution, and several tables around them had moved. I continue to observe the unfolding scenario as the gangly boy addresses the table, smiling and clearly asking them something. The man is trying to push him away, but the woman holds her husband's hand and forces him to talk to the boy. While this is going on, the small blond girl deftly grabs the woman's purse, which is hanging on the back of her chair.

Within a second, they are gone.

And I am right behind them.

The chase lasts for over a mile.

I am grateful for Inelia's taxing physical calisthenics because I am still in great shape, and no matter how hard they try, the thieves can't shake me. I don't even know why I'm chasing them, but I know that I am supposed to. I have a feeling. The minute I first saw the little blond girl, my voices returned, instructing me to pay attention. Even before they stole the purse, I had already taken my last bite of steak, put down my currency chip, and gotten up from my table.

As the pair slips into the heavy foot traffic outside, I follow them, staying within a few feet. Immediately sensing me, they pick up their pace and dart in and out of the Casino Towers. I easily stay in pace with them, slipping in and out of crowds and keeping them directly in my sight. After several attempts to shake me, they slow down and lead me straight toward the Caesar. Toward Sobek's estate.

Yet, rather than crossing the street and going into the palace, the pair join a group of tourists who are gazing at an enormous fountain that seems to be dancing on the large manmade lake. Music blasts and the water shoots up in complicated patterns. Many of the tourists are taking vids and holos with their identity watches. They are oblivious to the young couple with the stolen purse who walk directly up to the fountain . . . and disappear.

It is impossible.

I watch as the boy disappears first. Then the girl looks around until she finds me, winks, and then disappears behind her cohort. I run up to the spot and, sure enough, they are gone. I watched them vanish right in front of me. I look around the area; but there is only the ornate fountain shooting water into the air against the backdrop of an ancient song that was popular long before the war. Where did they go? An older couple disrupts my concentration and asks me to take a vid of them. I reluctantly comply, arranging them just in front of the fountain where I saw the kids disappear. I focus the techno-camera and then, just to the couple's left, I see a small indentation in the granite. I quickly take the picture, return their camera and go to the irregular spot. I am sure this is the spot where the pair disappeared, although I still cannot figure out how they did it. I bend down to examine the granite, quite aware that mist from the fountain is slowly drenching me. I am about to give up when I hear a familiar voice just behind me.

"I was wondering when you were going to finally show up, Beanpole."

CALIX DIDN'T KNOW WHICH WAS WORSE, being choked or being drowned.

He was able to tolerate the hanging upside down, but the other methods were more painful. What he hated even more than his own punishment was the torture Sobek and the Protectors were inflicting upon Sarayu. With each of Sobek's "lessons" she became weaker, more frightened, more beaten down. She clung closer to Calix, hanging onto him for dear life even when they weren't bound together. During many of the sessions she had passed out, and he couldn't get over the sensation of seeing the fear in her eyes.

What he also couldn't comprehend was that as she grew weaker, he felt stronger.

Calix hated that feeling, as if somehow he was drawing strength from Sarayu's pain. He tried to ignore this new primal need and simply succumb to the torture, but he could not. And with his intended partner's every tremble, every shake, and every quiver, he felt more alive. It was as if he was breathing in her essence. He could smell her. And it wasn't the usual scent of gardenia and oranges which Sarayu emitted . . . it was something else. An unseen static electricity which seemed to be charging him. He was somehow drawing out an invisible power from her and using it to charge himself. He tried to stop.

But Sobek's nonstop chatter made it worse. So much worse.

As Calix and his partner were suspended, choked, and drowned, Sobek stood nearby narrating the experience.

"I've created abuse to force you to dissociate from reality," Sobek whispered in his ear. "Look, Sarayu's already dissociating. It's a natural response when people are faced with unbearable pain. People react two ways to the torture. It's how we identify, at a very young age, who the Protectors are. So you have two options: You can dissociate or you can feed. What will you do, Son?"

Calix tried to ignore his father, but as he felt himself getting stronger, he knew which path he would invariably take.

15.

I am thrilled.

I didn't realize how much I had missed Kai until he is grabbing my hand and pulling me up. But there is no time for a reunion as his eyes dart around to make sure that no one is watching us before he maneuvers me to walk to a specific area at the side of the fountain.

"Where are we going?" I ask, not letting go of his hand.

"I'll explain everything once we get there."

"Where?" I demand, but he has already disappeared. I do a double take, realizing that he has slipped behind what appears to be the actual fountain, but is really a holo of a shooting fountain. I follow him through the mirage. Now we can see the tourists milling about, but they cannot see us.

"This is amazing. How many people know about this?"

"Only a handful. Most everyone down here was initially drugged to get here, so they wouldn't know the coordinates of the actual location."

"Down here? Down where?" "I ask as Kai inches around the side of the fountain to the indented rock and pushes it open. It shifts to the side, allowing us to enter a wide tunnel. I look around. There are candles dripping on the dirt wall. Otherwise, there are no discernible landmarks. We could be anywhere in the world.

Kai talks as he leads me deeper into the mouth of the tunnel. "The Underground. Taj built this place before the Great Technology War. She knew exactly what Sobek was planning. She's a genius."

"She is, huh?" My words are tinged with jealousy. "Are you and this Taj . . . close?"

"As close as she is with anyone," Kai says, as he leads me down a complex web of passageways. I have no idea where we are going, just that we are going down. "Luckily, she had one of her operatives intercept me on my way home. I took the motorglide to camp because I only lived an hour away. Next thing I knew there were two cyclists speeding alongside me, trying to veer me off of the road. It was Taj's extraction team. They liberated me just before I made it home." Kai stops at a large metal door with timepieces all moving in a counterclockwise direction. He pushes a button and the wheels stop and change direction.

The big doors open and Kai ushers me into the machine. "Going down."

"Wait. Why did they extract you?" I can't keep up with his story, and I've lost all sense of direction following Kai through the mazes and into this elevator contraption. I'm starting to feel dizzy. We are suddenly plummeting downwards, and I hold onto Kai so I don't fall. It is hard to hear him above the whirring and clicking of the elevator, which is making me nauseous.

"Because the Underground finds you before you find the Underground. Taj's people identified me as a revolutionary and recruited me before I could become one of Sobek's Protectors. One of his Spy Corps. The best of the best. The captains of his Protectors. That's what Sobek does with Anomalies. He trains us in order to turn us against our communities, our families, our friends. And it started at Monarch Camp. We were being prepped to be Sobek's spies, nothing more. What kind of life is that?" Kai stops and looks at me. "I can't tell you how worried I was about you. But Taj said you'd be safe."

"This Taj certainly knows a lot about me."

"You'd be surprised," Kai smiles and gives me a quick hug. "I've really missed you, Keeva."

"You did?" I say shyly, new emotions continuing to bloom.

"Absolutely." His answer is more polite than emotional.

When the elevator finally stops and the mechanical doors open, Kai gives me his arm and escorts me onto the ground floor of the enormous Underground City. "Welcome to the decentralized global network. Welcome to our self-sustaining community.

"Welcome to the Labyrinth."

CALIX ENDURED HIS FATHER'S TORTURES for the entire week.

Sobek did not see his methodology as evil. To him it was merely a way to educate his son. So that he knew, from the inside out, how a population could be manipulated.

With each night, the programming got worse. It lasted longer. As Calix suffered the programmers' abuses, his focus was threefold:

Stay alive. Protect Sarayu. Kill his father.

The only trouble was the hundreds of stupid butterflies that kept flying around him, distracting his focus.

"Butterflies begin their lives as worms," Sobek said as he stood beneath his spinning son. He made it a point to stand within earshot of Calix during his training, knowing that it would be nearly impossible for his son to tune him out. "After a period of cocooning, which you are now doing, they are reborn as beautiful butterflies."

Calix wished his father would shut up. He could see the energy draining from Sarayu as she went deeper and deeper into herself. Her subconscious was slowly releasing her life force. Letting go of the energy needed to keep her alive and sustain her. What he couldn't understand was why he continued to grow stronger as she grew weaker.

"I named Monarch Camp after the butterfly because it's one of the few creatures capable of passing knowledge through its genetics onto its offspring." Sobek held out his hand and a half dozen colorful butterflies rested on it. "One day, there will be no more need for Camp because this conditioning will have been through enough generations that it will be permanently etched in the citizens' psyches. They will be born completely pliable and compliant."

"Stay strong, Sarayu," Calix whispered as he tried to ignore his father's lesson.

"She feels lightheaded right now. Like she's fluttering. Like a butterfly. Don't worry, she won't remember this. She's dissociating from reality and going deep into a fantasy world in her head and will create a barrier of amnesia to protect herself. It's what they all do. Except the rare few, like you, Son."

Calix looked in Sarayu's eyes, but there was no one inside. Indeed, she had retreated deep inside her mind so that she could escape the pain. Calix wanted to scream at his father, to flail out and hit him; but his arms were pinned to his body as he and Sarayu continued to hang upside down, spinning.

"You can't help her, Son. Her alternate personality has been created. She will now be an obedient citizen who should not," Sobek corrected himself, "who will not get out of line."

"Why are you doing this to her? I love her," Calix screamed.

"You love the *idea* of her. She is disposable. There are plenty more Sarayu's out there. Prettier, smarter, better equipped to be your Queen." Sobek smiled, "Your training is almost over, Son." He began to walk away but stopped when Calix finally asked what Sobek was waiting to hear.

"How am I able to tolerate this torture?"

"Because you, my son, are not human."

16.

I am overwhelmed.

The first thing I see is an enormous airship.

I've read about them in history books, but I have never seen one before and it is awe-inspiring. The enormous craft is directly above my head, floating above the Underground City. The dirigible's metallic exterior shines off of the field of reverse solar panels high above. The experience is dizzying as I look up and try to gauge my whereabouts. The elevator must have dropped several miles underground, because not only is the airship floating high above us, there are several birdlike vehicles darting around it in the makeshift sky. I tilt my head back, dizzied by all the movement above me.

I'm brought back to reality when I almost get run over by a cyclist.

"Look out," a man on a three-wheeled cycle whirls past, almost clipping me in his wake.

I quickly jump back, realizing that I am standing in the middle of a small roadway where people are whizzing by on their wheelers. Safe on the curb, I watch as a pack of riders streams by, most of them on prewar cycles ranging from one to six wheels. They look so strange. Other than a few people dressed in the requisite community colors, everyone else is decked out in weird vintage styles. Women wear corsets and big skirts with tough-looking boots. Men wear waistcoats and hats. Many people wear goggles. It is as if I have stepped into a dream—someone else's dream.

"Kai, what's going on? Who are these people?"

"This is the Underground, Keeva. The place Inelia talked about."

"But . . . I didn't think it was real."

"Oh, it's very real. It's where the entire resistance is based. You're safe now."

With the cyclers now ahead of us, Kai guides me down the road that leads to the center of the Labyrinth. There are colorful tents everywhere, and everyone we pass smiles and welcomes me. But their salutations are cursory as they all seem intent on their tasks at hand. Everyone seems to have a purpose. Individuals with purpose. I shudder. Was it only a few weeks ago that I was questioning how docile everyone at camp had become? Here, everyone is so fired up, so passionate. I can feel their infectious energy.

Suddenly, the blond girl appears, and she's no longer wearing black. Now she is dressed like an old-fashioned princess. She wears a teal taffeta-and-lace dress, fuchsia boots that lace up to her knobby knees, and she carries a bright orange parasol. There is not one requisite color in her wardrobe. I'm stunned and feel weirdly inadequate in my solid colors. I've spent a lifetime relegated to the color blue which never bothered me until . . . until, suddenly I see the possibilities of so many colors together. Although it's a shock to my system and hard for me to visually comprehend, I have to admit it is unbelievably beautiful.

And, remembering how much Blue and I had laughed when we illegally painted our nails, I want to celebrate the uniqueness. I cannot understand why people should be defined by one color when there is a rainbow of possibilities.

The little girl interrupts my thoughts as she wraps her arms around me. "I'm so glad you found us."

I'm taken aback. I'm not used to so much affection. Especially from a stranger.

"I'm Zilli," she says, hugging me even tighter. "I'm so glad you're finally here. I've been waiting forever."

"Nice to meet you." I can't help but laugh. The little girl won't stop hugging me.

"You're going to save humanity. They said you'd come." Her little face is so earnest. Her big brown eyes are so innocent.

"I think you have me confused with someone else," I say gently, slowly prying her away from me.

She just smiles and slips her hand in mine.

"Zilli, are you supposed to be somewhere?" Kai asks.

"No. I did my job. I watched her and brought her here. I deserve a rest."

"Whoa." I look at Kai. "I was being watched?"

"Taj will explain everything, soon," Kai says.

"Why don't you explain everything to me now?" I demand.

"Keeva. You haven't been safe since you left Monarch Camp. Taj has kept an eye on you, the same way she's kept an eye on all the Anomalies. She has agents in every community assigned to watch us until we can be liberated. Zilli was your agent."

"She's, like, eight years old?" I say.

"I'm older. I'm just small for my age," Zilli says emphatically.

I'm too tired to argue, so I walk between Kai and Zilli, taking in the surroundings. To our right is a large open area with several tables on which people are busy crafting objects, fashioning various devices out of both recognizable and strange materials. There is an entire armory: bows and arrows, body armor, and old-fashioned pistols. A blacksmith uses a fire machine to craft swords and rapiers and scimitars and sabers.

"This is amazing," I finally say and Zilli squeezes my hand. "Who are these weapons for?"

"Everyone," Zilli says, "look." She opens her parasol, and it is decorated with three small shuriken, tiny throwing stars. "My aim is really good," she boasts.

"Do you have a weapon?" I confront Kai.

He lifts up his shirt and pulls out a dagger. "We all have one."

"And I'm supposed to feel safe here?" I roll my eyes.

"You haven't seen anything yet. Look." Kai points just to our left, where a garden sits on endless acres of ground.

"Is this—" I can't even finish my sentence. I didn't think it was possible.

"An underground garden? Yes," Kai says proudly as we stop in front of a row of bright red tomatoes that look so ripe I can feel my mouth salivate.

"Can I?"

Kai looks at the nearby gardener who wears black boots, gray slacks, and a long burgundy overcoat. Attached to one of the pockets is a long chain holding a dangling timepiece. "Can she, Lachlan?"

"Sure, it's hers for the tasting." The blondhaired man chivalrously tips his bowler hat and smiles. Other than his strange outfit, he looks a lot like my father, and it makes me homesick.

"Do you know everyone here?"

"Practically. Taj has made us a family. There are about two hundred of us."

"Is everyone an Anomaly?"

"Some of us are. Some of us are simply committed to the revolution."

"She's not even old enough to go to Monarch Camp yet." I nod to Zilli, who is on her knees with Lachlan chasing a ladybug.

"Zilli is special," Kai says, leaving it at that. "There are some regular citizens here, too, ones who have discovered the truth. There are those who have been enlightened. We are the unofficial seventh community . . . only in our community no one has to wear the same color and be confined to the same job. We don't have to be blindly committed to our intended partner and live the life Sobek picked for us. We can choose the life we want to lead. We have autonomy."

I join Zilli in the garden so Kai doesn't see my face. He has no clue how much I feel his words have stabbed me. First I lost the blue-eyed boy, and now the person who I feel most connected to wants nothing to do with me? I can't even begin to think about what is going to happen to me. I will be all alone. Annika and Rane will be living perfect lives with their intended partners and I will be an Anomaly forever.

"Where's Genesis?" I ask as I pluck a tomato off of the vine.

"Here. We're all here, except for Burton and Blue," Kai says. "No one knows where Burton is, and Blue's been hard to extract since she's in the palace. Taj thinks she's safe there, but I'd feel more comfortable if she were extracted."

I shrug. It's not that I'm unhappy to see Genesis; he's a great guy, but I'm immediately annoyed that Kai seems so worried about Blue. I pop the tomato into my mouth. My anger quickly melts away as the sticky wetness leaks down my cheek. It is sensational. I can taste the nuances in the fruit, its micronutrients, the sweetness of the seed, the texture of the ripe skin. I thought the steak I devoured earlier was good, but it has nothing on this tomato, which is absolutely delicious. One row over are mounds of multicolored firm peppers, which a girl in a tall hat and wide leg trousers with a topcoat is delicately cutting from their stems. "How does this work? It hardly seems possible."

Kai smiles, "Everything is possible down here. We're able to be self-sustaining. The food in this garden feeds the entire underground. Think about it. Above ground, even after the war, the ecosystem is being pounded day and night by pollution and resource depletion. Here, we have two hundred acres of fertile garden growing without soil."

"But how? I mean, don't you need sun and water?"

"Taj set up a system of recycling water."

"Seems like Taj can do everything," I say, no longer bothering to swallow my jealousy. I resent this woman whom I've never met. Resent the fact that Kai has so quickly become a committed member of her world and has left mine.

"She can," Kai smiles, oblivious to my distress. "And Taj's water is clean water. So we have a forever food source. Of course, we supplement it with foodstuffs from above land, but this stuff is uncontaminated . . . unlike everything above ground."

"Hold on." I'm getting a little irritated at Kai's blind obedience. "I've been eating food every day of my life. Fresh fish which I've caught with my own hands from the ocean, meat which is raised on local farms, organic vegetables grown locally in the Ocean Community. My food is not contaminated." How dare he, and Taj, say that everything I've ever known is toxic.

"You're right, the food definitely isn't contaminated. I'll give the Global Governance that. They successfully figured out a way to get rid of the prewar pesticides, insecticides, and chemicals. The food definitely isn't tainted." Kai pauses.

"So what are you talking about?" I demand. "What's tainted?"

"The water. Sobek's contaminating it with chemicals which alter our personalities, making us docile and compliant so he can take over our race."

"That's insane."

"You're right. He is. Sobek and his followers have been feeding off of the human race for centuries, making us docile and compliant. Feeding off of our negative energies to make themselves stronger."

"You're not making sense. Sobek saved us after the war. He made the oceans swimmable."

"No. He used the Great Technology War to make himself invaluable to us so that he could have us exactly where he wants us."

"Which is where?"

"As his slaves. His compliant slaves who he can subjugate and feed off."

My world is spinning. Everything I've ever been told has been a lie. Or is this a lie?

"How do you know all this?" I am almost crying now.

"Taj."

"Why would you believe this Taj? What makes her so special that you're all following her blindly?" I'm starting to shout now and making a scene. "If you say Sobek's controlling us, how can you prove it? How can this Taj prove it?"

"Because this Taj *can* prove it." A stunning woman materializes out of the crowd. As she glides toward me, I see that one half of her face is that of a beautiful regal woman with jet-black hair, the other half of her face is a shimmering silver. A luminescent metallic silver, which is dominated by light lavender eyes.

It is only a matter of seconds before I pass out.

"I'M A WHAT?"

After a week of MC-5 torture, Calix was returned to the Caesar and Sarayu was sent home. Calix was fairly sure he would never see her again. She was just a shell of her former self and hardly fit to be his wife. Sobek had confined him to the penthouse, declining to let Calix socialize with his friends or spend time with his mother. He was being fast-tracked to take over and Sobek refused to let him have any distractions.

The first order of business was to finally reveal the facts to Calix. The truth of his identity, the truth of his origin. "You are a Lacertilia. A suborder of an alien race."

"What are you talking about?" Calix demanded.

"You are a Lien," Sobek said simply.

"Um, yeah. And you're a monkey," Calix rolled his eyes.

"I'm serious, son. You are of a higher species. A stronger species. You live among the humans, but you are not one of them."

Calix just stared at his father. He was fairly sure a prank was being pulled on him.

Sobek stared back. He was slightly amused by the way his son was taking the news. However, this might be his own fault. He wasn't sure if he had delivered it correctly. Subtlety was not one of Sobek's strong suits.

"So, you're saying that I'm not human," Calix said.

"Indeed."

"I look human."

"You do. But you can also morph into your true Lien shape if necessary."

Calix's laugh took his father aback. "My true Lien shape? Father, I'm the holo game player, not you. Liens, aliens, Lacertilia . . . whatever you call them are just another name for made-up monsters who my friends and I fight in my games. Is this your way of trying to be hip?"

Sobek, who had little sense of humor, could not understand his son's jesting. "No. I am not trying to be hip. I am being truthful."

"Right. So I'm some big, creepy, superhuman immortal monster from a different planet who is stronger and smarter than the average human?"

"You are." Sobek was losing patience. Why was his son being so difficult?

"Prove it," Calix flippantly challenged as he crossed the room and went out onto the balcony. He hoisted himself on the ledge, which overlooked Sabbatical City. "If I'm not human, it must mean I'm immortal. So, if I jumped what would happen?"

"You would probably die on impact," Sobek said flatly as he followed his son to the balcony.

"But if I'm so advanced, doesn't that mean I can live forever?" Calix easily walked along the ledge as if it were a balance beam. He loved the thrill of danger. He lifted up one foot, precariously balancing himself.

"You've seen too many vids. Our people live long, but not forever."

Calix shifted his body, teetering on the six-inch slab of concrete.

"Prove it . . . Father."

And for the first time in Calix's life, he saw his father instantly morph into a ten-foot Lien with a shimmery metallic body, radiating a silver glow. Sobek's light lavender eyes stared unflinchingly at his son, as if daring him to make his next move.

And Calix fell off the balcony of the hundred-story building.

17.

I am confused.

"What happened?" I blink a few times trying to orient myself.

The first thing I see is Taj's face, the less disturbing side. She's smiling.

"You fainted." Taj hovers over me. She maternally wipes a strand of hair away from my face, and I suddenly think about Annika's mother. I pull back. I don't trust this woman . . . this monster.

I'm lying on a bed made of reclaimed wood and galvanized pipes that is covered in a mound of blankets made of shiny satin, luxurious velvet and intricate lace. Trying to look anywhere but Taj's monstrous face, I examine the room and am surprised by the tent's pretty decor. The large tent is beautifully appointed, filled with copper torch holders, bronze cabinets, and several trunks. Against one wall is a dark wood roll-top desk accompanied by an ornate wooden chair. Against the second wall, there is a dark leather sofa where Zilli is curled up asleep, clutching onto her parasol as if it is a stuffed animal. A metallic bookcase takes up the final wall. It is filled with books, antiquities in today's world where all reading is done on tablets. I want to go touch the paper and sense what an actual book feels like; I've never seen one up close. The whole tent has an industrial aesthetic with subdued colors contrasted with bright metallics.

The walls are filled with linen maps of the world before the Great Technology War and even earlier. These maps are outlawed above ground, as the Global Governance insists that the world began anew when they came to power and that clearly we cannot learn from our past mistakes. The Global Governance dictates that history is a hindrance rather than a help.

"Would you like some water?" Taj's voice is rich and thick and I am compelled to look at her.

"Yes, please."

Even sitting down, Taj seems tall. She is regal and her long, jet-black hair gleams against the emerald green corseted dress she wears. All of her fingers are bejeweled, and a metallic gold octopus hinge-cuff bracelet rests on her left wrist. Her walk is so graceful and fluid, it is as if she is gliding across the room.

"I'm sure you have many questions." Taj hands me a copper cup filled with cool water. I drink greedily.

Where's Kai?" I demand.

"Just outside the tent. He's very worried about you, but I wanted you to rest."

"Why did he stay outside if she's here." I nod over to the sleeping girl.

"Because Kai obeys orders. Zilli does not."

I stare defiantly at Taj. I don't care if she's the leader of the revolution. I don't care if she is half monster. "I want to see him."

"Fair enough." Taj nods at Lachlan, who is lurking in the doorway, almost blending in with the decor. He leaves and seconds later returns with Kai.

"I was so worried, Keeva." Kai rushes over to the bed.

"I just fainted, no big deal," I say with false bravado. Really, I am shaking inside.

"I've never even seen you stumble. At Monarch Camp you were always so tough. So brave. When you just crumbled like that, I thought . . . " He trails off.

"What?"

"I thought that you died."

"Don't be ridiculous." I force a laugh, "I've just never seen a person with half a creature's face before."

Taj is standing behind Kai. Her laughter is loud and silvery. "You mean a creature with half a person's face. I can lose the Lien if it would make you feel more comfortable."

"It would." I don't mean to be rude, but the Lien half of her face is really freaking me out. It's that light lavender eye. There is something so disconcerting about looking into it. It is as if she can see straight through me. And I hate it.

And just like that, she morphs: Her face shape shifts and the beautiful woman replaces the shimmery silver and lavender. No trace of the metallic creature remains. Instead, she has smooth, milky skin, bright green eyes, and a huge toothy smile. She is beautiful.

"How did you do that?"

"My family has been able to do this for centuries."

"Your family?"

"My race," she corrects herself. "We can easily shape shift into the human species. It is an effortless transition for us as we are not that different from you physically. Perhaps we are a bit taller and stronger, but our basic features are the same. The biggest difference is our eye color and our essence, which we wear on the outside instead of the inside. But I should start at the beginning, yes?"

"How far back does the beginning go?" I ask.

"About ten thousand years."

"Sobek and I come from a race of Lien known as the Lieniux," Taj begins. She pours us tea from a brass kettle, and the hot, smoky chai soothes me as I listen to her strange story. We sit around a makeshift table. Lachlan has put a tablecloth on the trunk and he, Taj, Kai, and I have tea. To an outsider, we would look like a family sitting down to afternoon tea: Mom, Dad, and their three kids. It's all quite civilized even though it feels anything but. Zilli has moved from the couch to my lap. I halfheartedly try to push her off of me; but she is determined and won't budge. Admittedly, it feels a little comforting to have her there to hold on to, so I don't protest too much. When Taj finishes pouring the tea, she sits down and continues her story.

"Ten thousand years ago, our home, Lieniux, was dying. It was a tiny planet. But it was our home. We were technologically advanced—far more than this planet is even today. But our race was expiring. Our energies were being starved to death."

"Whoa. Energies?" I am confused.

"Yes. Our race feeds on energies. It gives us life . . . immortality. Yet, without these energies, we cannot survive. And we were running out of energies to feed on. There were not enough living organisms on our planet to sustain us. Not enough specimens."

"Specimens? You mean like animals? Cows, chickens—"

"On our planet, yes. We fed off animals and plants. However, after we discovered your planet we began to feed on humans. It is a much richer . . . diet. When we found Earth, a large enough system with enough specimens to feed ourselves and thrive, fifty of us were chosen to make the exploratory trip, including me and Sobek. We were carefully selected: the children of leaders, thinkers, and pioneers. Twenty-five females and twenty-five males. Each of us no older than you, Keeva." Taj sighed and for a moment it looked as if she were succumbing to nostalgia. Yet it was only for a moment. "We did not know that we would be the only ship to successfully leave Lieniux. So, Sobek and I traveled here along with the surviving members of our race—"

"Ten thousand years ago?" I can barely whisper the words.

"Correct. When we realized we were the only survivors, we had to rethink our game plan. It was no longer an exploratory mission, but a permanent one. Earth would become our home, although we knew that we couldn't just take over. That would ruin the ecosystem and the balance of power. We had to wait. The Lien are a patient species and ten thousand years to us is merely a decade for humans."

Taj pauses, waiting to see if I have another question, but I don't. I am stunned. This woman . . . this creature in front of me is ten thousand years old. It doesn't seem possible, yet it is.

"As the older member of our party, Sobek was our appointed leader. By two minutes really," Taj added with a hint of disgust, "as he is my twin brother. But two minutes can mean everything in situations like this. We collectively put our trust in him and pledged our loyalty. He then guided us how to sustain ourselves. To survive, we fed off the energies of those nearest to us. We started in Mesopotamia, feeding off the energies of the native peoples. We were then based in Egypt for several centuries and fed off the energy of Egyptian slaves. Then we moved to Africa and fed off of the indigenous peoples there. Then we went on to Asia and South America.

"Although we fed, it was not enough for us to just exist. We wanted power. Well, my brother wanted power, and it was easy for him to persuade the four dozen remaining Lien to follow him. I was less convinced, but I pretended to go along with the plan. My brother is greedy. He is also a narcissist who becomes so intent on one thing that he is blind to anything else. That is his greatest weakness. So, as he set his designs on world domination, I slowly began to build a resistance. He had no idea I was doing this as he was so committed to his own vision. Hungry for power, the others all followed him blindly. After all, we Lien are not prone to sympathy. It is not in our nature, so we had no problem using others to benefit ourselves. Sobek laid out his master plan: He knew if he could wait long enough for the world to need him the way he needed them, then he could control the entire planet."

"Like a dictator," Kai chimes in. "Mussolini, Stalin, Hitler."

"Exactly. When my brother started having these megalomaniacal visions a few centuries ago, I knew the human race would be in trouble. Perhaps living so long among the humanoids, some of your feelings wore off on me. So I quietly started to prepare. Long before Sobek instigated the Great Technology War, I began building the Labyrinth."

"He started the war?" I am stunned.

"Yes, it was my brother who supplied the new technologies to the Americans and the Chinese and the Russians. He pitted them against each other so that, inevitably, their peoples got greedy and wanted what they did not have. He advised them and manipulated them so that, eventually, each side pushed its respective button." She laughed. "Well, it wasn't really a matter of too much manipulation. Decades earlier, Sobek had positioned Lien into the roles of power—"

"Wait," Keeva was astonished, "so the American President and the Russian President—"

"And the President of the People's Republic of China," Taj added. "All Lien. My cousins, in fact. So, it was easy for them to convince their peoples. My brother is quite brilliant. Sick, but brilliant, and his plan succeeded. Subsequently, the triangle of nuclear reactors went off, melting the polar ice caps and drowning half of the world, and Sobek stepped in."

"Making everyone dependent on him." I was starting to finally understand.

"Nothing like creating the problem so that you are the one with the solution. Sobek perfected the Third chip to link the survivors to the Lien, he introduced all of our advanced technologies to prevent disease, he dissected the world to prevent acrimony, and . . . ." her voice trails off.

"What?" I am equally disgusted and fascinated by Sobek's cunning and narcissism.

"He figured out a way to make humans compliant."

"How?"

"It's twofold," Taj continues, "he is contaminating the water with what he calls a tasteless fluoride solution that is allegedly good for you."

"It is," I say dumbly, "it helps build strong bones and teeth." Even as I am saying it I realize how silly it sounds.

"That's what my brother wants you to think. It's really a chemical that makes people relax and keeps them docile. It also blocks and calcifies the pineal gland so that the gateway from the physical to the spiritual world is blocked."

It is hard for me to digest this. I've spent my life in the water, and now I am learning it is contaminated. The water I drink, swim in, bathe in, cook with . . . all toxic. I am guessing, no, I am hoping that Sobek's second method of control is more humane.

I am wrong.

"Sobek's second method of control," Taj continues, as if reading my mind, "is the invented concept of intended partners so that humans are completely dependent on each other. He has manipulated your species so that you don't feel like you can exist without the companionship of another."

"I can exist outside Genesis."

"That is because you and Genesis were not originally intended for each other. Your intended partner Dorian—"

"With big blue eyes?" The boy I keep dreaming about.

"Yes, Dorian died when you were at Monarch Camp. His little body could not handle the torture from Sobek's Protectors. Most young bodies can. His was too frail and could not. If he had survived, you would have possibly been reunited with him at camp and you would have been completely dependent on each other."

"How?"

"My brother uses trauma-based mind control on the young, to both feed off of their fear and to make them feel incomplete except in the safety of their partners' arms. By feeding off their fear, he gets stronger and by making them feel incomplete from a very young age, he is able to control them better."

I think about Annika and Rane. Taj has summed up exactly what is wrong with them. They both seem as if they cannot survive without their partners. My friends have become shells of their former shelves because they no longer believe in themselves. "If he feeds off energy, why does it have to be fear?" I ask, trying to ignore the muddy vision in my subconscious of hanging upside down and screaming. "Why can't it be something happier?"

"It can be. We can feed off of any emotion . . . anger, happiness, sadness, tenderness, disgust or fear."

"Then why is the system at Monarch Camp fear-based?"

Taj smiles, placating my ignorance. "Simply said, fear tastes better."

"That's disgusting."

"Be that as it may, it does. There is nothing tastier than feeding off of an innocent because their fears, their terrors, their horrors are so pure. Once you get a taste for caviar, you no longer crave tunafish." Taj waits as I digest this analogy.

"But Zilli—" I start, feeling the child shift in my lap.

"Zilli never went to Monarch Camp. Part of the revolution's agenda is to save what children we can from the torture. Especially the special children. To extract them from their families before they can be chipped."

"What's the difference between a special child and a regular one?"

"The Lien have been breeding with humans for centuries. The bloodlines of the offspring are diluted: the Lien genes are recessive and most of these children have normal DNA. Yet, in a few of them, the Lien DNA becomes dominant and the children have an innate power even stronger than Lien."

"So then, what happens to these special children?" I jump up, knocking Zilli to the ground.

"Ouch," she whines.

"Sorry." I help her up, my eyes never leaving Taj. "What happens to these special children?" I am almost screaming. This is the closest I have ever been to finding my sister. To finding Sun.

"They are brought to safe houses around the world. They are raised to believe in themselves, to fight for themselves, to think for themselves."

"But you take them from their parents—"

"Do I?" Taj hesitates for a flicker of a second. "Or do the parents search me out and ask me to save their children?"

"Where is my sister?" My hands are around Taj's throat before I realize what I am doing. Within seconds, her entire face morphs back into its Lien form and her forked tongue darts out like a weapon, forcibly pushing me away. I look up. Lachlan is standing, sword drawn and ready to protect his Queen. Zilli has her throwing star aimed at me. Even Kai has his dagger aimed at my heart. I can hear their thoughts: I am a threat who must be neutralized.

I am astonished by their devotion to this woman. To this creature. Only Taj remains seated, her shimmery Lien face morphing back into her human one.

"Calm down everyone. It is fine." She turns to me, "I am not the enemy, Keeva."

Flustered, I sit back down.

"Your sister is safe. She always has been. Your parents entrusted her to the revolution. We needed her—"

"Why? Why did you take her? I needed her too."

"Keeva, what is happening to this planet is much bigger than just you and me. And it is not just the youth who are being systematically tortured. Sobek's plan isn't limited to five-year-olds. He runs experiments on the other end of the age spectrum as well. Sobek is also stealing energy from the elderly, from the handicapped, from the mentally ill. When humanoids get too old or too sick, Sobek subtly steps in. Every retirement home is secretly run by Sobek's operatives. Think about it, Keeva. Why don't you see old people anymore? It's because when they are close to dying, they are rounded up and taken to Elderly Villas where they are cared for. Cared for? This is more like Governance-sanctioned neglect. In the villas, Sobek's people can more easily consume life forces because the elderly are already going to die. Why do you think so many people get dementia? It is Sobek sucking their minds empty until they are no longer of use to him. He has been doing this for centuries."

I remembered Annika's grandfather dying in an Elderly Villa. He was not in any pain, but I watched as his mind just slipped away. There was no reason for it. His body was still in perfect health. He was simply old. No one questioned his memory loss, they just blindly accepted his fate. I remember the way the home was decorated. There were tiny painted butterflies in every room. Butterflies on every bed.

"So we have a choice," Taj continues. "We can stay ignorant, continue to allow this abuse and let Sobek finish off humankind as we know it, or we can wake up and fight back. If you want to go find your sister, I won't stop you. Lachlan will take you back up the elevator and you are free to go where you wish. If you want to stay, you have to be deprogrammed so that you fully understand the lie that you have been living. So that you can wake up. Everyone down here has already been awakened. They have accepted the truth and are willing to fight. To join our revolt.

"The question is, Keeva, are you?"

S OBEK SAVED HIS SON'S LIFE.
It was not the first time nor would it be the last. With lightning-fast reflexes, he caught Calix by the ankle, and his superior strength allowed him to lift his son back up to safety. When Calix finally caught his breath, he demanded that his father explain everything.

"Many lifetimes before you were born son, our planet was dying," Sobek began. "Lieniux was an extraordinary planet, far more technologically advanced than Earth. Yet, Earth had one thing that we did not–humanoids. Our race was expiring because there was no diversity. There were only Lien. Everyone was the same so we had no one to feed off. Our energies were being starved to death."

"Energies, seriously father?"

"Indeed. We feast on the energies or auras of other species. The more complex the species, the more satisfying the feed. Siphoning energies gives us enough sustenance to survive. And Lieniux was dying: we were running out of hosts to feed on. So, we found this planet filled with humans, weak creatures whose auras we could dine on. My sister and I traveled here–

"You have a sister?" Calix was shocked. He never knew he had an aunt.

"My twin, Taj. She and I don't exactly see eye to eye. Approximately ten thousand years ago, we traveled here along with the surviving members of our race–"

"Ten thousand years ago?"

"Approximately. Give or take a decade. When we arrived here, we quickly determined that we were a superior species; however, we knew that if we immediately invaded this planet it would destroy the ecosystem and the pyramid of power. So, we had to bide our time until the opportunity for world domination presented itself. It wasn't hard to survive. There were so many disposable people. Countries were overpopulated, so sucking the energy from lower classes was simple enough. We preyed on the people whose minds would not be missed. We traveled through Egypt and Africa and South America, growing stronger—"

"But how?" Calix interrupted.

"Do we feed?" Sobek smiled, amused by his son's stupidity. "We simply get within close proximity to our prey and breathe in."

"You mean, you just breathe in their energies?"

"Their auras. Yes, of course." Sobek was getting irritated at his offspring's ignorance. "Keep up, Son. It's not difficult. We breathe in and our auras do the rest. It is like an electromagnetic force. Everyone has auras, unseen fields of subtle, luminous radiation. Lien can see auras and when we focus and breathe in, we can suck just enough force to feed. Of course, the more immature we are, the less we can control our power, and it sometimes gets out of control." Sobek sighed. He thought educating his son would be easier; he would have to go slower. He tilted his head and studied Calix. "Remember when you and Sarayu were bound together?"

"It was last week, Father." Calix bit the inside of his cheek to control his anger. He would never forget the torture. He would never forget the process that drained his intended partner's personality and energy.

"Good. Well, have you bothered to question why, when you were bound together that she was getting weaker and you were getting stronger?"

"No . . . I . . . ." Calix's mind was swirling. Deep in the recesses of his mind, he knew the bitter truth but he did not want to admit it. Instead, his father said it aloud for him.

"You were siphoning her energy, son. You were feeding off her," Sobek said proudly.

"I didn't mean to," Calix shouted, horrified that he was responsible for Sarayu's weakened state.

"Of course not," Sobek said, each word dripping with disgust. "No one can control their energy when they are young or untrained. But I have learned to manage mine as you will learn to control yours. Anyway, where was I?"

"I have more questions," Calix demanded.

"Of course you do. But I have a story to finish. A history lesson, so to speak. So, as we fed, I realized how easily we could rule this planet. We could use others to benefit ourselves. I laid out my master plan: I would create a situation in which the weak humanoids would crave my expertise the way I craved their energies. I would mastermind such circumstances where they would beg me to control their entire planet."

"Like a dictator?" Calix was disgusted.

"Why such a negative word?" Sobek didn't wait for his son's response. "Anyway, when I started the Great Technology War—"

"You?"

"Guilty." Sobek allowed himself a slight chuckle. "I supplied the new technologies to the Americans and the Chinese and the Russians. I cleverly pitted them against each other, manipulating them by whispering words in their ears. Their leaders were already Lien, and they helped me manipulate their underlings. We promised them power beyond their wildest dreams if they were the sole proprietors of my technology. Their cabinets and committees and politburos fully stood behind their leaders as they pushed their respective buttons. And when the nuclear reactors went off, melting the polar ice caps and drowning half of the world, I magnanimously stepped in."

"Making everyone dependent on you." Calix started to understand.

"Rule one in leadership: create the problem so that you are the one people turn to for the solution. Trust me Son, the people who sell the cures are always the ones who create the disease. But I digress. I perfected the Third chip, which enabled me to link the survivors to the Lien. And as the planet's new benefactor, I generously gave the humanoids the advanced technologies to prevent disease and then put a few systems into place to ensure the humanoids' complete cooperation."

"What systems?" Calix demanded.

"I augmented the water with a tasteless fluoride solution which makes them more docile and I—"

"Sent them to Monarch Camp's MC-5 program." Calix finished his father's sentence.

"There may just be hope for you yet, Son. Yes, I created a groundbreaking trauma-based mind control which both feeds off of young humanoid fear and fractures their sense of self. They feel inadequate except in the safety of their partner's arms. By feeding off their fear, I get stronger, and by ingraining a strong sense of insecurity, I am able to control them more easily."

"Why does it have to be fear?" Calix asked, remembering the terror in Sarayu's eyes.

"It's simple. Fear tastes better."

18.

I am conflicted.

I need to find Sun. But first I must gain Taj's trust and become part of her revolution. How can I not? Sobek is a monster, and I am now one of the few informed citizens who has been enlightened to his master plan. Because I am an Anomaly, I'm not susceptible to his mind control. Because my link to my original intended partner, Dorian, was severed by his death, I am not a fractured person without him. I am a free individual. I can think for myself. My sister has waited for me for the last eleven years, I'm sure she can wait a little longer. Plus, being deprogrammed is the only way I am allowed to officially enter the Underground City. To quote Taj, I must remove my blindfold of ignorance and be reawakened. Only, it's not as simple as taking a test or listening to a lecture. I don't have to raise my hand in the air and pledge my allegiance to the rebellion. Like everyone else in the Labyrinth has done before me, I now have to be reeducated. Awakened. Deprogrammed.

And it involves needles.

"Don't worry, it doesn't hurt," Lachlan says. It didn't take me long to learn that he is in Taj's trusted inner circle. Her second-in-command. Lachlan's gentle voice belies his urgency as he ushers me from Taj's tent, directly across the expansive tent village to a large, boldly striped, black-and-red tent in the distance. I walk slowly, frightened by what may await me. Unconcerned by my terror, Zilli skips behind me, humming. I feel like I am on display as I march in my odd formation. Lachlan, then me, then Zilli. As we pass by the tents, I stare straight ahead, although I can feel the revolutionaries looking at me. As they whisper among themselves, I know that I am blushing. I have red hair and a red face. I must look like a tomato. I hate being on display. Worse than that, I hate feeling like I don't belong.

Everywhere I go, I seem to be an outsider. I suppose I have felt like that my entire life, although I've never really admitted it to myself until now. Something has always been just a little bit off. Sure, Annika and Rane were my best friends, but I always felt different. Maybe because of my sister. Maybe I always felt like I was hiding something and because of that, I could not fully embrace who I was . . . who I was supposed to be. I remember that when the turbaned man, Harijiwan, took my sister, he told me I needed to look within myself to discover truths. Yet I have never really looked inward. Perhaps I have been too afraid to find whatever is inside of me.

I was so desperate to blend in, I always ignored anything which might have made me stand out.

As we pass rows and rows of tents, I cannot help but feel jealous. This is yet another place where everyone seems to belong. Everyone except for me. Like Monarch Camp, I am a freak. I wonder if I will always be an Anomaly, an outsider in a community of people who seem to naturally fit in. Even Kai seems at ease here. Perhaps I shouldn't have come. I just want to disappear, but there is nowhere left for me to hide. A small hand slips into mine. Zilli looks up at me and smiles. The small girl has turned out to be oddly comforting to me. She accepts me for who I am without judgment. I feel a gentle squeeze of encouragement and I squeeze back.

However, once we arrive at the front flap of the large striped tent, she gives me a quick hug and skips away. I hesitate outside the slightly comical tent, which sits quite a distance away from the rest of the olive and brown tents. This tent looks like it should be part of an antique circus, where animals used to perform for humans. Lachlan opens the flap, beckoning to me. I take a deep breath and enter.

Inside, the perimeter of the tent is filled from floor to ceiling with computers. An entire wall of flickering holos show vids from across the universe. There is one of a man near the pyramids. Another of a woman swimming in the Great Barrier Reef. Hundreds of vids projecting people and places flash before me. A scientist, who is monitoring the operation, turns and quickly comes over to me.

"Welcome, Keeva. How are you? We've been busy here expecting you. I'm Holly, pleased to meet you, by golly." Her salutation is singsong and her soprano voice is so high, I have to struggle not to laugh.

"And don't forget about me; my name is Ivy. I'm Holly's twin. It's nice to meet you. Shall we begin?" a second scientist sings. Her voice is equally as high-pitched. I stare at this strange scientific duo and quickly realize that they are completely identical. They have hazel eyes, close-cropped white-haired bobs, and aquiline noses. Both women are similarly dressed, wearing large oculars like headbands and long brown coats, which have *Lab Rats* stenciled on the back in white paint.

"What does that mean?" I point to the back of their coats. I'm procrastinating. Trying to make small talk because I am petrified of what is about to happen.

"Just a little scientific humor," Lachlan chuckles. "These are the Ilex sisters. They are going to take you on a bit of an eye-opening adventure."

"Adventure. Super," I say unenthusiastically as I look around.

Other than the computers, the only piece of furniture in the tent is an operating table—a cold, hard, shiny, metallic slab in the middle of the room, and Lachlan is leading me straight to it. One of the sisters, Holly or Ivy, I've already forgotten who is who, is preparing a fairly long syringe filled with amber liquid while her twin pats the uncomfortable looking table, suggesting that I hop up.

"That's a really big needle." I panic. I hate needles.

"It's OK. Let's not delay," she sings softly as she helps me up, strapping in my arms and legs with tight leather restraints. "It's just a sedative to help you snooze. I promise I won't leave a bruise."

Is this woman for real? If the situation weren't so terrifying it would be downright comical. I look anywhere but the needle, fixing my eyes on the tent's ceiling where a tarp is held up by a maze of copper piping. I need to calm myself down, so I imagine myself swimming through the pipes. My thoughts are interrupted by the woman's lilting voice.

ANOMALIES

"No doubt, it will put you out." She puts a buckwheat pillow underneath my neck and tilts my head back. "Trust me, nothing's amiss, but you won't want to be awake for this."

"I only wish I knew what *this* was," I say bitterly as the other Ilex twin rolls up my sleeve and wraps a tight band around my elbow, finding my vein and plunging the syringe into it.

"Just a little prick, it's really quite quick," she sings. Her voice is getting lower.

I barely have time to panic. Everything is happening so quickly.

And the Ilex sisters keep singing. It gets faster and weirder. Their voices are getting progressively lower. They sound demonic.

"Just sleep," sings Holly, *"count sheep."*

"You'll be out," Ivy harmonizes, *"no doubt."*

I struggle to get up, but the restraints are so tight it is hard to move. I've changed my mind. I want to leave. The sisters keep singing faster and faster.

"Go back in time."

"You'll find the crime."

"See what is true."

"Unshackle a clue."

"It will be revealed, what has been concealed."

"I wan . . . wa." I look at Lachlan, trying to formulate words, but my tongue is thick and I can barely get any words out. These rhyming women are truly crazy. Why did I agree to this?

"Just relax, Keeva." Lachlan's eyes look worried behind his spectacles. He has been where I am going. He knows the terror which awaits me. "This will help you remember. To go forward, you must go back."

I doubt a little serum and a macabre lullaby is going to make me remember anything, but this upside-down day has made me realize that anything is possible.

"1 . . . 1 . . . " I stop struggling, close my eyes and quickly drift into a dream-filled sleep.

I'm spinning around and around, suspended from a vaulted ceiling, watching the world turn around me. I close my eyes because I'm so dizzy, and I call out for help, but no one is listening. There are grown-ups nearby, tall people in crisp black uniforms, who are laughing and ignoring my cries. I try to move my hands to stop myself from spinning, but they're stuck; they're pressed to my sides and swathed in silk, as if I am in a cocoon. Terrified, I finally open my eyes, which immediately rest on him. His name is Dorian. He told it to me earlier when we met at snack time. He gave me an extra cookie. Dorian is smart and he can already read from his older brother's tablet. He is tall, like I am, but he is very, very skinny. I find strength as I look into his bright blue eyes. Silently, Dorian's look encourages me. He will be there for me. He will protect me. And, although I can't stop spinning, I know that I am safe.

But Dorian starts crying. Suddenly, the pain is too much for him. I see hands choking him, large hands. I look at the face of the person who is hurting him. It is Claudia Durant. And she is smiling, as she feasts on his terror. I see her breathe in his life force as it leaves his body. I feel hands choking me. It is torturous, but I know if I can just focus on Dorian that I will be OK. But Dorian's little body is now lifeless. Something has gone wrong. The hands that are clenched around my neck let go and rush over to Dorian. They pound on his chest, trying to revive him, but he is dead. I feel my own tears dry up as I try to be still, wishing I were invisible so that no one will kill me.

I am lowered to the ground, and a large hand envelops my small hand, leading me back to the bunk. They think I am sleepwalking, Yet I am fully conscious. In fact, I feel stronger . . . stronger than I did before Dorian died.

The large hands tuck me into a lower bunk bed in Bunk 4. I open my eyes and see Rane sleeping on the bed next to me. I don't have to see Annika to hear her snoring in the bunk above Rane. We are all five years old and we are all being systematically tortured. I see the large hands pull Rane out of bed. It is her turn to be wrapped up with her intended partner, Edward, who is also from our community. They will be tied together and hung upside down, their energies siphoned from them like gasoline, giving energy to Sobek's people while their own souls are fragmented.

I want to warn Rane, but somehow I realize I am dreaming. After Rane, Annika will be tortured and then every girl and boy at the Summer Solstice session of Monarch Camp. During the day, we run and swim and play. During the night, we are systematically tortured in the stone building. We are part of operation MC-5. Everyone will survive the ordeal except seven people. Along with me, others have lost their intended partners. Kai Loren and Genesis Kraft have also been marked, unknown to anyone, as Anomalies.

Ten years later, our names, along with four others, will be announced by Claudia Durant, the monster responsible for killing our intended partners a decade earlier.

My eyes open suddenly, shocked by this new information. I see Lachlan and the Ilex sisters peering at me. I want to speak, but I can't articulate anything.

"Shhhh. Just relax, Keeva," Lachlan says. "Ivy, give her another shot."

Ivy. That is the name of the Ilex sister. Ivy. Ivy and Holly.

And I'm out.

I'm now in the ocean. My ocean. Swimming. Today, I'm visiting my father at the Desalination Plant. He is busy in meetings, so I decide to go for a swim. Just beyond the heavily protected plant is a series of labyrinthine pipes that run several miles under the water. I am aware that this matches the drawing in my father's notebooks and I see the pipes from a new perspective. Rather than seeing them up close, I am like a bird surveying the entire operation from above. I now know where the heart of the operation is. It is the red-capped carbon chamber in my father's drawing.

Ever since I was a little girl, I would swim in and out of the pipes, challenging myself to stay underwater as long as I could. Usually, I swim alone, but today there are several men working on the pipes. At first, I think they are my father's colleagues. As I swim closer I see they are not wearing the requisite blue uniform. Instead, they are wearing Protectors colors. What are the Protectors doing here? As I swim closer, I see their black webbed fins and the snorkels, which allow them to breathe.

The workers are busily swimming back and forth, putting some sort of liquid in the mainframe's carbon chamber: The pipe with the red cap. What are they doing? I swim closer, and suddenly I can see how they are swimming so quickly. There is a black aura around them, a shimmering energy which allows them to move faster underwater. It encapsulates them and propels them. I look behind their masks, and instead of faces looking back at me, there are metallic orbs with light lavender eyes. These things are not human. One spies me and I race to get away. He chases me through the pipes.

There is one section of the pipeline that is tighter to get through than the others. If I can only swim there, I may escape. I reach the compact area and swim through, my skinny torso and head just making it through. The Lien man is behind me. He swims toward me. His head makes it through the pipe; his body does not. He is stuck. I watch him screaming, but I do not help. He lasts for a minute, maybe more, until all the oxygen in his lungs has been replaced by carbon dioxide and water. He finally stops struggling. His enormous eyes bug out. He is dead.

I blink my eyes. I have to wake up. This alternate reality trip down memory lane is both enlightening and terrifying. I had suppressed the dream of watching the man drown. I hadn't been back to the pipeline since it happened. It was too traumatizing. I have to tell Taj what I have seen; just then I feel another injection in my arm, dragging me further under to the time in my life I most want to forget . . . and I most want to remember.

Screams pierce through the early morning ocean air. My mother isn't due to deliver her baby for several hours, but I sense the baby is coming right now.

Voices inside my head tell me to hurry because I will only get to briefly meet my infant sister before she is taken away from me, and it will be over a decade until we are reunited. The wails become deafening as I race up the shore. When I push open the wooden door, the first thing I see is my mother lying on the bed in a pool of blood. Her eyes are being closed by a man in white clothes and a large turban whom I do not recognize.

My mother is dead. A tiny blond baby lies quietly on the bed next to her, unaware of what is happening around her. My father, my rock, kneels on the floor next to my mother's corpse. He is sobbing.

"Mother," my voice cracks. My life is over.

"You must listen to your heart, Keeva," the turbaned stranger warns, lowering his accented voice and forcing me to come closer to hear him. I instinctively know that he is a good person. A wise man.

"Why?"

"Understand, Keeva, that there will come a time when you are called upon to save this world. And it will not be an easy choice because sometimes you have to make great personal sacrifices for the greater good."

"You mean like hiding my sister?"

"Yes, if we prevent her from being implanted with a Third chip, she could be a great help to us in the future."

"But I won't see her?"

"Not for a long time. However, she will be safe. I promise that I will keep her safe. When you are ready, when you are enlightened, you will know where to go."

"How will I know?"

"Because that which we travel the world to seek is always in our own backyard. And when you are ready, the beacon of light will guide you toward your Sun."

I am now fully awake. And I think I know where my sister is.

LIFE AS CALIX KNEW IT would never be the same.

Now that he was privy to the information about his heritage, now that he knew his father was responsible for secretly manipulating and exploiting humanity for ten thousand years, he needed to decide what to do with that information.

His father refused to discuss his sister Taj. Perhaps if Calix could find his aunt, he might get a different perspective. Yet, Sobek had no intention of introducing him to her, who he said was dangerous. Dangerous? Calix wondered what the world leader could possibly fear.

Sobek knew his son was wavering. That his loyalties were conflicted. And as the consummate puppeteer, Sobek knew how to ultimately manipulate his son to the right side. To his side.

To the side of power.

19.

I am awakened.

The first thing I want to do with my newfound knowledge is to get out.

I need to get to the elevator. I need to get above ground. I think I know where to start searching for my sister, so I can no longer commit my time to the Underground. I have to find Sun. But Taj made it very clear that once I am deprogrammed, I am supposed to stay in the Labyrinth and train before I can return above ground. I am not supposed to leave. I need to be indoctrinated to the revolutionary mindset before my reentry, and what Taj says is law down here.

It makes me wonder if I'm just trading in one dictator for another.

Still, I try to make a run for it. Once I wake up after the deprogramming, I pretend to sleep as the Ilex sisters chatter endlessly, discussing minutiae with their singsong rhymes before they finally decide to go to dinner. Once I am alone, I creep out of the tent and head toward the elevator. The main thoroughfare through the Labyrinth is empty: the revolutionaries are all at the dining tent. I make a beeline to the elevator, determined to leave. I wish I could say goodbye to Kai, but I need to find my sister. I arrive at the base of the elevator and realize that one needs a code to enter.

To get in. To go up. To get out.

There are number and letters on the holo keypad. I have no idea what to push. Frustrated, I tap several buttons, but nothing happens.

"You need a code," a small voice informs me.

I spin around. Zilli is standing just beside me.

"How did you . . . what are you doing here?" I sputter.

"I followed you," she says simply, "from the tent."

"Why?"

"Because you are going to save humanity."

"Listen, Zilli. I really wish you'd stop saying that. I have to go somewhere."

"Where?"

"Somewhere."

"You can't go." Zilli starts to pout.

"I have to."

"That's not the plan."

"The plan's changed." I am losing my patience. "What's the code?"

"I'm not telling you." Zilli crosses her arms in front of her.

"Zilli, please. I have to find my sister. She's like you. She needs to find her family."

"This is my family," Zilli says stubbornly, "and you are supposed to help us."

"I can't, I have to go."

"But I don't want you to go."

I've never argued with a child before. There's no logic behind their reasoning. I crouch down to her level, "Listen, Zilli. It's very important that I go. I promise that I'll come back and I'll bring you someone to play with. Someone close to your age."

"How do I know you'll come back?" Zilli pouts.

She has a point. I don't know myself that I'll want to come back. I can't enter the elevator without her help and she is too young to reason with. I remember Rane's constant fights with her baby brother. The only way she could get what she wanted was to bribe him. I have nothing to give, except . . .

"Zilli, what if I give you something very special. Something that is so important to me that I will want to come back for it." I look at my wrist. The bandanna my father gave me is still wrapped around it. It gives me both strength and a tangible memory of him. I untie it and wrap it around her tiny wrist.

"This is a present from my father. It is the most precious thing I own. Will you hold onto it until I get back?"

Zilli nods. She is thrilled with her new present, although still reluctant to let me leave.

"Do you know the code to get into the elevator?"

She nods.

"Can you please tell it to me?" I am trying very hard to be patient.

"OK," she finally says. "The code is PROTECTORS333." Zilli turns to leave.

"Thank you," I call behind her and punch in the letters and numbers. As I tap the last number three, I expect the door to hiss open. Instead, a loud wail emits from the elevator. An alarm. I've been fooled by an eight-year-old. I stand, hands in the air, as the first people on the scene approach, weapons raised.

And deliver me back to Taj's tent.

"I must say, Keeva, I've never had someone try to escape from the Labyrinth. You are the first."

"I want to go up," I say. Even though Taj has offered me a seat, I stand.

"I appreciate your spirit," Taj chuckles. "Sometimes what we think we are looking for, isn't what we are looking for at all."

"What does that mean? Why do you talk in so many riddles?"

"Because humans have gotten intellectually lazy. You expect the answers given to you instead of working for them." She sighs, "It's why it was so easy for my brother to take over. He specializes in instant gratification."

"I just want to go." Now I feel like a petulant child.

Taj walks over to the large bookshelf and pulls out an ancient leather bound book. "Have you ever read this?"

I can't help myself as I grab the book from her. I've wanted to touch a real book my entire life. I inhale the musky scent and greedily touch every inch of the leather binding. I turn the pages, touching the smooth paper, thrilled to see the printed words neatly typed across the pages. It is *The Art of War* by Sun Tzu.

"No."

Gù yuē: Zhī bǐ zhījǐ, bǐizhànbùdài; bùzhī bǐ ér zhījǐ,
   yī shèngyī fù; bùzhī bǐ, bù zhījǐ, měi zhàn bì dài.

"I have no idea what you just said."

"It's the ancient language of the Asias," Taj says. "*It is said that if you know your enemies and know yourself, you* can win a hundred battles without a single loss. *If you only know yourself, but not your opponent, you may win or may lose. If you know neither yourself nor your enemy, you will always endanger yourself.*"

"So, you're saying I don't know myself."

"Not yet. You will."

"How?" I demand. I am so frustrated. I feel like I've spent my entire lifetime trying to figure out who I am and I'm not anywhere closer than when I started.

"Trust yourself. Trust your instincts," Taj says as she unhinges her octopus bracelet and puts it on my newly bare wrist. Suddenly, tiny eight legs shoot out of the octopus's body. The legs seem to have a life of their own as they mechanically wind up my arm before locking shut. It is as if I am wearing a piece of medieval armor.

"Whoa. How did they do that?" I say, looking at the eight legs, which now cover my forearm. "When you wore the bracelet, the octopus's legs were curled around the metal cuff. Now they're extended onto my arm."

Taj grabs a stick and calligraphies a word into the sand.

"C-E-L-P-H?" I say, spelling the word slowly. "What does that mean?"

"This Celph is an ancient artifact from Babylonia. It is a talisman with unique powers which only its wearer can unlock."

"Is it magic?" I wonder, trying to manipulate the bracelet; yet it stays fast.

"*Any sufficiently advanced technology is indistinguishable from magic.* Arthur C. Clarke said that, and he's right. From my multimillennium of lifetimes, I can testify to that."

The Rise of the Underground

"You said it's an ancient artifact. So, how can it be advanced technology?"

"Indeed." Taj smiles but elucidates no further. Another riddle.

I touch the cool metal, entranced by its beauty. "Why are you giving it to me?"

"Why did you give your father's bandanna to Zilli?"

"So she would trust me."

"Exactly." Taj smiles, "Your instincts are strong, they just need to be honed. You think you're a guppy, but you are really an octopus . . . one of the smartest warriors on this planet and a defender of the sea. Like their arms, they are not limited to a couple of strategies; they have eight ways to defend themselves against their predators. Octopi can do everything to defeat their enemies, from offensively squirting ink to defensively camouflaging themselves to hide. Like you, they are fast swimmers. Take the artifact, Keeva. It will help you when things look most bleak."

"How will it help me?" I am entranced by this stunning piece of jewelry.

"It has powers which can only be unlocked when you truly know yourself."

"Then I'll never unlock it," I mutter.

"You need to start believing in yourself, Keeva. You have two options . . . you can be a great leader, or you can disappear. If you choose to embrace your greatness, this bracelet will help. It allows the wearer to access bits of unused DNA . . . giving access to extra memory, unrivaled speed, ultra-strength. You name it."

"How will I know when it starts to work?" I ask.

"You'll know. The Celph will show you." She walks to the tent entrance and opens the flap, suggesting that our conversation is over. "Spend a couple of weeks down here, Keeva. Watch. Listen. Learn."

"Do I have a choice?"

"No." Taj smiles as she ushers me out.

I have to give her credit. At least she didn't sugarcoat it.

CALIX SULKED IN HIS ROOM. It was another Saturday night and he was stuck in his father's penthouse.

Calix's misery was interrupted by a buzzing at the door. He entered the main room just in time to his father opening the door for his four best friends.

"This is so awesome," Calix's best friend Rao said, looking around as he entered.

"Wait. What are you doing here?" Calix asked, as Rao was followed by Byron, August, and Emmet.

"What are they doing here?" Calix demanded as Sobek graciously ushered the boys in.

"I know I've been hard on you, Son. So, I thought I'd organize a little surprise sleepover. Something spontaneous and fun for you."

"A surprise sleepover?" Calix felt himself parroting the words back to his father. Something was wrong. Something was very wrong. Sobek didn't have a spontaneous bone in his body. Everything he did was calculated.

"Don't look so surprised." Sobek uncharacteristically put his arm around his son, leading him to the couch where his friends had already settled themselves. "It's time for you to relax a little. Let go."

Calix was shocked. His father hadn't let him hang out with his friends since he had returned from camp. In fact, Calix couldn't remember a time when his friends had been invited up to his father's penthouse . . . to his father's lair. Calix's best friends always visited him at his mother's apartment, which was warm and inviting. While many of them had asked about Sobek's penthouse, none had dared to visit. And now Sobek had invited them for a sleepover. "Seriously?"

"Absolutely. I have access to a few new vids they might enjoy, including the new Sickled Blade trilogy."

"Epic!" Rao and Byron high-fived.

"It's my pleasure, boys." Sobek smiled. He had come up with a surefire plan to ensure that his son would join him.

Even if it meant possibly killing a few of his friends to convince him.

Sobek had spared no expense to make Calix's friends comfortable. He brought in big black leather couches, which the boys sunk into, ready to watch the promised double feature. The ever-present Rika diligently handed the four boys big bowls of popcorn and large thirst quenchers as they settled in for the evening. They would be the first of their friends to see it, as the vid hadn't yet been released to the public. But World Leader Sobek had access to all the pre-release vids being made in West America.

Calix dug his hand into a large bowl and settled in to watch the coming attractions. The last few days had been a disturbing blur, and his friends brought him an admitted sense of normalcy. Rao, August, Byron, and Emmett were sprawled out in front of the projection. The teens were Calix's closest friends. They had all grown up together in Sabbatical City; they played holo tag together and were in the same class in secondary school. Byron and Calix had acted in theater together. Emmett and Calix had been on the debate team together. August and Calix had run on the track team together. And Rao was Calix's best friend, his closest confidante. Calix had known them since they all went to Monarch Camp when they were five years old.

The boys were thrilled to watch the horror vid. Each was on the brink of manhood and would soon be leaving his Community. This would be one of their last bonding experiences before real life took over. Shy Rao, a science prodigy, had been matched with a girl in the Academic Community and would be moving to East America, where he would apprentice in a physics laboratory. Brawny August and talkative Byron had both been matched with girls from Ocean Community and would be moving west. August would apprentice at the Desalination Plant and Byron would apprentice in the fishery. Only Emmett and Calix would be staying in Sabbatical City. Emmett had been matched with a local girl and would work in the family business distributing Thirds, and Calix, the only Protector in the group, had to stay put to fulfill his destiny. Both Emmett and Calix would follow their fathers' footsteps. Calix shuddered; only he knew that his father's footsteps were made of a shimmery metallic from an alien planet.

"How are you enjoying the vid?" Sobek's booming voice echoed throughout the room. No one heard him enter, they had all been too engrossed in the climactic first murder in which a teenager's belly was sliced open by a masked man wielding a sickled blade.

"Excellent, sir," Byron stumbled as he tried to stand up. "This is some sick stuff."

The other boys nodded in unison. Although Calix still hadn't forgiven his father for his lessons at Monarch Camp, he was grateful for the time with his friends, which Sobek had orchestrated. He chimed in, "It's really cool, Father. Thanks."

"Of course, Son. I may be the world leader, but I still like to think of myself as cool." Sobek smiled at the boys. "Now, relax and enjoy. Prepare to be scared beyond your wildest imaginations."

"Awesome!" the boys screamed in unison before turning their attention back to the screen.

"Calix, may I see you for a moment?"

"But Father," Calix protested, "It already started."

Sobek didn't respond, rather, he turned and went into his inner office. Calix groaned and got up from his seat next to Rao. He had no choice but to obey.

""What do you want, Father?" Calix stood in the doorjamb craning to watch the vid. On the screen, the masked man was sharpening his blade. The surround sound made each scrape of the knife sound like nails scraping across a chalkboard. It sent shivers through his body. Calix glared at Sobek, repeating his question. "What do you want, Father?"

"To continue your education, Son," Sobek said. "In fifty seconds, I am going to need you to close your eyes."

"Huh? Can't we do it later, I don't want to miss the vid."

"Don't be ridiculous. It is a silly pretense. Actors pretending to be students on a camping trip, systematically and brutally murdered one by one. It is just make-believe. The blond actor is really the killer."

"Did you just ruin it for me?" Calix was furious.

"It is not about a contrived story, Calix. It is about your ability to drink auras. I need you to start practicing."

"On my friends? No way. I'm not letting them turn out like Sarayu," Calix said defiantly.

The Rise of the Underground   **229**

"And they don't have to . . . if you can control yourself and only take what you need. Just steal a little bit. They won't feel a thing."

"No." Calix stood his ground. His father was a sick man.

"It is not a request, Son." Sobek glared.

"I am not going to practice on my friends," Calix insisted.

"Not all, just one. Pick one friend."

Calix was stunned. He thought his father's gesture of inviting the guys over was a kind one. He should have known better; his father was never kind. He was a cold-hearted monster, and Calix would never be rid of him. He wanted to run, to escape, to get as far away from his father as possible; yet he also knew it was far easier to obey him than to refuse him. The last time he'd resisted his father's request, he found himself hanging from a ceiling with butterflies dancing in front of his eyes. But he could not choose one of his friends to hurt. He simply would not do it. He would fake it. How hard could it be to pretend? Calix smiled at his father and nodded compliantly.

"Good, Son. Now, close your eyes and breathe. Feel the energy of the room around you."

Calix smiled. He would focus on his father, not his friends. If Sobek wanted someone's aura siphoned, he was fair game as well. "Now what? My eyes are shut."

Sobek looked at the screen in the other room. The first student had wandered into the forest, seconds away from getting killed. He could smell the terror of Calix's friends. Rao was a bit nonchalant, but the other three were lapping it up. Emmett was the most absorbed in the picture. He had stopped eating popcorn, and both his eyes and mouth were wide open, as if transfixed in fear. Sobek grinned; this would be an easy choice. Calix could pick the low-hanging fruit, starting off with the easiest of the four and picking them off one by one. Emmett's fear was so strong it was palpable. It would be so simple, a child Lien could do it. Sobek could see the boy's aura—he could almost taste it, even from the other room. He only hoped his son's senses were strong enough to detect the same.

"What do you feel?" Sobek whispered.

"Nothing. I mean . . . wait." Calix paused, eyes closed, and breathed in. He tried to focus all of his attention on his father, although he could feel something in the other room. It was muted at first, but then it grew in intensity. As another victim was killed on the screen . . . the sound of the serrated knife brutally cutting him apart, Calix sensed the fear in the room. It flushed over him like a wave, empowering him with a newfound strength. Calix tried to ignore it, but it was hard to control his feelings. He answered his father honestly, "I feel . . . I feel . . . electricity, like my fingers are buzzing."

"Good, Son. Good," Sobek encouraged. "Now, keep your eyes closed and continue to focus."

Again, Calix tried to concentrate on his father and breathe in Sobek's aura, which was right next to him. But he couldn't sense anything. Sobek didn't give off any emotion, and if he did, it was way too nuanced for Calix to feel. Instead, he continued to feel the lure of the terror from the other room. Calix could sense his friends' energies and almost read them. Rao's energy was amused. He was mocking the film, clinically wondering how it was anatomically possible to slice open a gut and pull out entrails. Byron and August were scared, terrified even . . . but it was

Emmett who was completely petrified. His whole body was quivering. Without opening his eyes, Calix could taste his friend's terror.

"What do you feel, Son?"

"Power," Calix whispered. His hands were shaking. Even from the next room, he could sense the aura. It was exhilarating.

"Good. Now, you are going to harness that power."

"How?" Calix's whole body felt alive as if something had been awakened in him. He tried to fight it, but it was too strong.

"Go sit down next to your friends."

"Please, Father. I can't," Calix said weakly, but even as he was protesting, he felt himself drawn into the other room. Shaking, Calix sat on the couch next to Emmett.

And he breathed in.

20.

I am adjusting.

Life underground isn't as bad as I'd imagined and I am learning. Both about the revolution and myself. There is an entire subculture down here and although I feel like I am an intruder, I am fascinated by the revolutionaries' passion and dedication to their cause. They are advocates for change and fully committed to make the world a better place and saving humanity in the process.

Other than Kai, Genesis is my closest friend in the Labyrinth. It's great to reconnect with him, especially without the pressure of being each other's intended partner. We can just be friends. Genesis is far more laid-back than most people down here who are eager for revolution: he is content just to garden. He's grateful to be a part of the Labyrinth and he feels like his purpose is cultivating the soil and providing food. Genesis is good with his hands, and because he grew up in the Ecosystem Community, his skills have made him an integral part of the Sustenance Brigade, one of the three Brigades that operate the Labyrinth. The Sustenance Brigade is composed of people like Genesis and Lachlan, who know how to live off the land. They provide our food and maintain the city's daily operations.

The Bandit Brigade, the elite brigade that Kai belongs to, is made up of revolutionaries whose job it is to go above ground and steal materials to keep the Labyrinth working. They work in pairs, with one person distracting the intended mark and the other grabbing their material goods. Running a city costs money, and Taj has no compunction when it comes to stealing from the wealthy to support her cause. Yet there are only six members of the Bandit Brigade: Kai and his partner Gina, Zilli and her partner Troy, the gangly boy I saw her with above ground, and Lachlan's younger brother Fergus and his partner Suguru, a pretty boy with long hair. Taj's Underground cannot be infiltrated because no one besides the six members of the Bandit Brigade—and Taj—are allowed to go above ground. The chance of discovery is too dangerous; plus, if Sobek has any spies or plants in the Underground, they cannot get word to him, as the entire Underground is cut off from electronic communication with the outside world.

The coordinates of the Labyrinth are protected.

The last group is the Craftsman Brigade, made up of scientists, builders, and philosophers. They use both their minds and hands to craft the master plan to stop Sobek and create the weapons of revolution for when the time comes to fight. These are the real underground warriors who are skilled in the art of warfare, both mental and physical.

As I adjust to my life in Underground City, I divide my time between the Sustenance and the Craftsman Brigades.

Taj does not trust me to go above ground, nor should she. I still want to find my sister and I am constantly tempted to escape. But sometimes it's easier to obey than to refuse. So I bide my time by obeying and learning. In the Sustenance Brigade, I learn how to survive without relying on technology. There are no processed foods down here. Everything is fresh. I work side by side with Genesis in the garden, tending to the vegetables and learning about irrigation. When I kneel in the dirt and prune the plants, I feel at one with the earth in the same way I used to feel when I swam. My mind and my ego are uncluttered and I just . . . am. I'm not worried about schoolwork or boys or following the rules. I am in the moment and it feels wonderful. I look around; no one knows what I am feeling because it is inside of me. I don't have the need to run to tell Annika or Rane. I just enjoy the moment for what it is. It is in this state of mindful bliss when I feel one of the octopus legs around my wrist loosen and slide back into place on the cuff. I look down. How did that happen?

"Keeva." Lachlan approaches and gives me a hand, helping me up.

"At your service." I wipe the dirt from my hands.

"Ready for a lesson?" he asks, smiling.

"I think I just had one, though it was weird," I say, touching my octopus bracelet.

"Good. Lessons often come when you least expect them. Oftentimes the answer has always been within." He looks at Genesis. "Mind if I borrow her?"

"Only if you promise to bring her back." Genesis blushes. Is he flirting with me? He has been so nice to me, so constant. I feel safe with him. Unlike Kai . . . and even me, Genesis has no ego. He puts his work for the good of the community above himself. "I won't be gone long." I smile at him and lower my eyes, suddenly embarrassed by our proximity.

Wait? Am I flirting back?

I walk with Lachlan down a long row of pepper plants to the far end of the garden. Despite being underground, the self-sustaining garden is in full bloom and I marvel at the colors and smells.

"I understand your father is a bigwig at the Desalination Plant," Lachlan says.

"He is. He was," I add uncertainly. I don't even know if my father is still alive. I wish I knew where the Protectors took him. What they did with him.

"How often have you been to the plant?" Lachlan interrupts my thoughts.

"Hundreds of times. I often went there after school to visit my father before I went swimming."

"So then you know how to purify water." He waits, expectantly.

"Um, no."

"Why not?"

"It never interested me. It was just numbers and machines and . . . why are you asking me?" Was it just minutes ago that I was feeling at peace in the garden? Now I feel like a scolded child.

"Information is power, Keeva. That's one of the reasons Sobek is so successful. He parcels out information on a need-to-know basis. His race has access to so much technology; yet humans are not privy to it. Humans merely follow the rules, they don't impose them."

"What do you mean they?" I ask. "You're one of us, too."

"Am I?" Lachlan stops and pulls his timepiece out of his coat and consults it. He then turns to me, and within seconds shifts his shape into a Lien. Although he is still wearing his burgundy coat and gray slacks, his skin has been replaced by a shimmery silver. Underneath his bowler hat, his face has completely morphed into a Lien head. Gone is the Lachlan I have come to know. His pale skin, blond hair, and warm smile have been replaced by a shimmy metallic mask that is broken up only by the indentations of two light lavender eyes. His whole face seems to move, but he is not hideous. I stare at him, unflinching. I am starting to see the beauty in these creatures. There is a simple beauty in their mercurial form. They move effortlessly, as if they are gliding.

"You're one of them?" I try to contain my surprise even though I am taken aback.

"Many of us are." He effortlessly shifts back into his human form and readjusts his hat. "The best way to stop Sobek is from within and many of us are working from the inside. We are everywhere. The Americas, the Asias, Australia. We are both above and below ground."

I look around at the people in the garden. "Who else is a Lien?"

"Does it matter, Keeva?" Lachlan asks earnestly.

I look around the garden at the workers busily committing to their tasks. Across the main thoroughfare, I can see artisans constructing weapons. On the other side of the city, select revolutionaries go up in the elevator, risking danger daily to do their part to help the revolution. And I realize that it does not matter who is in fact from another galaxy. I have accepted that the Lien species lives among us, and now I must accept that they do not all have evil agendas. There are good ones. Like Lachlan.

"So, what's this about a lesson?" I change the subject.

"I'm going to teach you how to purify water."

"Right," I laugh. "I mean, we can't. We need machines." I say looking around. My father's plant is so enormous, it would take up over half the Labyrinth.

"Do we?" Lachlan chuckles and leads me to his gardening shed. Inside there are a few things laid out on the table, including a pitcher of water, a blue cup, a glass bowl, and a roll of plastic.

"Almost everything we need is right here," he says confidently.

"OK. . . ." I say tentatively. Where are the machines? The filters? The pumps and the holding tanks?

"Take a sip of the water, Keeva." Lachlan pours a little water from the pitcher into the glass.

I drink the water and immediately spit it out. "It's salty."

"Indeed. I just wanted to show you what ocean water tastes like."

"Oh, I've tasted plenty of it. Growing up, I've swallowed many waves."

"Good. Then you are aware that it is undrinkable. Now, take the small glass cup and put it in the middle of the large glass bowl."

I dump out the remaining drops of salty water from the cup I am still holding and put it in the middle of the clear glass bowl. "Now what?"

"Fill the large glass bowl with the saline water and stop filling it when you are approximately one inch from the top of the cup."

I do so, careful to pour the water to Lachlan's specifications. "Done. Now what?"

"An eager student. I like it. OK, wrap the plastic over the bowl, cup and water and allow for a little bit of slack in the plastic."

Once I do this, Lachlan picks up the bowl and goes outside. I follow him and watch as he places it directly under a reverse solar panel, with the light hitting the top of the bowl.

"Now we need one last thing," he says.

"What?"

"A marble. Do you happen to have a marble?"

"No." Is he crazy? Why would I have a marble of all random things.

Lachlan reaches behind my ear. "What's this?" he teases, producing a red marble in his hand.

"Aren't you a little old for magic tricks?" I playfully chastise him. I feel very relaxed around this man. Around this Lien.

"One should never be too old for magic tricks." Lachlan puts the marble on the plastic just above the glass cup. The heaviness of the marble creates a makeshift draining system.

"Now what?"

"Now, we wait." He ties two hammocks to nearby posts and beckons for me to sit. "By placing the marble on the plastic, it allows just enough condensation to collect on the plastic which will then drain down into the cup."

Lachlan and I swing on our hammocks for the next several hours, watching the water. When it's time to eat, he instructs Genesis to go to the dining tent and bring us our dinner in the garden. Genesis brings thermoses of soup. One for Lachlan and me, one for himself, and one for Zilli who is lurking nearby. Genesis sits on my hammock with me, and we drink in comfortable silence. Later, as we wait for the water to desalinate, Lachlan tells us stories of ancient days.

Stories my father told me as bedtime stories.

Stories I read about in history books.

Stories Lachlan lived through.

"Wake up Keeva," Lachlan gently shakes me awake.

"Where is everyone?" I'm disoriented. I slept in the hammock all night.

They've already started their days. Look at your water." He removes the plastic and hands me the blue glass cup, which is now filled with water.

"Can I drink it?"

"I'd expect nothing less."

Slowly, I bring the glass to my mouth and sip. It tastes fantastic, crisp and fresh. "It's delicious."

"And you made it, Keeva. Without any big machines. Just some plastic and a marble."

"What about that water?" I point to the collected water in the bowl.

"That is still salty. The desalination process works because salt cannot evaporate with the water that collects on the plastic. All the salt from the water is left in the large bowl."

"This is fantastic." I feel empowered by this newfound skill. I feel like I have access to important knowledge, which I am now capable of imparting to someone else.

As I feel this extraordinary rush of joy, I feel a click on my wrist as one more octopus leg disengages on my bracelet and snaps back into place.

CALIX COULDN'T STOP.

As the vid progressed and the teens in the room became increasingly terrified, Calix's entire body was alive. It was tingling with power as he greedily drank Emmett's aura.

As he breathed in, siphoning Emmett's aura, Calix could feel his friend's energy draining. It was too addictive to stop, a delicious rush of everything he had ever enjoyed: the thrill of a holo tag win, the triumphant hacking into a computer's mainframe, the warmth of his mother's hug. Everything Calix relished intermingled as he siphoned the aura. And with each breath in, he felt stronger. After a while, Calix's thirst was replaced by panic as he realized that he could not stop. He was a slave to the feeling; it was controlling him . . . he was not controlling it.

"Father," he croaked out, begging him with his eyes.

Sobek didn't come. Instead, he sat in his office watching his son from the other room. He was pleased at how quickly Calix had picked up the skill. Now, he needed to ensure Calix's devotion. To him. To the Lien race. Sobek had felt his son wavering when he was first given the task of siphoning energies. Now Sobek would play his final card . . . in this round.

The world leader went out to the living room, sat down and placed himself as a barrier between Calix and Emmett. Once the connection between the boys was lost, Emmett's eyes rolled into the back of his head and he fainted.

"What did I do?" Calix whispered, hoping that his other friends hadn't noticed. He needn't have worried.

They were completely engrossed in the climactic ending of the vid.

"Nothing a little time and rest won't cure." Sobek pulled Emmett's sleeping bag over him and rested the boy's head on his pillow. "Look, it is like he is sleeping with his eyes opened," Sobek chuckled.

"Does he know what happened?"

"Of course not," Sobek snapped. "Humans are often unaware of everything but themselves."

"Did I . . . kill him?" Calix was trying to control his breathing. He felt hysterical, yet he also felt strong . . . hungry . . . greedy for more. And it terrified him.

"Not yet." Sobek turned his attention to the screen, just as the blond murderer was having his comeuppance. As the end credits rolled, he looked at the other boys and said, "Are you ready for round two?"

"Oh yeah," Rao said smiling.

"Bring it on," Byron and August said in unison.

Sobek punched a code into his identity watch and the next vid started immediately. It was entitled *Revenge of the Butcher's Knife*. The remaining boys were glued to the holo and didn't even notice that Emmett had "drifted off to sleep."

Sobek sneered. The human race was so weak. It was no wonder they had been easy to conquer.

21.

I am learning.

I quickly settle into a comfortable routine. I spend my days switching off between the Sustenance Brigade and the Craftsman Brigade. Apparently, I'm still not ready yet for the Bandit Brigade. Maybe Taj still doesn't trust me. Maybe she doesn't think I have the guts. But I've already learned how to live in the moment and survive off of the land. I am a fast learner, but I'm not without my flaws. Including jealousy. I miss Kai. I wish I could spend more time with him, but he leaves first thing in the morning and is up the elevator and working above ground before the rest of the city awakes.

Kai's partner, Gina, is an elfin girl who used to be in the Academic Community. She is smart and brave, and at first, I was resentful of her, but then I met her girl-friend Rezz, and I realized that I had nothing to be jealous about. My first night in the Labyrinth, they invited me to bunk with them in the teen girls' tent.

Tent living is unlike anything I have ever experienced. It's run on the ancient Kupah system, where practically everything is shared. We each have our own beds, a series of olive hammocks hung in ten rows of three across the long room. Gina and Rezz both have top hammocks next to each other, but there is an available middle one below Rezz and above Patel, a shy girl who works in the Sustenance Brigade. My first night in the dormitory environment, I am unsure if I will be able to sleep . . . until Patel's snoring reminds me of Annika and I drift off.

In the morning, I watch in amazement as the girls get dressed. All the community clothes and necessities are on a huge shelf, and we may take what we want. At the end of the day, we throw the clothes in hampers where members of the Sustenance Brigade collect the washing as part of their duties. For someone who grew up limited to wearing only blue, I now have a lot to choose from. I never realized having a choice could be so wonderful. It is freeing to be able to select what I feel like wearing rather than being told what to put on. I gravitate toward a wardrobe of green equestrian pants, a crisp white tuxedo blouse, brown high boots and a leather vest. I love my new, dynamic garments, which aren't limited to one color, and I love my new, dynamic friends who are unique and think for themselves.

The revolutionaries are universally curious and behave the way my friends used to before they were brainwashed. Gina and Rezz are only a couple of years older than I am. The three of us become instantly close, and they accept Zilli, who is our little tagalong. These girls couldn't be any more physically different from Annika and Rane. Gina has beautiful ebony skin and a shaved head. She is petite and extremely agile, important skills that help her thieve above ground. Rezz is a redhead like me, only she's very brawny. A former Labor, she has clearly been working with her hands her entire life and has highly developed muscles. She works in the Craftsman Brigade forging swords. One day, she shows me how to build a sword from scratch. The Brigade has its own series of work tents, and I follow her through each part of process.

"OK, Keeva, pick a piece of steel," Rezz says once we enter the first tent.

There are several pieces to choose from. Some are heavy and some are light. I choose a sheet of thick metal and hand it to her. Rezz then puts on goggles and gloves and uses a laser to cut it into an 18-inch piece.

"Cool," I say watching the red laser beam easily cut through the metal.

"It's Lien technology. Taj is teaching us all about it."

"What about the technologies Sobek is cultivating on the outside?"

"Oh, we have access to those as fast as he does. Remember, we're everywhere."

"OK, by we . . . do you mean that you are a Lien, too?"

Rezz laughs, "No, I'm a boring old human. But I grew up with the Lien. They're everywhere."

"How do you know who they are?" I'm still having trouble adjusting to the notion of Lien living among us as humans.

"You don't," she says, handing me a mallet. "We have to hammer this into shape."

As I pound the metal, Rezz educates me about the Lien race. "The Lieniux have been here for over ten thousand years, Keeva. You don't think just the originals are here, do you? Sure, Sobek and Taj and Lachlan and maybe a few other ancients, but ten thousand years is a long time. They procreated and bore offspring, which are usually full Lien, even though half human-half Lien have managed to slip through the cracks. Most of these absorbed the recessive Lien gene and are nearly full-blooded humans; however, there are a few Hybrids who got the dominant Lien gene. These unique Hybrids have been living among us since before we were born."

"What's the difference between full-blooded Lien and Hybrids?"

"Hybrids are far more powerful." Rezz takes the hammer and examines it. "Hybrids have the strengths of both humans and Lien. They have human compassion, plus they have gifts Sobek is working on to exploit for his own needs."

"Wait, so now in addition to Lien, you're saying there are Hybrids in the Ocean Community?"

"They are few, the Hybrids, and many of them remain hidden from the general population, either by Sobek or by us. The ones who slip by us are discovered at Monarch Camp when they are five. That's when their DNA is classified. Every Hybrid is identified during the torture process and then matched with a fellow Hybrid or Lien. This keeps the bloodline going. Even though it's a bit diluted, it still keeps the Lien stronger. Sobek then manipulates these people into power. Keep your friends close and your enemies closer. The heads of old governments were all full-blooded or Hybrid Lien, past presidents, queens, and prime ministers. Every top-tiered member of Sobek's Governance is a Lien."

She examines the metal. "OK, you can stop hammering. We're ready to move on."

It shocks me how cavalier Rezz is as she discusses the Lien. This species has infiltrated itself into our planet, so much so that no one knows who is who: human, Lien, Hybrid. No one knows except for Sobek.

I follow Rezz to an area with a series of fire pits. She places the metal in the fire.

"How hot is that?" I see the blue flames eagerly licking the metal.

"Eighteen hundred degrees. The high temperature is necessary for me to harden it." She deftly turns the blade back and forth over the flame. She glances up at the elevator, which can just be seen entering the shaft as it descends into the Labyrinth. "Gina should be done soon. She had the early shift today."

"When did you first meet Gina?" I ask.

"Monarch Camp. We were in the Winter Solstice session three years ago."

"My friend Rane's brother was in that session."

"Yep, Cannon. I didn't know him very well, but his intended partner, Jo, grew up with Gina in the Academic Community. She was always really kind to us . . . even though we were Anomalies."

"You and Gina both were?" I ask.

"Yes. Both of our intended partners had died sometime between their first and second visits to Monarch Camp. So we were classified as unmatched individuals and labeled as Anomalies. Trust me, we dealt with the same ridiculous mental and physical tests you did. Claudia Durant, Max, Inelia. From the moment I met Gina, I knew that she was meant to be my intended partner, but Sobek's system doesn't allow for same-gender intended partners."

"Why not?"

"Sobek needs breeders. One man and one woman. His system of compliance is dependent on it. Needless to say, Gina and I didn't fit his cookie-cutter society."

"So what happened?" I am fascinated that Rezz is in love with a girl. I didn't know that happened. Ever since I was a little girl, women were paired with men. That is the way it has always been done. But now I have met a woman who has chosen to be paired with another woman. My eyes continue to be opened to new possibilities. Like the restriction on my wardrobe, Sobek has put a gender restriction on pairs to suit his needs. It is not fair. People should be paired with whom they want to be paired, not just to serve a megalomaniac leader. I'm equally enthralled by Rezz's story and by the red-hot piece of metal she pulls out of the fire and quickly dunks into a barrel of oil.

"Now I'm quenching the sword," Rezz says as she pulls it out of the barrel and hands me a scrubbing brush. "You polish, I'll talk."

I polish the metal, slowly watching it change from a dull dark color to bright silver.

"Like everyone else who is down here, we both found our way to the Labyrinth. Back then, Sobek wasn't as paranoid as he is now. He didn't go after the Anomalies right away. Instead, he waited to see if we would buy into his system. Become his super spies. His Protectors. Most did. I didn't. Whoever didn't conform had two options; wait to be recycled or run. I ran. There was another girl from the

Labor Community who was slightly older than I was. And she was like me. When she got back from Monarch Camp, she warned me that I probably wouldn't find an intended partner under Sobek's limited system.

"So, I started researching the revolution. Watching, listening, paying attention. One of my teachers was fairly subversive and I speculated that he was part of the revolution. I kept hinting at it; yet he never took the bait. The day I got back from camp with my new Anomaly brand, he confessed that he was a revolutionary, and he told me to how to find the Labyrinth. And how to let the Labyrinth find us. I left my friends and my family and came to a safe house here, stopping first in East America to collect Gina, who was more than happy to join me. A member of the Underground collected us, drugged us, and we woke up in the Labyrinth. We've been together ever since."

Rezz takes the sword from me and turns it over, examining both sides of the polished metal. "This looks great, Keeva. Now for the fun stuff."

We return to the work tent as Rezz puts the final touches on the sword. She assembles the handle and pommel by drilling holes through the blade and attaching it to the handle with a blowtorch. It is a long process, but it is fascinating to watch an innocuous piece of metal develop into a deadly weapon. She is quite an accomplished blacksmith and I'm impressed.

"Any regrets?" I ask as she finishes up.

"None." She looks at me curiously, "Why, do you?"

"No. I mean, I'm not sure. I want to stop Sobek, but I'm still not sure why I'm here. Everyone seems so clear about their role in the Labyrinth. I've been here three weeks, and I still don't know what my purpose is. I don't feel special in any way; in fact, I feel quite the opposite. I almost feel like I'm . . . trespassing."

Rezz smiles and hugs me. "Patience, Keeva. Your purpose is being revealed to you . . . you just don't know it yet."

"How can you be so certain?"

"I'm an Anomaly. I can think for myself. And one of the greatest gifts of individual thought is self-empowerment. We don't have to let anyone cut us down a notch or make us feel bad about ourselves. We are strong, brave, beautiful, vibrant women who are going to stop this megalomaniac."

"You say it with such passion, I almost believe it."

"Start believing it, Keeva. Self-esteem is the only route to revolution."

She hands me the sword we just crafted. "This weapon is not one-hundredth as powerful as your brain."

"Wait, are you giving this to me?"

"I am. You have to learn to defend yourself. Just remember what I said about believing in yourself. Confidence will take you a lot further than anything else." Rezz brings me over to the Weapons Master, a pasty-faced man who wears small spectacles and is dressed in a formal tailcoat with suspenders and a bright red cravat.

"Mick, can you please teach my friend here how to wield her new weapon?"

I master the weapon in three days. It's not all fun and games. Mick is a serious teacher whose appearance belies his skill. When I first meet him, I'm not threatened in the least. After all, he is a doughy-looking man who used to be a history professor in the Academic Community. He is at least four inches shorter than I am. I soon learn that appearances can be deceiving.

"What is the most important thing to do when you confront an opponent?" Mick asks when we draw our swords and face off.

"Run," I say jokingly, and before I can blink, he knocks the weapon out of my hand and pins me to the side of a tent. The sword's sharp blade pushes into my neck, just nicking my carotid artery. After a few precarious seconds, he pulls the weapon away.

"Hey, you could have killed me." I press my fingers to my wounded neck.

"I know. Pick up your sword." Mick waits for me to collect the fallen object and begins the lesson again. "What is the most important thing to do when you confront an opponent?"

I remember what Taj told me, "Know my enemy and know myself."

"Excellent. Now, the reason I disarmed you so quickly is because you did not know your enemy. You immediately judged me by my slight stature and glasses. You underestimated me and were reckless, and I used that to my advantage."

Mick teaches me how to draw my sword quickly, and we practice this move over and over until I can draw as quickly as he can.

"Once you draw your sword, the most important thing you can do is to relax." He instructs, "You are already in a hazardous situation; everything around you is tense so you can't afford to be. You must stay in control. Assess the situation. Stay calm and breathe."

Mick shows me different ways to stay calm. Most of them include taking meditative breaths so that I can regulate my breathing. "There are many mantras you can say. All of them will help you focus, but you should choose one to help protect you in this situation. Repeat after me, *Aad Guray Nameh*."

"*Aad Guray Nameh*. What does it mean?"

"It's over three thousand years old and will surround your magnetic field with protective light. Say it three times before you go into battle."

"OK," I say tentatively. I am not quite following his methodology, but he seems to know what he is talking about, and I'm willing to try.

Once I master the breath work and the chanting, he shows me how to keep my balance so I can strike or parry without being hit.

"Keep your feet shoulder wide, and when you move, always make sure that your legs stay apart." He pushes me, and I fall down.

"Get up. Your feet should never be too close to each other." He pushes me again, and I fall.

"Get up. You need to focus, Keeva. Your footing is imperative for balance. The more the sole of your foot touches the ground the more grounded you are." He pushes me again, but I manage to hold my ground.

"Good, now you need to assess the situation. Warriors always need to be aware of their surroundings and their assets and liabilities, as well as those of their opponent. Everyone has a weakness, Keeva." He grins and then hits my legs repeatedly with the broad side of his sword, "For instance, tall people have a longer reach but often leave their legs exposed."

"OK, OK, I get it," I protect my legs from his parry of blows until he is satisfied.

We continue with the tough-love lesson as I learn to focus, balance, protect myself, keep my elbows bent, and learn to be sure of my attack. The entire time I am fighting, I practice controlling my breath and silently chant my mantra.

On the third day, I fight Takumi, who is Mick's best warrior. I remember all of my lessons as we face off. The Craftsman Brigade has all gathered to watch the event. Most of them stand on Takumi's side. He is their hero. Rezz and Zilli stand on my side. I appreciate their vote of confidence, even if it's misguided.

I look at Takumi. He is fit and lithe. His long black hair is pulled back into a slick ponytail, and he moves like a tiger. Before we draw swords I assess him and the situation, observing how he smiles to the audience, clearly showing off. He is both overconfident and a bit of a clown as he postures for his friends. These are weaknesses I can use to my advantage. I am calm and confident as I quickly draw my sword. He has experience over me, but I have Mick's tutelage.

If I can just wait for him to make a mistake, I can win.

Our fight is like a chess game. We parry, attack and counter each other. His overconfidence has been replaced by determination as he delivers a series of blows, which I deftly deflect.

Takumi has better stamina than I do and as the fight continues, I have to work harder to stay focused. We circle each other, eyes locked, waiting to see who will make the next move, and without warning, Inelia's voice enters my head.

Inelia repeats the message that she first imparted at Monarch Camp, "If you erase the self, there is no you, just infinite possibility."

Suddenly I no longer see myself as the attacker or the defender. I am neither afraid of striking nor of being struck. Takumi looks at me strangely, aware that something has shifted within me. I wait as he lunges in for an attack. I take advantage of his unbalance and step to the side while disarming him.

I barely register the group's applause as Mick announces me the victor.

I am too busy feeling another octopus leg click back into place.

"HOW DO YOU FEEL?" Sobek asked Calix after his son reluctantly left his friends watching the double feature and joined Sobek in the inner office.

"Alive," Calix admitted. He felt guiltily drunk with his newfound power. "But what will happen to him?" He gestured to Emmett who now looked slightly comatose, just staring at the television. He appeared bizarrely calm for a teenager who had just seen a brutal film.

"It's an expected reaction because you siphoned so much of his energy. You must learn to control your power. Emmett was just a tiny taste of what is available. There is more, oh so much more, out there . . . but you have to be willing to taste it."

Calix had sampled the power of siphoning energy. It was intoxicating.

Yet his moral compass started to go crazy as he realized the ramifications of his actions. Even though the taste was addictive, it would hurt other people. He would get stronger feeding off their weaknesses. It wasn't right. This was against every belief his mother had indoctrinated in him. It was wrong. But he had to placate his father. He had to outsmart him.

"So, how does this work?" Calix asked. "Do I just go up to random Sabbatical City tourists and siphon their energies? Getting close enough to them to feel their auras and tasting just a little bit so that they don't pass out?"

"Yes, that is exactly how you will hone your skills."

"Stealing from strangers . . . it seems so cruel."

"Then you don't have to."

"I don't?" Calix was confused.

"No. Why feed off of strangers when you can practice on friends."

"What?" Calix wasn't sure what he was hearing.

"Don't play stupid, Son. You are not finished your training for tonight."

Calix's heart sank as he suddenly realized what his father was going to say before he said it. "No. Absolutely not. I can't, Father."

"You can."

"But you said I had to choose so I chose. I chose Emmett. I'm done."

"It is a world leader's prerogative to change his mind."

Calix and Sobek stared at each other for several minutes, neither one wavering. In the background, they could hear the screams of Rao, August, and Byron. Emmett was still silent.

"Father—"

"It's not up for discussion. There is approximately an hour left of this vid. Just enough time to taste the nuances of three new energies."

Calix felt sick. "I can just go down to the commissary—"

"You can stay right here." Sobek glanced at his watch. "59 minutes."

Calix bit the inside of his cheek to prevent himself from crying. It was the only way he knew to calm himself down. He turned and looked at his friends who were engrossed in the vid. Calix didn't think it would be possible to hate his father any more than he already did.

"Oh, and Son," Sobek said putting his hand on Calix's shoulder, noting the almost imperceptible flinch, "Do be careful. Daddy's not going to save your little friends this time."

As Calix sat down next to Rao, preparing to breathe in the energy of his best friend in the world and praying that he could control his thirst, he was certain of one thing.

One day he would, without a doubt, kill his father.

22.

I am exhausted.

Taj has kept me on a strict training regimen and even though I know I am getting stronger and smarter, I am tired all the time. My body aches from the nonstop running and fighting and conditioning. Every night, I am asleep mere seconds after my head hits the pillow. I crave my soft hammock and look forward to sleeping seven solid hours before the training begins again.

One night, after a particularly grueling day, I have been asleep only a few hours when my hammock shakes, and I feel a tug which wakes me. It's Kai and Genesis. What are they doing in the girls' tent? I'm having a bit of a déjà vu from the time when Kai woke me up at Monarch Camp in the middle of the night. That feels like a lifetime ago. I blink a few times to adjust to the darkness. Why are they both here? They don't even really get along, or do they?

"What are you—" I barely manage to say before Genesis puts his hand over my mouth. Kai puts his finger to his lips, motioning for me to be quiet. They both nod at the door, expecting me to join them outside.

Still wearing my sleep shorts and T-shirt, I slip on a pair of boots and creep out of the girls' tent. No one stirs as I leave. They are all fast asleep . . . just like I should be.

Both Kai and Genesis are waiting silently outside the tent flap. When I come out, they turn on their head-lamps and hand me one. It is a tight leather headband with a small light attached to it. I strap it on my head and turn it on, giving me a bright red beam to illuminate my path. I follow them nearly a half-mile past all the tents to a section of Underground City where I haven't yet been. Beyond Lachlan's garden, I can make out enormous mountains of dirt, remainders of the dry earth that was cut away when Underground City was created. The red glow from my light makes the place appear ominous.

"Whoa." I walk through the forest of dirt hills which are at least twenty feet tall. It is surreal. "What is this?"

"Pure, unadulterated soil," Genesis says as he rubs some of the dirt through his thumb and forefinger. "It is soil from before the war. Nothing here is genetically modified or infused with Sobek's fluoride solution."

"Wait, I thought it was just in the water?"

"It is, but think about it, Keeva. Where does rain come from?"

"Huh? What does that have to do with anything? I don't know." Suddenly I feel stupid. Why is Genesis quizzing me? Why isn't Kai saying anything?

Genesis continues, "The water that is in our lakes, rivers, and oceans eventually evaporates. It goes into the sky and it makes the clouds. Eventually, the clouds become so full of water they let some of it go onto the. . . ." He lets the sentence hang, expecting me to finish it.

"Earth," I say.

"Exactly. The rain, which originated in the ocean, hits the ground and sinks into the dirt. And while most rainwater is pure, because Sobek has manipulated the water, everything is slightly contaminated. So we're stockpiling dirt down here for when the time comes."

"The time comes for what?"

"For us to return above ground and start society anew," Genesis says proudly.

I keep walking, in between talkative Genesis and silent Kai. It is a strange role reversal. I had no idea Genesis was so well-informed. He is clearly passionate about his work on the land and committed to the revolution as much as Kai.

"So, where are we going?" I direct my question to Kai.

"Another test. Courtesy of Taj." He leads me beyond the last hill of dirt to a clearing. There is an enormous ditch and even though it's dark, I can see it is filled with water.

"What kind of test?" I have a strange feeling of apprehension. Even though I am flanked by my trusted friends, there is something odd about their behavior.

"Taj wants you to work on your swimming," Kai says matter-of-factly.

"It's a well." Genesis nods to the dark ditch. "The walls are made of stone and impossible to climb."

"Why are you telling me this?" I am starting to get a bit freaked out.

"To prepare you," Genesis says. He sounds . . . apologetic.

"So, she wants me to go swimming. In a ditch?"

"A well," Kai says.

"Whatever. Is she crazy? It's the middle of the night," I stammer.

"Sometimes the best time to train is when you're not at your most alert. It forces you to go into survival mode," Kai offers.

"Thanks, but I've had enough of survival mode lately. I just want to go back to sleep." I turn to head back to the tents, but Genesis blocks my way. He is large and immovable.

"Get out of my way," I demand, but he holds his ground.

"Kai," I plead, "this is ridiculous. I'm exhausted. I'm going to be of no use to anyone if I drown."

"Exactly." Kai grins. "So don't drown." And with that glib statement, he and Genesis push me over the edge of the pit.

I've been down here for two days and it is clear that no one is coming to save me.

Once my friends betrayed me and pushed me over the edge of the well, I felt like I was falling forever, even though it was just a few hundred feet before I felt the cold water splash, enveloping me as I sunk under the surface into the thick water. I immediately kicked off my boots, not worrying that they wouldn't end up on the community shelf the next day. When I managed to swim back up to the surface, I sputtered a bit as I caught my breath. Luckily, the headlamp remained on my head so that I could make out the walls of my water prison; slick and tall mud and stone packed walls which contained the water. I was furious. How dare Kai and Genesis trick me. Of course, Taj was behind the test and they were only acting on her orders, soldiers following blindly. I wondered if all initiates have to plunge into this well of water or just me.

I swam around the perimeter of the pit, biding time until the morning when someone, anyone would come and collect me, but no one came. I shouted out, but no one answered. Remembering my journey from the tents, I calculated that the pit was at least two miles from the center of Underground City. There was no one within shouting distance. After a few hours, I stopped screaming to conserve my energy. How was I ever going to get out? While the well was not as large as I originally thought— I could easily make it from one side to the other in less than ten minutes—there is nowhere to rest.

After another several hours, I am getting tired of treading water. There is nothing to hold on to. I am falling apart mentally and physically. I don't really see the point of Taj's master plan. Is she planning to push me to my breaking point? Or slowly kill me? Kai and Genesis wouldn't let that happen. Or would they . . . if Taj ordered it? Perhaps I am not as strong or special as everyone thought. After yet a few more hours of treading water and floating, I am ready to give up. I want to fall asleep and not wake up again, I am that tired. I am resigned that I will never see my father again. I will never see my sister again. As the second night falls, I stretch out and float on my back, looking up into the blackness.

Suddenly, the water rushes around me. I am turned over unexpectedly and I am pulled under the surface. I feel something slimy rub against my leg. I am not alone. I try not to panic as I swim furiously toward the side of the pit. Yet, there is another splash and another. Eight splashes in all. Either something is attacking me or it is determined to invade my space. Whatever it is, the creature is faster than I am. I pick up the pace; however, the thing is right beside me. Finally I turn, beaming my light directly on it.

It is an octopus, a highly intelligent creature Taj told me about.

Something happens to someone when they are at their worst. When all is lost and there seems to be nothing left to lose. When you realize that no one is going to save you and the only thing you can do is to save yourself.

I start to laugh and I can't stop. Maybe I am having a nervous breakdown, or maybe I just don't care anymore. My fear completely evaporates. A calm washes over me as I stare at the beast, who seems more afraid than me.

The ugly creature bobs in front of me, waiting. I speak softly and slowly, "Hey there, where'd you come from?"

As if he understands me, the octopus dives down before resurfacing.

"From below?" I wonder if he is trying to tell me something. There is no possible way I can climb out. Genesis had told me that. Wait, had he been giving me a hint? Why hadn't Kai said anything? Instead, it was Genesis who told me exactly what I needed to do. Sometimes, you have to go backward to go forward. Sometimes you have to go down to go up. And I can't go up. Even if I had the strength, I no longer have the energy. I'm running on no sleep, and I know I have to get out of the pit to survive. I smile at the realization.

I want to survive, I really do.

"Lead the way," I instruct my slimy friend as I take a deep breath of air and dive under the surface.

At the bottom of the pit is a netted opening. I easily swim through the net and out into an underground room. There, I find a copper ladder built into the wall, which leads me back up to the surface. I climb out a trap door which is located behind one of the mountains of dirt. Exhausted, soaked, and filthy, I trudge back through Underground City, feeling the fourth octopus leg click into place as I climb back into my hammock.

Just in time for the bugle to wake us up for breakfast.

SOBEK SPENT THE NEXT THREE WEEKS instructing his son on the nuances of siphoning energies. He taught Calix to walk up to strangers at the apothecary and grocer. He challenged his son to steal energy from a waiter while she was taking his order at a restaurant. Sobek even tutored Calix how to sidle up to children who were waiting at the sweet shoppe. Calix got so good at stealing energies that the victims barely knew what happened. Sure, they were a bit dizzy and light-headed at first, but Calix only took what he needed.

And it was delicious.

But nothing tasted better than fear, and Calix spent his nights honing his tastes in dark alleys when he could smell fear on people's auras. He especially enjoyed hanging around the cinema when there was a horror vid playing. Fear did taste better than embarrassment, excitement, or misery. Lien could survive on all emotions, but fear was definitely top shelf.

Sobek was thrilled with his son's enthusiasm. Once Calix developed a taste of what it felt like to feed off of energies, he became an apt pupil. He was insatiable and Sobek had him exactly where he needed him.

Even though Calix was learning quickly, and put up a good front for his father, he was constantly miserable. Calix hated that he relished the taste of energies so much. He hated that he needed his father's tutelage so that he could feed without killing anyone. The thing he hated the most was that he would need his father until he could completely

ANOMALIES

master the skill. Until the time when the student could surpass the teacher.

Calix eyed his father's identity watch. It held all of Sobek's secrets, all the keys to unlock the world leader's plans. Yet it never left his father's wrist. To gain access to it, Calix would need to convince his father of his loyalty.

"I want more, Father," Calix said easily. "I am ready to step into my role as heir apparent."

"All in good time, my son." Sobek looked at a feed coming in on his tablet. There was word of a possible dissident in the Asias. Sobek grimaced. It was not the information he was waiting for. Months ago, he had managed to get one of his agents picked up by revolutionaries and taken to Underground City. But he had heard nothing since. It was as if the agent had disappeared. But Sobek would practice patience, one of his greatest gifts.

Sobek turned back to his son. "Before you assume your place, we first have a resistance to quash."

"Aunt Taj."

"Yes, it will soon be time for my beloved sister to pay the price for her treason."

Calix smiled, hoping that his father would take his eagerness as a sign of loyalty. "Let me know what you need from me, Father. I am ready."

23.

I am ready.

After not talking to Genesis and Kai for a few days, I realize that I need their friendships, so I forgive them. Taj is another story. She may be the head of the revolution, but I don't trust her and her warped way of schooling someone. Plus, I've mastered two of the three Brigades. I am discovering who I am and of what I am capable. And I know how to save myself. I want to tell Taj that I am ready to go above ground with the Bandit Brigade, but I can't find her. Lachlan tells me that she is rarely in Underground City; she usually takes a flying machine through the Labyrinth and visits her captains in different parts of the territory.

I'm impatient.

I want to help, I really do. Maybe tending tomatoes is the best use of Genesis and Patel's skills to aid the resistance, since they are both from Ecosystem. Rezz and Mick are born to represent the Craftsman Brigade, but I know that I am meant for more, and the only Brigade I haven't tried is the Bandit Brigade.

At the end of my fourth week as a rebel, I notice candlelight in Taj's tent, and I finally summon the courage to talk to her. But before I can, word spreads through the city that Taj has called a mandatory meeting. All of Underground City collects in the dining tent where the elusive Taj holds court. She is back to her half-human, half-shimmery-Lien face and wears a top hat, a lavender taffeta gown that matches her eye, and a long silver glove on her right arm.

I stop in front of her, "Hi Taj, can I talk to you?"

"What do you want?" she snarls. She is in a bad mood. A very bad mood.

"I was hoping that I could get some experience with the Bandit Brigade."

"Be careful what you wish for, Keeva." She sighs, "Please sit down. I'm a little busy."

I obey. Perhaps I'll approach her later about going above ground—when she is in a better mood. I head toward the back of the tent and grab a seat between Kai and Gina.

"What'd she say? Can you go up with us?" Kai whispers.

"I don't know," I admit. "She speaks in riddles. I can barely understand her."

Taj clears her throat, and we immediately quiet down as she says, "Enlightened Citizens, the time for Phase One of our revolution has begun."

A cheer goes up from the crowd.

"Isn't this too soon?" I whisper to Gina.

"You've only been here a month, Keeva. Most of us have been here a lot longer."

I nod. It's easy to forget that I am just a tiny piece of this puzzle, if I am even a part of it at all. Around me, everyone's cheering finally settles, and Taj continues her speech.

"I've appointed two reconnaissance teams of six for the initial attack on the Global Governance. Team One's job is to neutralize the toxins in the Desalination Plant. Once this team has completed their mission, Team Two will be standing by to blow up the MC-5 building at Monarch Camp. When these missions have been accomplished, we will be able to wake up humanity and begin the end of my brother's totalitarian rule. Team One's mission will begin tomorrow at dawn. The zeppelin is standing by and ready to go."

Everyone turns and looks at the dirigible, which is sitting on the ground. The murmurs then start as the revolutionaries look around expectantly. Who will be chosen? I see some of the bigger boys sitting in the front, posturing expectantly. Takumi is with them. They are all in the Craftsman Brigade and are the biggest and the strongest members of the Labyrinth. It seems fairly obvious that some, if not all of them, will be selected.

"Team One will be lead by Lachlan and Keeva."

A silence settles over everyone as all eyes turn to the back of the dining tent.

The entire resistance is staring at me: the girl who spent her lifetime trying to be invisible is now the main attraction. I blush and lower my eyes. Is Taj kidding? I am the newbie, the last one to join the revolution. Clearly there has been some mistake.

Whispers run through the group. Most of them don't know who I am, let alone feel thrilled that a skinny redhead will be jointly leading the first phase of the revolution.

"What makes her qualified?" one of the biggest boys in the front stands and shouts out.

"Are you questioning me, Omri?" Taj's face suddenly turns hard. Any pretext of softness and beauty is gone, and her true nature reveals itself. Like her brother, she does not like to be questioned. I see her long forked tongue snap out. A predator threatened.

"Just asking." Omri sits down shakily, his bravado quickly emasculated.

"Keeva is more qualified than everyone in this city. Including me," Taj says severely. "She and Lachlan will be joined by Kai, Rezz, Magnum, and . . . ," her eyes return to her inquisitor, "Omri. Team Two will be led by . . ."

But I am no longer listening. How am I going to lead a rebellion? What did she mean I am more qualified than everyone else? I barely got out of the octopus pit and now I'm leading a rebellion. I feel sick to my stomach. Somewhere in the distance, I hear Taj finish her speech, " Meeting adjourned."

Everyone gets up and splits into their respective Brigades to begin their day's work. I linger with Kai, to ask Taj why she put me in charge. We approach our leader who gives us the once over. Something is bothering her, and she turns and walks quickly to her tent. Kai and I scramble to keep up with her.

"Um, Taj," Kai persists.

"What is it?" She stops, clearly irritated. Something is distracting her, and she wants to go.

"I'm not sure Omri is right for the job."

"Why not?" she snaps.

"It's just a feeling," Kai mumbles.

"Well, why don't you keep your feelings to yourself, and I'll keep mine to myself. Deal?"

She doesn't wait for a response before storming off.

"I JUST GOT A CONCLUSIVE TIP on the revolution," Sobek confided to his son a few days later.

Calix had been studying with his father, learning the tools necessary to be a strong future leader. And as a reward every day, Sobek brought one of his human staffers into the penthouse. He slowly tortured them and let his son feed on their fear.

Each day Calix grew stronger, and each day Sobek became prouder of his heir.

"Can I fight?"

"No. But you can observe. I have a sleeper operative on the inside. The rebels will rendezvous at a safe house that our people have been observing for weeks. The Protectors will be waiting to infiltrate their plan."

"Won't we just kill them and stop them?"

"Then we lose our advantage because we don't know their end game. No. We will cripple them by decreasing their numbers and then once we learn of their ultimate plan, we will crush them. And then my sister and I will be able to have a little discussion for the first time in several hundred years. Oh, will it be lovely to see her again," Sobek sneered.

"Will I be on the front line?" Calix said eagerly.

"You are too valuable to be a mere pawn, Son." Sobek put his arm on his son's shoulder, giving him a rare sign of affection. "Remember how I taught you to beat an opponent at chess?"

"Stay at least two moves ahead."

"Indeed. Well, I happen to be an excellent chess player . . . which means I can stay five moves ahead of my opponent as well as use the element of surprise." Sobek spoke into his tablet, "Rika, you may send your sister in." He turned to his son, "Sarayu has served us well, but I don't think she will be a suitable queen for you. I believe that I have found someone who will . . . better suit our needs."

Calix's eyes popped open as he watched the gorgeous girl with the long hair and thick bangs enter the room. He couldn't help but stare at her emerald eyes.

She smiled shyly, "Hi. I'm Blue."

I am strong.

I stand with my team and prepare to board the dirigible. This airship will take us underground the entire way to the coast of West America. Rezz and Gina stand off to the side, whispering softly to each other, holding hands with their heads nestled together. This is the first time they will be separated for longer than a day and, last night I heard the usually tough Gina crying in her sleep. She made me give her my word that I would protect Rezz.

I agreed, wondering who was going to protect me.

Of the six of us heading out on the mission, I am the only variable. Omri, Magnum, and Rezz represent the Craftsman Brigade. They are skilled weapon makers and fighters. Kai is from the Bandit Brigade and is sneaky and fast, and Lachlan of the Sustenance Brigade is a natural-born leader, and he has the distinction of being Taj's second-in-command.

And then there's me.

"I'm going to miss you," Genesis comes over to me. He hands me a pink orchid. It is fragrant and quite beautiful.

"Thanks." Suddenly, I feel very shy around him.

"I always knew you were special and tough," Genesis adds. "Ever since that first day at Monarch Camp when you and Kai were yelling at each other at the flagpole. You are so brave."

"Trust me, I'm not that brave."

"Then you don't see what I do," Genesis says before kissing me. The kiss comes as a shock. We only kissed once before and it was more of a performance for Claudia Durant.

This is on the lips and it's real. It's very real.

"Come back safely," Genesis murmurs before turning and slipping into the crowd.

I look out at the ship and see Kai watching us from the deck. I can't quite make out his expression. Anger? Amusement. He is so hard to read.

I am wearing my usual wardrobe: tall boots, equestrian pants, a leather vest, and a white shirt. My sword is hanging at my side and I wear the octopus bracelet with half of the legs now back in their original positions. I also have a canteen, a bathing suit for the mission, and now Genesis's gift. I gather up my belongings and prepare to board. Omri hasn't even attempted to leave. He is off to the side posturing with his friends, showing them the duffel bag filled with weapons that Mick has crafted specifically for our mission, including dynamite and a steel basin wrench to open the carbon chamber in the Desalination Plant.

"Good luck, Keeva." Mick hugs me just before I board, whispering in my ear, "Don't forget, *Aad Guray Nameh.*"

I look around. There is no one left to say goodbye to. Taj is standing far away from the gathered crowd. She and I exchange a look before I hear her voice in my head.

"You are meant for great things, Keeva."

I nod, acknowledging that I can hear her message. I don't like her being in my head, but at the same time I know this intuitive ability to read thoughts is a gift, and I do not fight it.

"You've already begun to find yourself. Continue to believe and your possibilities will be endless. Remember, this is only the beginning."

"What if I can't?" I silently question.

"But you already have, Keeva. You have learned to live in the now, which is no easy feat. You must always focus on the present and be in the moment to see the opportunities in front of you."

I step onto the aircraft where Kai, Magnum, and Lachlan are already preparing to lift off. Omri and Rezz follow me. The airship slowly begins to rise. As Magnum steers the craft, the rest of us wave goodbye. Everyone has gathered below to send us off.

"I don't see Zilli," I say to Kai as I wave to Gina, Patel, Takumi, and Genesis.

"She was so mad you're leaving her that she's been sulking in her tent."

"Poor kid," I say, realizing that I will miss my little shadow.

As we fly away from the Labyrinth, I explore the ship. The holding area is made of wood, and there are few frills. Food supplies and a large pile of blankets take up one end of the ship, and Taj's desk and supplies sit on the other end. The main platform is a large, open area with two long benches. Our journey will take six hours underground. Once we arrive at the coast, the tunnel ends at a defunct volcano, and we will fly the airship into its holding cell and climb the ladder through the mouth of the volcano. This will deposit us just off the coast near a deserted road about two hundred miles away from our destination. About two hundred miles away from my old home.

Suddenly, I hear music. I turn. Kai is playing with an old-fashioned, Victrola-like machine.

"What's that doing here?" I wonder. I've seen pictures of record players, but have never seen one in person.

"Maybe Taj listens to music to relax when she's out on her reconnaissance missions." He pulls out a flat circular disk and puts it on the machine, gently placing a needle on top of it. As the music begins to play, Kai bows.

"May I have this dance?"

"Seriously?"

"Hmmm. Well, Rez is reading in the corner with her headlamp, Lachlan's sleeping, and Omri and Magnum are up front. I don't see anyone else around. It's just you and me, kid."

"Kid? We're the same age."

"Age is relative. C'mon, Keeva. Dance with me."

"You sure you don't want to push me over the side first?" I jokingly nod to the side of the craft. "Any more lessons left for me to learn?"

"That's a cheap shot."

"Sorry, I couldn't help myself." I smile, take Kai's arms and dance with him.

"What song is this?"

"One of my favorites. Years ago, when my grandpa was a boy, he used to listen to this group, the Beatles."

"Like the bug? Gross."

"Keeva, once upon a time music wasn't regulated by the Governance. It wasn't considered subversive . . . well, OK, maybe it was . . . but no one stopped people from listening to it. There used to be so many different groups that could all express themselves through their music. It is where they found their voices."

"Blue's in a band," I say offhandedly.

"I know."

"You do?" Why am I jealous? I don't understand my feelings when I'm around this boy. Sure, we've become better friends, but that's all we are. Friends.

Kai pulls me closer. "This is called 'Sexy Sadie,' it's a classic."

I keep up with him as he spins and turns me. Annika, Rane and I used to dance together in anticipation for the day when we would dance with our intended partners. Now they will dance with Dante and Edward in an oppressive society where they don't even know they are prisoners. As I keep discovering more truths about Sobek's rule, I am even more determined to free them.

When the song is over, Kai and I flop down on the floor; flushed and exhausted. We lay on our backs, looking up at the makeshift sky. Eventually, I ask what no one has broached, "How hard do you think this is going to be?"

"I don't know," Kai sighs. "So far we've been lucky. All the Anomaly extractions have been fairly easy. Now we're moving it to the next level. I suppose it depends on whether we have the element of surprise. I've been thinking. Taj has so many double agents embedded in Sobek's world. Who is to say that he doesn't have traitors in the Underground?"

"Who?"

"I don't know. Maybe, Omri. I'm just speculating. What if someone knows that we're coming?"

"Omri seems too—I can't figure out the word to describe him . . . simple. He doesn't feel like someone who is undercover. I think what you see is what you get with him. All brawn, little brain."

"Maybe, but he rubs me the wrong way."

"What about Magnum?" I ask. "Do you know anything about him? I'm surprised Taj chose him instead of Gina or Takumi."

"He's also Craftsman Brigade. He's quiet. Quiet but effective, even though he's so big. He's just a teenager, but he already looks like a man, and he knows how to use his size and strength to his advantage. Always beware of a boy with a man's physique."

"I'm better off trusting a boy with a boy's physique?" I joke, pushing Kai.

He pushes me back, and we get into a wrestling match, laughing and fighting until we fall over, exhausted.

"Save it for the mission," Lachlan yells from across the ship, never opening his eyes.

"Sorry," we giggle and lay back down.

We're silent for several minutes, and I have yet another déjà vu as I remember lying with him on the salt flats our last night of Monarch Camp. It was the last night before everything became so complicated.

"What would you have done if you weren't awakened?" Kai whispers in the darkness.

"What do you mean?" I roll over and face him. Our faces are so close that they are almost touching. "Like, if my house hadn't been blown up and I hadn't found the Labyrinth?" I shrug. I wonder if I would have gone on with my preplanned life and married Genesis. Then again, that wasn't really my preplanned life.

"I dunno. I mean, I don't think I would have been happy," I admit, enjoying the feeling of laying so close to Kai. "I would have tried to be happy, and I would have followed the plan. But I think I always would have known that something was off."

"Do you have regrets?"

"No. Not yet. I want to find my father. I want to find my sister."

"We will," Kai says earnestly.

"Is that the royal we?" I joke.

"We're a team, Keeva." His eyes are so kind. He is genuinely supportive. "Do you know where your sister is?"

"I didn't. I do now. At least, I think I do."

"Where?"

"In one of the safe houses. I'm not sure exactly which one, but it's on the way to the Desalination Plant."

"We can't, Keeva. We have a mission."

I raise my voice a little, "We're not going out of our way and like you said, it should be an easy extraction. Easy in, easy out."

"You think you can have your cake and eat it too?" He shrugs, "Look, let's see what happens when we dock."

"So it's not a no," I say hopefully.

"It's not a no, but it's not a yes. Hey, can you grab us a couple of blankets?"

I reach over to the lump of blankets next to me and start to pull one over to me, but it won't budge. I try again, it is heavy. I pat down the blankets and begin to pull them off one by one until I can see the whites of the eyes of a little girl staring up at me.

"Hey Keeva."

"Zilli, you are in so much trouble."

"If Keeva is going to save humanity, I don't want to miss it," Zilli pouts.

"You know that you're not supposed to be here," Lachlan warns as we confront the headstrong girl.

"I can help," Zilli insists.

"How?" I counter. She is a child. I have enough on my mind with this mission. I don't need to add babysitting on top of it.

"I'm small and I'm fast and I'm smart. The enemy won't see me coming," Zilli insists.

"Look, there's no sense in arguing now. She's here. We're not going to turn around," Lachlan says.

"Good, so I'm staying," Zilli hugs him.

"Not exactly," Lachlan extricates himself from Zilli. "We'll drop you off at a safe house on the way."

I smile at Kai and mouth *safe house*. Looks like I will have my cake and eat it too.

CALIX'S JOB WAS JUST TO OBSERVE. But Calix was never one to just sit back and watch.

The elite squad of four Protectors allowed Calix and Blue to tag along on their mission; however, their orders were clear: do not engage.

They had docked the helicraft behind a thicket of trees and hiked ten miles to the edge of the volcano where the safe house was located. They spread out around the base of the volcano and waited.

Calix didn't really want to get to know Blue. Sure, she was pretty and smart, but so was Sarayu, and look what had happened to her. So he kept her at a polite distance. He wasn't even sure why Sobek wanted her to come along, Blue was hardly the military type, and even though she was a Protector, she still dressed like a fashionista schoolgirl.

Calix and Blue were stationed away from the rest of the group. They were on their stomachs, peeking through the boulders as the first revolutionaries emerged. Both he and Blue simultaneously let out a gasp as the first pair climbed out of the volcano's mouth–Calix, because he recognized the tall, sad-eyed redheaded girl he saw on his father's holo wall, and Blue because she recognized her intended partner.

"Kai."

25.

I am home.

Not my home per say, but the ocean.

Despite the appearance of our young stowaway, our flight is uneventful. There's nothing to look at when you travel five hundred miles in the dark. We wear headlamps and play cards, but everyone's mind is on the mission. Everyone except Zilli, who clings to me like an eager puppy.

We arrive at the volcano and slowly rise to the opening. Magnum docks the zeppelin on a makeshift platform. We carefully climb out, one by one, before scrambling up a ladder, which had been soldered to the side of the volcano. Kai is the first to get out and I am right on his heels. Once we reach the top, I let out a gasp. It is a virtually unobstructed view of the ocean, save a small lighthouse in front of us.

Feelings rush over me: nostalgia, loss, hope. I want to leave everyone and just plunge into the ocean; however, I realize I have a mission to do. Two missions. I have to find my sister and I have to stop Sobek.

"Well, young lady, looks like this is the end of the line for you," Lachlan says to Zilli.

"Where am I going?" Zilli pouts. She has perfected the art of the sulk.

"A friend of mine runs this lighthouse. You'll be safe here until we get back."

"This is the safe house?" I ask.

"Best place to hide something is in plain sight," Lachlan says.

"But I want to help," Zilli pleads.

"You will be helping. You'll be helping Harijiwan. The old goat gets lonely. You can keep him company for a few days."

"Harijiwan?" My ears perk up. "He is the lighthouse keeper?"

"Indeed. Been running it for the last few hundred years."

"So he's—"

"One of us? Yes, Keeva. He's one of the good guys."

"I'm coming with you."

"I'm only going to be a minute."

"Please let her come," Zilli pleads, batting her eyes at Lachlan.

"Fine. The rest of you stand guard. I will bring the ladies to the lighthouse. Keeva and I will be back in fifteen minutes."

"And if you're not?" Kai asks.

"Then something has happened," Lachlan says, "and you'll have to complete the mission without us."

"I'm coming too," Kai insists.

"This isn't a party," Lachlan groans.

"Let him go," Magnum speaks up. "It will be good to have someone from the Bandit Brigade with you."

"Yeah. Rezz, Magnum and I have to divvy up the weapons anyway," Omri says. They've already opened the duffel bag and are pulling out swords and daggers.

"Fine. Let's go." Lachlan turns toward the lighthouse.

"Keeva, wait," Rezz says. She runs over and hugs me, "Good luck."

I laugh, "You'll need it more than I do. I get to explore a lighthouse while you're stuck here with these lug heads."

Zilli takes my hand, pulling me away. "Be back soon," I say to Rezz, and I follow the other half of my team to the lighthouse.

"This is so pretty," Zilli shouts as we approach the tall stone structure. She lets go of my hand and runs ahead to the large door.

Lachlan knocks several times, but there is no answer. We go around to the back where a window is cracked open.

"Wait here," he instructs and pushes the window open further. But he is too big to squeeze in.

"I'll go," Zilli volunteers and squeezes herself through the small space before any of us can protest.

We walk back around to the front door.

After a few minutes, the door is still closed.

"What's taking her so long?" Lachlan asks. He starts to bang on the door, "Zilli. Let us in."

Seconds later the front door opens. "Welcome to my castle," Zilli curtsies.

The lighthouse is deserted. Someone has left there in a hurry. There are two plates with half-eaten breakfast on each and the caffeine is still tepid.

"Something's not right," Lachlan says, drawing his sword.

Kai and I draw ours as well and the three of us spread out to inspect the premises.

"Wait here, under the table," I instruct Zilli, who nods.

I climb the stairs of the lighthouse tower while Lachlan and Kai explore the rest of the rooms. As I ascend the steep stairs, I notice three small doors, almost camouflaged into the stone. I push open the first one. It is an old-fashioned library filled from floor to ceiling with books. I climb a few steps higher and push open the second door. It is a simple, unadorned bedroom. There is a double bed and a table filled with maps and charts. I climb to the highest door and push it open. It is another bedroom, only this one clearly belongs to a child. There are colorful drawings tacked to the walls. There are pictures of butterflies everywhere. Multicolored butterflies of every shape and size fill up the walls of the room. I tilt my head and see more pictures tacked up on the ceiling. These are of the water: bright, childlike re-creations of different views of the ocean from the lighthouse. They are magnificent. So simple. So honest.

I step into the room, careful not to disturb anything. I walk over to the small desk where an unfinished picture rests. It is a picture of a skinny redheaded girl wearing equestrian pants, a leather vest, and tall boots. Me. And I am standing just outside the lighthouse, on the volcano with my sword drawn. I don't understand. I look closer. The picture is unsigned. I look above on the wall at several of the butterfly pictures. They all bear one signature.

Sun.

Where is she? I race up the remaining stairs, up the catwalk to the lighthouse tower. It is similarly abandoned. Where is my sister? The light is automated, but there are so many footprints in the dust that it is clear people have been up here recently. There are two sets of adult footprints and one child's size footprints. Where is she hiding? I look across the water and over the terrain. In the distance, I can see Omri and Magnum sitting on the ground sharpening the weapons. Rezz is standing on the side of the cliff. I am about to turn when I spy a group of Protectors sneaking up behind them, ready to ambush them.

"Rezz!" I scream. "Rezz!" My cries are lost in the wind. I am too high up and too far away. "Rezz!" I continue to scream in vain as I watch the pair of Protectors creep up behind her and taser her to the ground. One of them throws her crumpled body over his shoulder. It is like watching my father get taken all over.

I race down the stairs to where Zilli is still under the table.

"Where are Lachlan and Kai?" I demand.

"Still looking around."

"Lachlan! Kai!" I scream.

There are sounds of heavy footsteps running toward me as Lachlan and Kai burst into the room, swords drawn.

"Are you OK, Keeva?" Kai asks.

"Our team is in trouble," I shout and race out the door.

The mountaintop is deserted.

"Where are they?" Zilli asks.

"I don't know," I say. "They were here ten minutes ago. I saw a team of Protectors coming up behind them."

"Are they dead?" she persists.

"I don't know," I snap.

Kai and Lachlan spread out to look for our missing teammates while Zilli and I wait on edge of the volcanic cliff.

"Keeva, what's that?" Zilli points downwards.

Sure enough, barely sticking out of a thicket, just a few feet down the cliff is a pair of black boots.

"Wait here," I instruct as I lower myself down, finding footholds in the rocks. As I get to the landing, I see Magnum's crumpled body. His lip is smashed and he has a bloody nose.

I shake him violently, "Magnum, are you OK?"

He nods, dazed before he finally mumbles, "Protectors. They surprised us."

"I know. I saw. What happened?"

"They thought there'd be more of us, but we told them it was just us. They didn't believe us."

"Where are Rezz and Omri?"

"They took them. Tased them and took them."

"Why didn't they take you?"

"I'm too big. Maybe they thought they couldn't lift me. They beat me and pushed me over the cliff. Didn't wait to see where I'd land. Luckily, I fell on the bushes here; otherwise, I'd be dead."

"Can you stand?"

He nods and I help him up. His body is not bruised other than the cuts on his face. He gingerly climbs the rocks and I follow. Kai and Lachlan are waiting.

"What happened?" Lachlan demands.

"Omri was one of them," Magnum finally says after drinking water from Zilli's canteen. "He was a traitor."

"I knew it," Kai shouts.

"He tipped them off and they were waiting for us. When I realized what was happening, I knocked Omri out so he couldn't tell them about you. They had already tased Rezz. Maybe she was a traitor too."

"She wasn't a traitor," I insist.

"Fine. Well, they took her. I was the only coherent one and they tried to torture me. I told the Protectors that it had been changed from a six-person to a three-person operation and we were the only ones left. That's when they punched me and pushed me over the side. They took Omri and Rezz."

"Where did they go?" I ask.

"I don't know. It all happened so fast and then the next thing I knew, you were helping me up."

Lachlan assesses the damage. "Well, they got the weapons and the food supply. We're going to have to hoof it from here. If Omri tipped them off about the safe house, he probably tipped them off about our contacts up the coast." He looks at all of us. "We're on our own now. So we really have to stick together as a team."

"Me too?" Zilli asks.

"I'm afraid so," Lachlan mutters before heading north.

CALIX COULDN'T STOP STARING at the bodies.
He and Blue had watched the events from a safe distance from the moment the redheaded girl, the older man, the little girl, and the boy called Kai went off to the lighthouse, and his team had immediately taken action. He had watched as the Protectors surrounded the three remaining rebels and violently threw the boy and the girl over the cliff.

Calix stared at the mangled corpses below. He had spent his entire life without seeing anyone die, and now he had witnessed three murders firsthand–the two rebels and the woman he had killed with a swipe of a few numbers on a tablet. Suddenly, he felt sickened. The past few weeks of training with his father seemed pointless if the end game was to simply kill the enemy. He had loved drinking energies, but death was not a solution he was comfortable with.

He wanted to scream out to the remaining rebels, "There is a traitor among you." He had watched quietly as the boy called Magnum climbed down the cliff as another Protector punched his face until he bled. They made Magnum seem like a victim. He was Sobek's sleeper. The one who had infiltrated the resistance and would lead the Protectors to Taj. Calix was confused. He could no longer tell who was good or who was bad. His father's ideologies didn't make sense.

"C'mon." Blue grabbed his hand. Magnum had told them that the rebels were heading to the Desalination Plant. The Protectors would take the main road to get there and be waiting for the rebels' next move, of which Magnum was still uncertain.

Calix allowed himself to be pulled by Blue toward their destination.

But he was conflicted about what he would do when he got there.

26.

I am angry.

My sister was there. At that lighthouse. I missed her by just minutes. Harijiwan probably caught wind that the Protectors had been tipped off and he and my sister left before they could be captured. I am now more determined than ever to find her.

Our bedraggled group walks for the rest of the day, sticking to the coastline. We daren't stop at the pre-planned safe houses or jeopardize the revolution by contacting Taj's allies in fear of compromising their safety.

We are alone, hungry and heartbroken. Lachlan uses his skill set to find edible roots and vegetables, and I help him desalinate water for our canteens. At night we make a fire to stay warm. Zilli and I curl up together and I think about my friend. Poor Rezz. What am I going to tell Gina? I promised her that I would keep Rezz safe, and I failed. I look at my bracelet. How are my instincts helping me now? I had no idea Omri was a traitor. I never saw it coming. One-third of our team is gone and it's my fault. I wiggle away from the sleeping Zilli and join Lachlan at the fire.

"What are our options?" I ask quietly. Everyone else is sleeping. Was it only a few months ago that I was excited to go to summer camp? Just an ignorant teen. Now, I am commanding a renegade mission, and I have lost two members of my team and let a third get injured.

"Well," Lachlan sighs, "with only the weapons we are carrying, we are now without our two greatest assets."

"What's that?"

"Power and the element of surprise. Omri and Rezz were our two of our three weapons specialists. They were our security. We are now without our primary soldiers."

"We still have Kai and Magnum," I say hopefully.

"True, but protection is not their skill set. They are an effective offense, but useless on defense."

"And our element of surprise?" I ask.

"Omri probably tipped the Protectors off to our final destination, and if they're not chasing us now, they will be waiting for us there."

"Omri didn't know what the final plan was."

"No," Lachlan nods. "Only you and Taj know that. She wanted it that way."

"So, we still might have a chance to complete our mission. As long as we can get to the Desalination Plant, I can destroy the fluoridation chamber."

"Without the skills of the Craftsman Brigade, it's going to be a tougher journey than we planned."

"So we're doomed."

"Not necessarily. I'm good for a trick or two, and we have you and Zilli."

"What good is Zilli?" I say nodding at the sleeping child.

Lachlan is quiet for a moment, deciding whether to speak. Finally he says, "Keeva, why do you think Taj assigned Zilli to track you?"

"I have no idea."

"There is one reason Sobek is so desperate to Third-chip all newborn citizens, and it is the same reason that the Underground is so desperate to keep them untouched. We can't save all the newborn children, so we target a few special ones."

"Special ones?" There is a gnawing pit at the bottom of my stomach.

"Hybrids. The rare children who are born of human and Lien with dominant Lien genes. They have powers beyond imagination. They are few, and they are extremely rare. Sobek manipulates this to his advantage, identifying the children when they are five and immediately grooming them for Protectors. Their psychic energy is much higher, their instinct is quicker, they can read thoughts, and they can more easily see the future."

"Wait," I stop him, "so, you're saying that Zilli is a Hybrid."

"Indeed. She is one of the many who has both Lien and human blood. She is one of the few who has the dominant Lien genes which gives her unimaginable power."

"So all the children who have been taken at birth are Hybrids with dominant Lien genes?" I dread where this conversation is going; and yet, I can't stop talking. "Which means my sister Sun is also Hybrid . . . which means . . . which means . . . which means . . . ." I don't even have to say it aloud.

The rest of the legs of my bracelet click into place.

I finally know who I really am.

"I HAVE NO IDEA WHO I AM," Calix told Blue as the Protectors celebrated step one of their successful mission.

"You are the heir," she said. Blue took a deep breath. She was walking a dangerous tightrope, hanging out with the son of the world leader. She needed to bury her own motivations deep, so no one, especially not Calix, would discover her ultimate plan. "Now start acting like it and stop sulking."

Having thinned out the revolutionary group, the team was bunking at the home of a Protector who lived in the Ocean Community. The Protector, named Dax, was completely bald and had been particularly interested in the redheaded girl among the ragtag group of revolutionaries. Calix and Blue remained quiet as Dax filled in the group on the two probable targets.

An attack on the Desalination Plant or an attack on the Protectors' Headquarters.

He recommended that the elite squad of four split up to cover the two possibilities and instructed Calix and Blue to stand guard near Keeva's old house. Dax guessed that there must be a specific reason the revolutionaries had included newbies in their plan, and wanted to give them the job with the least chance of screwing up. Keeva's most logical action would be to return to her homestead . . . even though it was no longer there. He guessed perhaps she had a hiding place or a friend nearby whom she might contact.

So, as the rest of the Protectors planned for a day of battle, Blue and Calix talked.

And waited.

27.

I am determined.

Our mission may have lost our strength and our element of surprise, but we will not be defeated. Sobek has forgotten one thing: he's now on my home turf and I have the home-field advantage.

We sneak into the Ocean Community in the middle of the night and go directly to my cave. It is the one place no one else knows about. It is the one place we will be safe. Our plan is to attack at dawn, before Sobek has time to amass his troops. As far as we know, Sobek thinks we are attacking the Desalination Plant. That is where he will station his Protectors. His Liens and his Hybrids.

I know differently.

The plan, all along, was for me to attack the heart of his operation, the carbon chamber with the red cap where the fluoride is being dumped into the water. The entire pipeline leads to the heart of the operation and it needs bypass surgery. My father always wanted to be a surgeon, to operate on people. Instead, when he was imprinted with my mother at Monarch Camp, he joined the Ocean Community rather than the Academic Community or the Protectors. But he never stopped learning. He would spend hours talking about different ways to save the human body. I was always bored during those lessons, but now I understand their purpose. He was educating me. The one operation he talked about incessantly was open-heart surgery, specifically bypass surgery. A surgeon takes a vein or an artery from your chest, your leg, or another part of your body and connects it to the blocked artery. The new artery then bypasses the blockage so that oxygen-rich blood can reach the heart muscle. That is what I am going to do to Sobek's pipeline.

I am going to give it a bypass.

The only person who knows about this is Taj. We plotted it out together. Although everyone else on the team thinks we are blowing up the pipeline, that would be an ineffectual solution, as our water still needs to be desalinated. It just needs to be done without adding Sobek's toxic chemicals to it.

Once we get to the cave, we split up: Lachlan checks out the security at the Desalination Plant, Magnum goes in search of dynamite and a wrench, and Kai goes to "borrow" some transportation: After the mission we will need an escape route back to the Zeppelin, and there's no one better to steal a few motorglides than Kai. Zilli and I go up to the cave.

I pull my father's knapsack from behind the rock and start to pore over his charts. When I was deprogrammed, his plan became clear to me. These aren't random scribblings; instead, they are a complicated maze to the red carbon chamber. I understand the map now and trace the best path for me to swim to fulfill my mission. I also realize Taj's "test" by throwing me in the well for two days had a practical value. She had to see if I could still keep my sanity in the water when put into a dangerous situation. She had to make sure that I could live in the now and focus on opportunities that presented themselves to me in the moment.

"What happens when you get there?" Zilli asks.

"I have to reroute the pipes to go around the carbon chamber."

"How do you do that?"

"Well, look at this drawing my father did. See the two pipes which lead in and out of the carbon chamber? I need to connect the pipe leading in to the chamber with this other one over here. That way, it goes around the carbon chamber that adds the fluoride instead of through it."

"Won't they just put it back?"

Why is an eight-year-old questioning me? We've come this far, and this is the plan.

"No." I say, but my voice has lost all of its authority. "It will take them months to realize the fluoride solution has been bypassed."

"Will it?"

"Do you have a better suggestion?" I am at my wit's end with this girl.

Zilli just smiles, ignoring my snarky attitude. She hands me the packet of vitamins my father left for me.

"I think it's a little late for me to worry about nutrition," I say.

"My father was a scientist," Zilli says. "Vitamins weren't exactly his priority. Creating an antidote to the fluoride solution was. What better way to sneak out potent chemicals from the plant without anyone noticing? You do it in plain sight." She smiles, "Vitamins."

"Your father?" I am speechless.

"My father," she insists.

"But you . . . you can't be."

"But I am," she announces. "Zilli means shadow. I was underground for so long, I was like a shadow. But now that I'm here, I can finally be myself."

"Sun?" I gasp.

"I've always been near you, Keeva. Watching my sister with the sad eyes. Harijiwan raised me in the lighthouse, but I was never too far away. And I saw Father many times. We just couldn't afford for you to see me. It would have endangered everything."

"I . . . saw your room . . . at the lighthouse." I am so stunned, I can barely get out my words.

"I know. That's why I ran ahead. To warn Harijiwan and Inelia. They went through the trap door. They're safe."

"Inelia?"

"Yes. She is Harijiwan's intended partner. She's been one of Taj's main insiders since Monarch Camp began. One of the reasons Sobek set up MC-5 was to identify Hybrids with dominant DNA. There have been so many pairings between humans and Lien over the years that the Lien gene is all but diluted . . . save for the few who have the dominant Lien gene. Not even the parents know if their children will have the gene. Inelia is the one who identifies the Hybrids with dominant Lien DNA for the resistance. When you were identified, after your intended partner couldn't handle the torture that you could, she reported back. She told Father, and the plan was all along for me to be extracted after my birth. Both to save me, but more important, to protect you."

"But, how?"

"I've been watching you my whole life. It's what I've been trained for. I've followed you since Father fire-bombed the house."

"What?" I am not sure I can handle any more truths. "He started the fire?"

"Yes, he had to get you to the Labyrinth. Sobek's men had been watching you as well. Hybrids with our DNA are in huge demand because of our power. Most of us get manipulated to the dark. You and I have managed to make it to the light."

"You're so little." I'm still babbling. I'm still unable to comprehend what is happening. I have to complete a huge mission in less than an hour, and all I can think about is being reunited with my little sister. If this is, indeed, my little sister.

"Like I said, I'm small for my age," Sun laughs, "but I can grow if you want." With that, she shape shifts, making herself almost as tall as I am. Her eyes turn light lavender. She is shimmery and metallic. But she is . . . beautiful.

"Whoa. How did you—"

"It's in our genes," she says easily as she returns to her original shape. "Dad is able to do it and so are we. You just need a teacher. Harijiwan taught me, and I will teach you."

I want to cry. I want to shout. I want to ask a million questions. Instead, I hug my sister as tight as I can.

"I've missed you so much, Sun." I don't know how I can miss something I've never had, but I do.

"I know. Me too. But we have work to do. You have work to do." She picks up the vitamin packet and hands it to me, "And these are not vitamins, but an antidote to the fluoride solution. If you can put it in the carbon chamber, it will neutralize any past and future toxins Sobek dumps in."

It is genius: a nonviolent act of rebellion, which the Protectors will never see coming.

"**W**HY DO PROTECTORS ALWAYS RESORT to violence?" Calix wondered.

He and Blue were huddled in the shadows of the cliffs near Keeva's former home. The rest of the Protectors were meeting with Magnum, the spy, while Calix and Blue were kept at a safe distance. Tomorrow, the rebels would be killed and he would be miles away. Completely ineffectual. Not that he minded. He had quickly developed an aversion to murder.

"You need violence to keep the peace," Blue said simply. "Look, I know Keeva and Kai. They are . . ." she hesitates, wondering which word will be most effectual and believable "dangerous. They were from the minute they entered camp. Curious. Individualistic. Headstrong. Most dominant-gene Hybrids are."

"Hybrids?"

"Descendants of Lien and Humans. Children of mixed DNA with a dominant Lien gene. You and I are full-blooded Lien." Blue said, "When I entered camp, I knew I was going to be a Protector . . . only my job was twofold. I was going to be matched with a Hybrid so that I could help manage him." She shrugged, "I just didn't think he would abandon ship so quickly to join the revolution. I barely had enough time to make a real connection with him."

"You were a plant?" Calix was shocked.

"Sure. An undercover. A lot of us are. Another one of my jobs was to gain Keeva's trust, which I think I did. That may help us in the future. She doesn't like me, but she trusts me. Look, Calix, there are very few full-blooded Lien. We are of the highest order. One of our jobs is to be matched with dominant-gene Hybrids so that they are easier to control and able to conform to our agenda. It's quite genius. So Lien plants are placed in camp as Anomalies to help identify who has the potential to help the Lien and who must be recycled. I was paired with Kai."

"But now you're paired with me," Calix said flatly.

"It's every girl's dream to be queen." Blue smiled, "It doesn't matter that we don't have feelings for each other, Calix. We look good together, we will have beautiful children, and we will rule this planet when your father gets bored of it." She squeezed his hand. "Try to get some sleep, Calix. Relax."

But Calix was anything but relaxed.

28.

I am confident.

It is an hour before dawn when Sun and I meet the team a half mile down the shore from the Desalination Plant. I'm wearing my bathing suit, and my sister has the packet of vitamins safely tucked into the bandana on her wrist. My father's bandana that he gave to me.

Which I then gave to my sister.

Lachlan and Kai are the first to arrive. I don't share the news with them about Sun quite yet. There will be plenty of time when the mission is over.

"There are over a hundred Protectors on site already," Lachlan reports. "They know we are coming."

"Then our only move is to get in and out before they notice us," I say.

"That's the plan," Lachlan agrees.

"I secured us two bikes," Kai says. "It was fairly easy to disable the tracking devices. I figured Magnum and I can drive and you and Keeva can ride pillion."

"What about me?" my sister asks.

"That's why I got a bike with a sidecar," Kai grins. "You'll ride in style. They're stashed behind the clump of trees behind us. The navigation is preset, so if we have any trouble, just jump on the motorglide and go. Although I think when we're done, we should head straight back to the Labyrinth. Some Protectors may be stationed near the lighthouse."

"Agreed," Lachlan says.

Magnum waves at us from the distance. He is limping. When he approaches, his lip has been split open again, and his nose looks like it's been broken.

"What happened?" I ask.

"Protectors. They're everywhere," he pants. "I broke into the emporium to get the steel basin wrench and the dynamite. They were waiting for me when I got out."

"How did you get away?" Kai asks.

"I used one of the sticks of dynamite to cause a distraction," he grins. "I think it worked; I took out three of them."

"Most people don't survive Protectors once, and you've managed to survive them twice," Sun observes.

"What can I say? I'm a lucky guy."

"Stop talking," Kai says, "we're running out of time."

"Fine," Magnum snarls and looks at me, "what's the plan?"

And then I hear Lachlan's voice in my head, *"Don't tell him, Keeva. Something's not right."*

I suppress the new panic inside of me and look at Magnum through new eyes. Why hadn't I noticed before? My instincts about Omri were correct. He wasn't the traitor, Magnum is. I see the large wrench in Magnum's hand. It is now a weapon, rather than a tool to open the chamber. And I am in my bathing suit, unarmed. I must think in the now. I must act quickly. Sun Tzu's lesson comes to mind: *The supreme art of war is to subdue the enemy without fighting.*

"Well, Keeva?" Magnum is markedly impatient. I notice his eyes are scanning the sky. That means that any second a helicraft will be descending. I need to save as many people as I can.

"Yes, Keeva. We're all waiting for your decision," Lachlan adds.

I take a deep breath and repeat Mick's mantra, *"Aad Guray Nameh. Aad Guray Nameh. Aad Guray Nameh."*

"What does that mean?" asks Magnum.

"We go ahead with the original plan," I say.

"What is the original plan?" Magnum asks. "You still haven't told us."

"Kai," I look into my friend's eyes, hoping that he will understand the message. "Remember what we did the last night of Monarch Camp? What you taught me?"

"Yes," he replies, completely confused.

"I need you to teach Zilli that lesson."

"Now?" Kai is baffled.

"Right now. Trust me." I turn to my sister, "Can I have my bandana back? When Magnum and I bomb the plant, I'm going to need something to cover my mouth to protect it from the smoke."

She nods and unties the bandana, rewrapping it around my wrist with the antidote pills securely in place. I give her a quick hug goodbye. "Now go."

"Keeva," Kai lingers.

"Go Kai," I say harshly, "I'm running this mission, not you."

I stall while she and Kai disappear into the thicket of trees.

"What was that about?" Magnum growls.

"She's just a kid. She shouldn't be involved in this."

"What about Kai?" Lachlan asks.

"I don't trust him. He never got us the escape vehicles. I think he's been working with the Protectors all along."

"I never trusted him either," Magnum adds.

"Good. So we're all agreed," I say and both Lachlan and Magnum nod. "We'll deal with him after we complete our mission. Magnum, strip down to your skivvies."

"What?"

"You want in on the plan or not?" I say with great authority. "You and I are going to do this. It is a two-person team."

"No. No way," Lachlan says. He is not happy. "I'm coming too." In my head, he says to me, *"He plans to kill you, Keeva. Let me help."*

"We don't need your help, Lachlan," I say aloud. I then silently communicate to him, *"Please trust me. I know what I'm doing."*

I figure if I can draw Magnum into the water, he will be the bait that the Protectors will follow. I can save my team, my friends, my family, and maybe even complete the mission as well. It doesn't matter if I die, for I will save many.

Except I know Lachlan won't let me go. His job is to protect me. Yet my job is to protect humanity.

"I'm sorry about this, Lachlan," I say.

"Sorry about what?"

"This." I grab the wrench from Magnum and swing it at Lachlan's leg before he can react. There is a crack of bone. I have just broken his kneecap. He crumbles to the ground, wailing in pain.

"Let's go, Magnum," I say, tossing the wrench back to him. I don't turn back. I can't bear to see Lachlan in pain, but it is the only way to prevent him from coming with us.

"What'd you do that for?" Magnum says as he plunges into the water beside me.

"He'd slow us down," I say cruelly. "This is a two-person job. He's too old and too weak. We need warriors. Like us."

As we swim further and further out into the ocean, we can still hear Lachlan's cries.

I reach the pipeline first. While I wait for Magnum, I scan the empty shoreline. My only hope with my brutal action is that Kai and Sun were able to collect Lachlan before the Protectors could.

"That's a long swim," Magnum sputters as he hoists himself up on a pipe.

"Try doing it every day of your life."

"What now?" Magnum is having trouble catching his breath.

"Beneath here is the pipeline to the Desalination Plant where the water is purified."

"I thought it was purified in the plant," Magnum says.

"It is. Then it flows through the section of pipeline below us where new ingredients are integrated into the water."

"Wait. I thought we were swimming to the plant."

"We are. This is the part of the plant."

"But I thought—

"What? That our team was going to blow up the actual plant? What good would that do? Sobek would just build another plant." I slide off the pipe, slightly distancing myself from Magnum as I tread water. "Besides, it'd be too easy for the Protectors to wait for us there. There are too many nooks and crannies for them to hide in before they take us down by tasering us and torturing us. Protectors are notorious for hurting their victims, not for letting them go." I'm hurling my words at Magnum.

"I don't know what you're talking about."

"Don't you?" We stare at each other. "It was never Omri. It was you. It was you all along. You killed Rezz. She was my friend."

Magnum realizes he's been caught. "I'm going to kill you too, you dirty Hybrid," he throws the wrench at my head. His aim is good, but my reflexes are lightning sharp, and I twist my body as the wrench misses me by millimeters. I then dive under the water.

Magnum is right behind me.

I weave through the maze of pipes below with Magnum on my heels. He clearly feigned being a slow swimmer before. Now, I can barely outswim him. I pick up the pace heading for a destination that I had never planned to visit again. En route, I pop up to the surface to take a long gulp of air before I dive under again.

I reach my destination and turn to see Magnum inches away from me. I let him grab me. His hand is wrapped around my arm, twisting it. His head has just squeezed through the compact area of pipes and his eyes are shooting daggers into me. He contorts his torso through the pipes until his body is wedged tightly between them. He cannot escape. He pounds on the pipes hoping to free himself. With each movement, he expels more energy and more air. Realizing what has happened, he thrashes his body violently in hopes of freeing himself. Eventually the fury in his eyes turns to fear. After a minute, his body stops fighting.

For the second time in my life, in this exact spot, I watch someone die.

"**W**HAT'S THAT?" Calix jumped up from his sleep as he heard a loud wail on the beach.

He and Blue raced from the cliffs around the shore just in time to see two rebels slowly moving up the shore. Kai was helping an older man who was limping.

"We have to stop them," Blue said.

"And then what?" Calix asked earnestly.

"I dunno," Blue shouted as she ran, "but we can't just stay here."

They approached the pair. "Stop," Blue said.

"Hi Blue." Kai grinned, "Fancy meeting you here."

"Kai."

"I see you've moved on." Kai eyed Calix warily. His hand was on his knife, ready to throw it at any sudden move.

"Where's Keeva?" Blue looked around.

"She's a little busy right now. Why don't you come back with us, and you can meet her new friends."

"I was actually going to suggest the same thing. I'm sure Sobek would love to see you again."

"And Taj would love to meet you."

It was a standstill as the pair looked at each other. Everyone had his or her hand on a weapon. Within minutes there could be a possible bloodbath; yet no one was willing to make the first move.

"Can I suggest a trade?" Lachlan finally said. Everyone turned to the older man who was grimacing in pain. "It will make this all go a lot faster."

29.

I am myself.

Fifteen minutes after a citizen dies, his Third goes off the radar. I'm sure Sobek's men are monitoring Magnum, so I have fifteen minutes to get the antidote into the carbon chamber and escape. The only problem is, I don't have enough time to dive down to try to find the wrench where Magnum threw it. If I go back for the basin wrench, there is no way I will be able to finish the job in time, but if I don't go back for the wrench, I may not be able to open the carbon chamber. I hesitate for a moment, deciding which course of action to take.

And I confidently swim directly to the carbon chamber.

If I am indeed a Hybrid with advanced powers, then I shouldn't need a wrench to open the chamber. I spot the red-capped chamber in the midst of the maze and swim over to it. It has an octagonal socket, which the basin wrench could have easily opened. I use my fingers to try to turn the bolt, expecting my newfound super strength to kick in and help me. But my fingers slide away from the contraption, which hasn't budged.

I go up to the surface to get more air and to think. Time is ticking away and I realize for the first time I may not actually complete my mission. I will be letting down the resistance. I will be letting down my sister.

I reach into the bandana to retrieve the pills. If only I could put them directly into the water and neutralize it that way. Of course the ocean is too vast. The only way to stop Sobek's poison is to get inside that carbon chamber. But I don't have any means to do it. I don't have an eight-sided wrench. The only thing I have with eight sides is . . . .

I quickly dive down to the carbon chamber and focus on my talisman. My Celph. Myself.

In the same way that the eight legs curled back into shape when I discovered who I was, the eight legs lock onto the carbon chamber and turn. It works, and within seconds the bolt is off and I am able to deposit the antidote into the chamber. I use the bracelet to retighten the bolt.

And I swim away.

Epilogue

I am home.

I find the motorglide Kai left for me and drive straight to Sabbatical City. It is close to midnight when I arrive at the fountain and I duck behind the holo and into the maze, which leads me to the elevator.

I take the long journey down and expect to find a big celebration waiting for me. As the door slides open, I hope to see all of my friends. Instead I only see darkness. Underground City is all asleep, except for one small face who is waiting by the elevator as it opens: my sister. My Sun. She is better than any celebration. I hold her tightly, never wanting to let her go.

"It's finally over," I say. "We can be a family now."

"It is now only just beginning," she sighs, wise beyond her years. She puts her hand through mine and walks with me me to our tent.

"How was the trip back? How is everyone? Was the motorglide ride fun? How's Lachlan's leg? Where's Kai? Has Taj started Phase Two?" I have so many questions and only Sun can answer them.

"We'll have plenty of time to catch up tomorrow. Tonight, you must sleep," she insists as we enter the dormitory tent and she tucks me into my hammock, the lost child becoming the found mother.

Patel's snores still comfort me but Rezz's empty hammock above me adds a foul bitterness to my victory. Tomorrow, I will comfort Gina. Tomorrow, I will reunite with Kai. Tomorrow, I will strategize Phase Two of the mission with Taj. For now, I am excited to finally enjoy uninterrupted dreams. I have won. I have saved humanity.

A voice enters my head and it doesn't belong to Inelia. Or Taj. Or Lachlan.

This voice belongs to Sobek.

"Congratulations on your success Keeva, I always knew you were special. Just imagine how much better you could be with a partner. Oh, I don't mean me, my darling, I'm too old. I've lived far too long already. I'm ready to give up my world to a deserving heir. A team of partners who can bring this world into the next millennium.

"Oh, yes, you must be wondering where Kai is. Poor dear. Well, the mystery is solved. He's with me now. I've captured him. Come find us.

"I'm sure we can work something out."

About the Authors

Photo by Savannah Bloch

SADIE TURNER is a Los Angeles-based producer and writer originally from Brighton, England, who works in business development with several Hollywood entrepreneurs. She has various projects in development and also teaches yoga.

COLETTE FREEDMAN is an internationally produced playwright, screenwriter, director, and novelist who was recently named one of the Dramatist Guild's "50 to Watch." In collaboration with *The New York Times* best-selling author Michael Scott, she wrote the thriller *The Thirteen Hallows*. Her critically acclaimed novel *The Affair* was published in January 2013, and the sequel *The Consequences* was published in February 2014. Colette's play version of the book earned great acclaim as it toured Italy from February through May 2013.

She has authored over twenty-five produced plays including *Sister Cities*, which was the hit of the Edinburgh Fringe and earned five-star reviews. It has been performed around the United States and internationally, including Paris (*Une Ville, Une Soeur*) and Rome (*Le Quattro Sorelle*). She wrote the screenplay that is currently in preproduction starring Jacki Weaver, Alfred Molina, Tom Everett Scott, Stana Katic, and Troian Bellisario. Her musical *Serial Killer Barbie* premiered at NoHo Arts Center in Los Angeles in November 2014 and opened in New Zealand in September 2015.

Colette has been commissioned to write several screenplays including an adaptation of the best-selling novel, *The Last Girls*, a modern adaptation of *Uncle Vanya* and the thriller, *Mystery of Casa Matusita*, starring Malcolm McDowell. She has co-written, with international best-selling novelist Jackie Collins, the play *Jackie Collins' Hollywood Lies*, which begins its regional tour in 2017.

As a director, Colette has won over sixty awards for her commercial work, including the International Summit Award, Telly, and Communicator Awards. She was also first place winner in Creative Writing at the Santa Barbara Writer's Conference. She just co-produced her first film, *Quality Problems*, starring Jack McGee, Jenica Bergere, Brooke Purdy, and Doug Purdy.

For more information, please visit
www.colettefreedman.com